Praise for Emma Lathen and her Books

RIGHT ON THE MONEY

"An enjoyable puzzler . . . brisk, smart dialogue."
—*Publishers Weekly*

"Lathen is a whiz at plotting and a wit at catching
dignified executives with their spreadsheets
down. . . . She takes relish in exposing the corporate
shenanigans that wend their way from washrooms to
boardrooms and sometimes to courtrooms."
—*The New York Times Book Review*

"*Right on the Money* is another winner."
—*Detroit News/Free Press*

EAST IS EAST

"As usual, Lathen provides an insider's view of the
financial world, some intricate fair play plotting and a
cast of interesting characters."
—*The Purloined Letter*

"One of the funniest confrontations of John Putnam Thatcher's delightful career."
—*St. Louis Post-Dispatch*

SOMETHING IN THE AIR

"Emma Lathen spins an observant tale of financial and criminal intrigue. . . . *Something in the Air* is far more pleasurable than a flight on any no-frills commuter airline. In fact, if I were forced to make such a journey tomorrow, I'd bring along a vat of water, a sweater, and another book by Emma Lathen. Maybe two—you never know about delays."
—*The New York Times Book Review*

"Still spoofing Wall Street with wacky, wild hilarity."
—*The Washington Post*

"Lathen's Wall Street novels, featuring banker John Putnam Thatcher, are among the most popular being written today. Lathen manages to instill suspense and fascination in her books by offering an insider's view of how high finance and low motives often intersect."
—*Newsday*

BOOKS BY EMMA LATHEN

*Available from HarperPaperbacks

RIGHT ON THE MONEY

A JOHN PUTNAM THATCHER MYSTERY

EMMA LATHEN

HarperPaperbacks
A Division of HarperCollins*Publishers*

HarperPaperbacks *A Division of* HarperCollins*Publishers*
    10 East 53rd Street, New York, N.Y. 10022

Copyright © 1993 by Emma Lathen
All rights reserved. No part of this book may be used or reproduced in any manner whatsoever without written permission of the publisher, except in the case of brief quotations embodied in critical articles and reviews. For information address Simon & Schuster, 1230 Avenue of the Americas, New York, N.Y. 10020.

A hardcover edition of this book was published in 1993 by Simon & Schuster.

Cover illustration by Danilo Ducak

First HarperPaperbacks printing: March 1995

Printed in the United States of America

HarperPaperbacks and colophon are trademarks of HarperCollins*Publishers*

10 9 8 7 6 5 4 3 2 1

ACKNOWLEDGMENT

≫

I would like to thank Jay Verner of the Fire Department in Wellesley, Massachusetts, for all his help. The expertise is his; the blunders are mine.

E.L.

CONTENTS

Chapter

OPENING BID

Wall Street loves a parade. Marching bands give everybody the opportunity to blow off steam. If the United States ever embraces soccer, all those fine minds in Lower Manhattan will relieve stress and tie up noontime traffic cheering primitives who use their heads to butt balls.

Weather permitting, a lunchtime parade pulls even program traders outdoors.

John Putnam Thatcher, senior vice president of the Sloan Guaranty Trust, emerged one mild December day to find himself immobilized against the wall of his own bank. Since surging masses of humanity are not respecters of person, Tom Robichaux, of Robichaux & Devane, was pinned down, too.

It was not easy to discover what the marchers were celebrating.

"I think it's some freedom fighters," said a vague

young paralegal. "From one of those places in Africa, or South America."

Given Tom Robichaux's low tolerance for discomfort and inconvenience, this should have set him off. Instead, as the last politician-filled convertible inched past, he waxed nostaglic.

"Parades aren't the same unless the boys are coming home," he said, conjuring up the golden past.

John Thatcher had shared much of that past with Robichaux, starting with their years in Harvard Yard. Knowing his man, he drew a natural conclusion.

"What's put you in such a good mood, Tom?" he inquired when they finally reached their table.

Robichaux defended himself. "Good mood?" he demanded. "Who says I'm in a good mood? For that matter, who in his right mind would be? My God, John, if you only knew what Houlihan is proposing! Francis is fit to be tied. Then there are those bloody Germans."

Minor squabbles at those eminently decorous investment bankers, Robichaux & Devane, did not divert Thatcher. Neither did the Bundesbank. When Tom Robichaux ignored the chance to excoriate freedom fighters, he had to be feeling on top of the world.

"So you're actually deeply worried by the look of things?" Thatcher said skeptically.

"Well, no," Robichaux admitted. As his complex marital history demonstrated, he was at heart an incurable optimist. "Actually, we just got some very good news."

"That makes a nice change," said Thatcher, speaking of things general rather than particular.

Robichaux scented irony. "Well, it should interest you, too," he said reproachfully. "You have heard of ASI, haven't you? You may not know it, but they're one of our clients."

"Splendid," said Thatcher.

ASI, as he recalled, was Aqua Supplies, Inc., a large

manufacturer of water-related fixtures for the kitchen. They sold only under private label to mail-order houses, contractors, and others. Why ASI should interest him, or the Sloan Guaranty Trust, remained obscure.

"ASI's finally made its decision," said Robichaux. "God knows they spent enough time narrowing the field."

"You mean they're looking for a merger partner?" Thatcher suggested helpfully.

Robichaux thought he had already explained as much.

"Exactly," he said with impatience. "They want to pair up with somebody who'll help them break into the retail market. When they came to us, they said they'd only consider blue-ribbon outfits. And if I say so myself, we came up with a list of candidates that knocked their eyes out."

"I'm sure you did," said Thatcher, pandering to institutional pride. "Who's the lucky one?"

"The Ecker Company," said Robichaux with a smirk of triumph.

"I see," said Thatcher, the light dawning.

He knew little about the Ecker company, except that it produced a line of small kitchen appliances—and banked at the Sloan Guaranty Trust.

"Who handles Ecker for the Sloan, John?"

"Milo Thompson's done it for years," said Thatcher. He did not feel obliged to add that Milo Thompson had retired months ago.

The original Ecker was still at the helm of the Ecker Company. Tradition had it that Conrad Ecker's hair had been rust-red when, as a new husband, he sat watching his wife scour a coffeepot. It was a matter of record that, before breakfast was over, he had roughed out some sketches. After that came a period of surreptitious tinkering at Bridgeport Engineering, where Ecker enjoyed a steady paycheck, job security and good prospects. Then he handed in his notice and went out on a limb.

The first self-cleaning Ecker percolator was developed, produced, and peddled from a shoe-string operation in a barely renovated mill. But one success led to another, and the Ecker Company grew into one of Bridgeport's larger employers.

Ecker's hair was grizzled now, but he was still marching to a different drummer.

"I never expected to have to sell out—oh, all right, they call it merging, but it amounts to the same thing. Still, conditions change and only a damned fool doesn't change with them."

Public speaking, even in his own living room, was not Ecker's strong point. He fussed with his pipe, then continued, "Now this feeler from ASI might be a possibility. I'm going to have to talk to the Sloan about it, and I'm not rushing into anything. But I'm inclined to treat it seriously."

The Ecker Company, which was family-run as well as family-owned, did not boast a boardroom. When anything resembling a conference was unavoidable, it took place in Conrad Ecker's old Victorian house, a few blocks from the plant. Today the homey surroundings were adding to his difficulties.

"Now I could have told you all separately. But," he justified himself, "I thought it would be better to break the news like this."

His audience of three remained tongue-tied.

"Well, it isn't such a big surprise, is it?" he demanded gruffly.

Alan Frayne was first to respond. "No. No, it's not, Conrad. Sure, we won't like seeing Ecker go. But like you said, time doesn't stand still. If you don't act now, you'll have to later. And later may not be better."

"That's how I see it," said Ecker, daring anyone to protest. Nobody rose to the bait. Arguing with Conrad when he had dug in his heels was, to say the least, counterproductive.

But there was another reason for the collective restraint. Although Ecker was surrounded by relatives, his own son and heir was not among them. After a nearly fatal heart attack, Douglas Ecker, aged forty-nine, had been forced into permanent retirement. This tragedy was not mentioned in Conrad's presence. Similarly, the subject of what would happen to the Ecker Company when Conrad himself was removed from the scene was strictly taboo.

Alan Frayne was one of the few people who could hold his own against the great man. Frayne had even managed to get through a divorce without hard feelings, even though his ex was Conrad's daughter. It said much about his value to the company that, after the breakup, it was Betty who left for California. Alan Frayne stayed in Bridgeport, everybody's strong right arm.

"ASI could be our best bet," he said, stroking ruffled feathers.

Bob Laverdiere finally found his tongue. "I'm not sure you're right, Alan," he said. "I mean, what makes it such a necessity to sell? There's still plenty of talent here at Ecker."

"I know that," Conrad snapped at his nephew.

There was little family resemblance between them. Bob Laverdiere was slight, whereas Ecker was stocky. Friendly and easygoing, Bob was a boyish forty.

"It would be a terrible shame to see Ecker going out of the family," he said earnestly.

"A shame, sure, but maybe it's a necessity," Alan Frayne said sympathetically. "Besides, Bob, merging doesn't necessarily mean somebody's going to ride herd on us. We've got a beautiful operation here."

"You can say that again," Bob Laverdiere rejoined.

Conrad Ecker agreed with both of them. "After all, it's the Ecker name and ideas and profits that they really want. Why would ASI go around making whole-sale changes in something that works so well?"

"Absolutely," said his nephew.

Amused, Alan Frayne relaxed and let the two inno-cent egotists hold the field. Conrad, an eccentric genius of sorts, approached everything idiosyncratically. Bob Laverdiere had less excuse for his self-confidence. Frayne, who suspected Laverdiere's limitations, could imagine disillusion ahead for him.

But then, Alan reflected ruefully, he had been fore-seeing the worst since Doug Ecker's departure.

Mrs. Robert Laverdiere could not afford to share Frayne's detachment. Tina was not only Bob's devoted wife and the mother of his two children, she was also the company's financial watchdog. A cool, handsome woman, she knew more about the business end of the Ecker Company than Conrad and Bob combined.

"When will you be talking to ASI, Conrad?" she asked without a trace of anxiety.

"I've put in a call to the Sloan," Ecker told her. "If they don't have any objections, we'll try to get together as soon as possible. Say the day after tomorrow."

"As soon as that?" Bob Laverdiere exclaimed.

His uncle ignored him. "That is, we won't be starting negotiations or anything. But ASI probably wants to send some folks up to look the place over."

With a flash of dark eyes, Tina kept Bob from saying more.

"When something's got to be done, I'd just as soon get cracking," said Conrad Ecker decisively. "I don't believe in letting the grass grow under my feet."

On this vintage note, their meeting came to an end.

Chapter

SOME RISK INVOLVED

There was nothing at all homey about Aqua Supplies, Inc. A large, impersonal institution, it had a rigidly defined chain of command. At headquarters, in Princeton, New Jersey, news of anything so important as a potential merger was a sacred mystery, to be shared by the chosen few. First among them was Gardner Ives. White-haired and distinguished, he was every inch the corporation president.

"Ecker's a damn good choice of yours, Phil," he told his executive vice president. "Naturally I knew about their solid reputation, but I never dreamed they had so much brand-name recognition. They're ideal for our purposes."

Philip Pepitone, built like the workhorse that he was, rarely let compliments go to his head. "Robichaux and Devane did the heavy digging," he said. "But when they came up with Ecker, I jumped. Of course we can't really tell anything until we get numbers on the table."

Ives was torn between caution and enthusiasm.

"It's a good sign that Ecker's willing to let us take a preliminary look. I'd like to get that done as soon as possible, Phil. But on the quiet. The fewer people in on this, the better, in case things don't pan out."

"We'll play it close to the chest," Pepitone agreed.

Having started his life at ASI on a lowlier rung than Gardner Ives, he should have known better. Access codes for computers are just as ineffective as the locked filing cabinets and limited-circulation lists of yesteryear. Gossip still zipped around the ASI grapevine with the speed of sound.

In a plant a quarter of a mile from headquarters, Victor Hunnicut was already listening avidly.

"The Ecker Company?" he exclaimed. "I never heard of them."

"They're big in retail," said his informed source. "All of a sudden, Ives is in a real hurry. It makes sense, that's where the growth is."

"It could really jazz things up here at ASI," said Hunnicut.

He was in a hurry himself. Armed with a chemical engineering degree and an M.B.A., he had launched himself on his career with single-minded determination. By the time he arrived at ASI, after three strategic relocations, he was eager to take off.

And a brand-new division might be just what he needed.

Of course, there could be risks involved, too, he told himself.

Fifteen minutes later he had consulted some business directories and was making the first of two telephone calls.

"Food processors and countertop appliances," he repeated uneasily. "Doesn't Ecker do any bigger systems, like ASI?"

His second contact was also unsettling.

"Just small electricals? Nothing at all in fixtures?"

This was enough to make him pause. What was good for ASI might not be good for Victor Hunnicut. Small appliances were a long way from his area of expertise. Worse still, they might be within the competence of some other assistant division manager. Having one of his contemporaries leapfrog over his head would make his own struggle upward that much trickier.

Most junior executives would have felt helpless at this juncture. Not Victor Hunnicut. Thinking deeply, he pondered ways to safeguard his position. Before he could do anything, he had to know who was pushing the Ecker merger and who was against it. Lunch in the executive dining room should take care of that.

At ASI the niceties of mealtime protocol were the same as elsewhere. Subordinates did not suggest lunching with their seniors. A senior, however, could join his underlings when nothing better was available. Accordingly, Hunnicut scanned the room before inserting himself into a table of young accountants. His strategy paid off. When the company auditor arrived ten minutes later he looked vainly for peers, then affably pulled out the chair directly across from Hunnicut.

The conversation, predictably, centered on the day's hot topic. Silently eating, Hunnicut listened for the all-important details.

"Ecker's kind of an offbeat choice for Phil Pepitone to make," the auditor commented. "Of course, nothing's really settled yet."

Good! Sullivan was no friend to Phil Pepitone.

"I thought it was Mr. Ives who was behind the idea of taking ASI into the consumer market," Hunnicut said.

The auditor was careful to draw a distinction. "Yes, and it's high time, too. But it's Pepitone who pulled Ecker out of nowhere. Now that could be a mistake the way I see it."

"They've got a pretty good track record, don't they?" said one of the accountants, deaf to undertones.

"What's past is past," pontificated the auditor. "Conrad Ecker's an old man now. But maybe Pepitone knows more about the Ecker Company than I do."

The auditor declined to say more, but Hunnicut had obtained the information he wanted. There was a pocket of opposition to the Ecker merger. It was not a bad beginning.

When lunch was over, Hunnicut found himself in the men's room, scrubbing hands next to one of Phil Pepitone's cronies.

"Everybody's buzzing about Ecker," he said conversationally. "But Wade Sullivan seems worried about the old man's age."

The derision was almost automatic.

"What choice do we have? ASI's got to have some new products, and Sam Bradley's operation hasn't come up with a single one in five years."

"I suppose that's what's tipped the balance," Hunnicut agreed. "But Ecker must be close to retirement, isn't he?"

"He's still more productive than Sam Bradley's ever been," Pepitone's ally snarled.

As he dried his hands, Hunnicut grew more thoughtful. Until now he had not even known there was an anti-Bradley faction. Surely, an astute young man could find some way to exploit these latent animosities. At midafternoon he got a sharp reminder of how important this might be.

Two other assistant division managers waylaid him in the hallway to present their own conclusions about the Ecker merger.

". . . a real break for one of us," said the tubby extrovert. "Too bad it can't be you or me, Vic."

This cheerful acceptance of the undeniable grated on

Hunnicut, particularly since he knew that tubby's companion was likely to be in the running.

"It's early days to talk about any opening," he replied with a smile. "Don't get your hopes up, Pete."

Pete had learned to be circumspect with good old Vic.

"Sure," he said amiably. "They could get an outsider or stick with whatever they've got in Bridgeport now. But then"—he paused—"that wouldn't make much sense, would it? Not if the idea is to bring Ecker into line with us."

Tubby threw in another possibility. "For that matter, Stan is betting the whole deal'll fall through. What does Fred think?"

Hunnicut's boss was out of town, he told them. Later that day he was saying the same thing to Philip Pepitone.

"I'm sorry, but Fred's in California. Is there anything I can do?"

The phone delivered fulminations from Pepitone. Then Hunnicut, as if he had been planning it for a week, said, "The trouble is, we're not expecting him back until next Friday. Of course I'd be glad to stand in for him."

After getting just the orders he wanted, Hunnicut took them straight to ASI's research division.

". . . so you see, I thought I'd better talk to you."

Sam Bradley, a tall, lean southerner, had created his own atmospherics at ASI. As befitted a scientist, he was in flannels and a tweed jacket.

". . . with Fred out of town, Phil Pepitone wants me to go along on this inspection tour," Hunnicut continued soberly, before going on to cast himself as a novice in need of guidance.

This flattery was wasted on a man sensitive to institutional slights. If Pepitone wanted anybody to assess the Ecker Company, he should have come to the director of research before he went to any assistant division manager.

"Phil's the expert about Ecker, not me," Bradley drawled. "I've never even met Conrad Ecker."

"They say he's a remarkable man," said Hunnicut. "Of course he's pretty old by now."

"Yes, I know," said Bradley indifferently.

When Hunnicut left, he was still not altogether sure where Sam Bradley stood.

Chapter

PROFIT AND LOSS

John Thatcher was just beginning his own quest for information. After lunch with Tom Robichaux, he lingered by his secretary's desk.

"The Ecker Company, Miss Corsa. Will you find out who's taken over from Milo Thompson?"

Although the Sloan held thousands of business accounts, Miss Corsa had the name at her fingertips.

"Mr. Nicolls," she replied promptly.

Thatcher accepted this as yet another instance of her inhuman competence until she added, "Mr. Nicolls wants to talk to you about Ecker when you have the time."

"Shoot him in," said Thatcher breezily. He was less schedule-minded than she was.

Furthermore, he was in a hurry. If the Ecker Company was envisaging a major transformation, Ken Nicolls was not senior enough to represent the Sloan's interest. No doubt, the Eckers felt the same way.

Ken Nicolls himself entertained doubts.

"I don't want to come running to you every time there's something complicated," he apologized. "But I talked it over with Charlie"—Charles F. Trinkham was Thatcher's second-in-command and, while the idea would have horrified him, an all-purpose mentor to the younger staff—"and he said I'd better check with you."

Thatcher did not affect omniscience for its own sake. "Robichaux and Devane's representing ASI," he explained. "I understand formal negotiations haven't begun, but as a matter of courtesy they informed me. Unfortunately I seem to know precious little about the Ecker Company."

"Me, too," Nicolls confessed.

His commendable forthrightness was not altogether accurate. Nicolls had arrived with bulging files of Ecker statements profiling a medium-sized firm of two-thousand-plus employees, located in Connecticut and Texas. Compared to giants in the field, Ecker was small, but in certain niche products it was the market leader. On paper, the Ecker Company was healthy as a horse.

As Thatcher had feared, Ken Nicolls could not flesh out these arid records. The recently retired Milo Thompson was the one who knew where the bodies, if any, were buried.

"Of course, Milo took me up to Bridgeport and introduced me around," said Nicolls. "But that's not the same as working with them for years and years."

"No, it isn't," Thatcher agreed.

Clearly, the Ecker Company was going to require some heavyweight Sloan attention in the near future. Deciding how to provide it would have to wait.

"Miss Corsa," he said, stabbing a button. "See if you can put me in touch with Milo Thompson, will you?"

Since the Sloan Guaranty Trust was still sending monthly payments to Thompson, this did not prove insuperably difficult. It was not even necessary to break into the golden sunset of Hobe Sound. Milo Thompson, on the brink of a European vacation, was staying at the St. Regis. He was delighted to leave the packing to his wife, and come downstairs.

"It's hell," he said jauntily in response to a civil inquiry about life after the Sloan. "How much golf can one man play? And I'm not crazy about cathedrals and museums, either."

Nicolls, serious-minded to a fault, assumed an expression of sympathy. Thatcher, taking in the tassels on Thompson's shoes, was less gullible.

"Itching to come back to work, eh?"

"Like a shot," said Thompson with a straight face. "Only Muriel won't let me. What's the story on Ecker?"

Thatcher filled him in, reflecting that they were in luck. Some redoubtable Sloan stalwarts underwent personality changes when they surrendered to time. Thompson had put off pinstripes; otherwise he was unaltered.

"A merger? Well, I suppose I should have seen it coming. It makes a lot of sense."

"Not to me, it doesn't," said Thatcher. "Nicolls and I have been over the Ecker financials and they look rock-solid."

"The financials don't really tell the story," said Thompson. "Let me give you some background . . ."

When Conrad Ecker started out, he had ambition, shrewdness, and vitality. But his working capital consisted only of his meager savings and the twenty thousand dollars provided by his sister's husband. No bank, including the Sloan, would touch him.

"So much for our contribution to American enterprise," Thatcher observed. "When did we join forces?"

"When Ecker got its act together," Thompson replied, looking back at one of his own prouder achievements. "That was when Doug Ecker came of age."

After years of struggling from crisis to crisis, the Ecker Company had tasted its first real management. Doug lacked his father's ability to churn out objects that captured the fancy of the American housewife, but he had a talent for marketing, organizing, and budgeting. Almost overnight, the Ecker Company became one of the most tightly run outfits in the business. Conrad retreated to his workbench and everybody was happy.

"Then came the son's first heart attack," said Thompson, shaking his head dolefully. "That floored them, especially Conrad, but everybody thought Doug would recover. Unfortunately, it didn't work out like that. When he came back, he collapsed again and they barely pulled him through. So, on doctor's orders, he's taken early retirement. It's been painful for the family."

"And the company as well," said Thatcher.

Douglas Ecker's systems and organization were, according to Thompson, still running well. But sooner or later they would require refurbishing, particularly when Conrad Ecker's contributions dried up. Change of some sort was inevitable.

In a family-owned firm, however, selling out was not the only option.

"Isn't there anybody else who can step in and take over?" Thatcher inquired.

"Apparently Conrad doesn't think so," said Thompson. "And he calls the tune because he hasn't ever parted with a single share of stock. The only other holder is his widowed sister with her twenty percent. It's her son, Bob, who's production manager in Bridgeport. He's been running the show, insofar as anybody has."

This was the first disparaging note in Thompson's account.

"Is the nephew a washout?" Thatcher demanded.

"You can't say that. He's a perfectly competent production manager. But otherwise he's just been coasting on Doug's decisions."

"A sure prescription for trouble in the future," Thatcher commented.

Thompson agreed. "Particularly since the other two are real specialists. Tina, Bob's wife, is smart as a whip. She's a CPA who just knows the financial end. A hands-on person she isn't. And Alan Frayne—he was married to Conrad's daughter for a while—he's a backroom boy. He's into design and testing and working with the pattern makers. His job is over when Bob Laverdiere's starts. My guess is that Conrad doesn't think any of them can step into Doug's shoes."

"Is that how you see it?"

It took a moment for Thompson to formulate his reply.

"Between Doug and Conrad, none of the others was given much scope. They're all good at what they do— Doug wouldn't have kept them on otherwise. But with the clock ticking the way it is, I'm not so sure I'd bet the farm on finding out if they've got what it takes."

Then, with the best intentions in the world, Thompson flattened his successor.

"Isn't that your impression, Nicolls?"

Momentarily Ken Nicolls, who had really formed no impressions at all, looked foolish.

"Don't worry," Thatcher advised him kindly. "After we've sent you up to Bridgeport to nose around, you'll know as much as Milo, if not more. In the meantime, what can either of you tell me about ASI?"

He had put them back on a level playing field. Both Thompson and Ken Nicolls drew blanks on ASI.

"Well, Robichaux should be able to fill me in," said Thatcher, although his expectations lay elsewhere.

Walter Bowman and the Sloan's indefatigable research staff would be getting an emergency assignment. And even though ASI banked elsewhere, Thatcher had well-merited confidence that Bowman would lay bare the truth.

At ASI, almost everybody was trying to camouflage it.

CNBC buttonholed Gardner Ives in the parking lot.

"No, there is no foundation to these rumors," he said, twirling his car keys from one aristocratic finger. "While ASI always considers new opportunities, at present we are not contemplating or actively pursuing any merger possibilities. Now, if you will excuse me . . ."

Like diplomats, CEO's are good men sent abroad to lie for their country. Victor Hunnicut was only a would-be CEO.

"So I'm going up to Ecker tomorrow with an absolutely open mind," he said. "Sam Bradley gave me some good tips on what to look for."

"Be careful about anything you get from Sam," his companion warned. "If ASI really does acquire Ecker, we won't have to waste money on more of Bradley's screw-ups. He's twisting in the wind."

"I'll watch it," said Victor Hunnicut.

Philip R. Pepitone and Dr. Samuel Bradley were leaving work at the same time.

"Hi, Phil!"

"Hi, Sam!"

After a companionable pause Bradley inquired, "Anything doing up in the front office?"

"Not a damn thing," said Pepitone heartily. "We're just plugging along."

Sam Bradley smiled benignly. "Good. There's nothing better than a quiet life."

Chapter

YIELD COMPARISON

The next morning, Phil Pepitone made Bridgeport ten minutes early. Nevertheless when he arrived, he found Victor Hunnicut already gazing at the massive old mill that housed the Ecker Company.

"I'm glad you're here, Vic," he said, putting the extra time to good use. "Now before we go in, remember the drill. I'm going to press the flesh a little while you keep your eyes on the physical layout. Just get an idea how up-to-date they are."

"Right," said Hunnicut, following him into a small modern room that defied its grim surroundings.

They were still too early. Alan Frayne, full of apologies, bustled out to explain that Bob Laverdiere was on the way over.

"Let's get settled while we're waiting for him," he said, ushering them through a door that still read "Douglas Ecker."

Pepitone had been expecting Conrad Ecker.

"You'll be joining him for lunch," Frayne continued. "But Bob's in charge these days. Anyway, as far as showing you around, Conrad would be the worst choice. He doesn't put in a lot of time over here."

"Off in his own private space, huh?" Pepitone responded. "Well, as long as he keeps churning out winners, that's the best place for him."

These preliminaries were interrupted by the arrival of Bob Laverdiere. After greeting his guests, he settled behind the desk and addressed Pepitone.

"Glad to have you up here. Conrad and I want you to see the whole operation."

Before Pepitone could reply suitably, Laverdiere continued, "I hope you don't mind company. We've got a new man at the Sloan and he wants to get up to speed. I told Tina to bring him along and join the tour, if that's all right with you."

"We go months without anybody," Frayne remarked, "and all of a sudden we've got a crowd."

Their trip to the production floor was occupied by sorting out the newcomers and establishing a pecking order. By the time they arrived, Phil Pepitone was flanked by Bob and Alan Frayne. Bringing up the rear, Tina escorted Ken Nicolls and Hunnicut.

Laverdiere had decided to start with geography. Taking them into his command post, he produced a diagram. Aside from assorted sheds and modest outbuildings, the Ecker plant consisted of one vast L-shaped structure. The longer wing still boasted the original brick-walled caverns, now home to all the manufacturing operations. Everything else had been shoe-horned into the shorter arm, which was a hodgepodge of offices, packing rooms, and storage facilities. The old railroad siding was still a shipping dock, but these days the Dickensian windows were sparkling clean.

Laverdiere's quarters were also a mixture of old and new. A battered desk overflowed with printouts, makeshift shelves were crammed with folders—but the communication system was state-of-the-art. Obviously this was where he really lived and worked, not at that bare mahogany surface over which he greeted the company's more distinguished guests.

"We'll start upstairs," Laverdiere announced.

Upstairs came as an eye-opener to Victor Hunnicut.

"Will you look at this!" he exclaimed. "You've got some really advanced stuff here."

Tina laughed. "Everybody's always surprised. After the outside, they expect the dark ages."

Ken Nicolls hazarded a guess. "You don't believe in cosmetics?"

"Oh, yes, we do," Tina replied. "Just wait until ASI takes a look at what we've got in Texas. It's beautiful."

Up ahead, Phil Pepitone was discovering that Bob Laverdiere was an enthusiast. As the perfections of one mechanical marvel after another washed over him, he let his attention wander long enough to overhear Vic Hunnicut's next remark.

"I expect Ecker's already considered closing down here and moving everything to Texas."

While Tina gathered her thoughts, Pepitone hurriedly intervened.

"Vic, come on up here, will you?" Turning to Laverdiere, he added, "Hunnicut's the one who'll understand you, Bob. I'm just a paper pusher myself."

Allowing the two younger men to proceed, he informed the others, "Vic's one of ASI's coming hopefuls. These days they've all got the technical stuff as well as the M.B.A.'s."

"Sounds like a high-powered bunch," Alan Frayne commented.

"Our recruiters don't settle for second best."

Ken Nicolls knew little about Ecker and less about ASI. But he knew something about people and that something told him that Phil Pepitone was frightening the natives. If cogs in the machine like Victor Hunnicut were so sharp, what was the rest of ASI like?

Startled or not, Tina did her duty by Phil Pepitone. While her husband and Hunnicut continued their unintelligible dialogue, she fielded questions about labor turnover, shipping costs, and energy consumption.

But even after they had covered three floors, the two tigers were still going strong.

"Of course, that's just a run-through, Vic," said Bob. "Why don't you come back to my office and let me show you some spreadsheets?"

"Great!"

Pepitone had had enough. "Later," he said decisively. "We don't want to overdo on our first go-round and—"

"Besides, it's time for lunch," Frayne interjected. "The driver's already waiting for you, Phil."

The tour resumed that afternoon with a diminished cast. Phil Pepitone was still being wined and dined by Conrad Ecker; Bob Laverdiere and Alan Frayne had discovered other calls on their time. This left Tina showing Ken Nicolls and Hunnicut the lesser nooks and crannies at Ecker. In her contained fashion, she was as thorough as her husband.

"This," she said, tugging at an oversize sliding door, "is our packing department."

Obediently they examined mountains of corrugated cardboard. Then they watched motherly women perform the usual magic with tabs and slots. Zip, zip, zip— and another Ecker coffeepot was snugly encased.

On the opposite side of the corridor, the shipping department was monitoring the weather station and the foreman was too busy to talk.

"Sorry," he said ten minutes later. "But I wanted to get these trucks up to Albany. There's snow heading that way."

No part of Ecker, it turned out, was too humdrum for Victor Hunnicut. Like a relentless child, he had questions about everything.

"Have you ever thought of subcontracting your transport?"

"Yes, indeed," said Tina promptly. "We costed it out and decided it wouldn't pay."

Minutes later he was back at her.

"I see you're picking up the full medical insurance."

"That's the way Ecker's always done it," she replied with a shade of constraint.

After health insurance came inventory control. This time Tina contented herself with a nod and hurried them on.

She was beginning to wonder if she had mistaken Hunnicut's role. It had seemed clear enough, when he was summoned to talk technicalities with Bob, that he was another faceless corporate aide. Then had come Pepitone's accolade. And now here was Victor Hunnicut tacitly passing judgment on every aspect of Ecker.

Fortunately their next move was on to her turf. The change could not have been more graphic.

"My offices are next door," she said, then continued blandly, "We'd better go back for our coats before we go outside."

Ken and Hunnicut alike were at a loss.

The boiler house, in the days of steam, had provided the mill with power. Nowadays the small circular building contained the computer center, Tina's accounting department, and a record depository. Outsiders were usually beguiled by its oddity, but with a biting arctic wind heralding sunset, Ken Nicolls could only say, "This must be wonderful in January and February."

Mischievously she replied, "It has its compensations. We get a lot of privacy over here."

Except for the masonry, Tina's domain looked like financial offices everywhere. There is very little to say about white collar workers shuffling memos and punching keyboards. When Tina began introducing Ken Nicolls around, Hunnicut shifted awkwardly, then remembered a more pressing concern.

"Say, there are a couple of things I didn't get to ask Bob. I think I'll see if he can spare me a few minutes more."

Tina, Ken, and one of Milo Thompson's old buddies were so deep in conversation that they barely noticed his departure.

It was brought to their attention an hour later when Phil Pepitone, replete with the best that Bridgeport had to offer—which was in Westport—arrived.

"They told me Vic was over here," he said.

Tina detached herself from Ken and the financials to reply that Hunnicut was once again closeted with her husband.

"Do you want me to call him?"

"Oh, don't bother," said Pepitone. "Just tell him I've left, will you? But before I go, Mrs. Laverdiere, I want to thank you and your husband for a really useful tour. It's been a very satisfying day."

Chapter

BAD PENNY

Phil Pepitone was long gone from Bridgeport when Victor Hunnicut finally called it quits. Emerging from Ecker, he sighted Ken Nicolls unlocking his car. And the Sloan Guaranty Trust, Hunnicut reminded himself, was also a player in the merger.

"Ken!" he yelled on impulse. "How about unwinding over a beer before we hit the traffic?"

"Oh, hell," Nicolls muttered under his breath. In Brooklyn Heights, his wife and children were waiting, but downtown was John Putnam Thatcher with his insatiable thirst for information.

"Fine!" he shouted back. "I'll meet you at the Holiday Inn."

The booth was comfortable, the lighting dim. Hunnicut joined Nicolls with a sigh of relief. Massaging the nape of his neck, he said, "Boy, I can sure use this breather."

"It's always a strain when everybody has to be so

careful not to step on toes," said Ken understandingly. "But by and large, things seemed to go pretty well, didn't they?"

"I suppose you could say so," said Hunnicut.

He waited until the waitress had unloaded the tray before elaborating. "Maybe I expected too much. I was glad to see that at least the plant's okay. But, by God, look at how they run it. From the way Laverdiere describes their think session about the merger, you'd take them for a Ma and Pa store."

After an ASI, Ken could see why Ecker might look amateurish.

"But you knew you were dealing with a family firm," he pointed out.

"Of course we'd all heard about Douglas Ecker," Hunnicut assured him. "But who could tell anything about these Laverdieres and Fraynes on the organization chart? If you ask me, even Phil didn't expect this mob of . . . of whatever you call them."

A career at the Sloan helped Ken supply the missing term. "Collaterals?" he suggested.

"Collaterals," Hunnicut agreed. "Take Laverdiere, for instance. You probably couldn't tell, but I got a real whack at him. He doesn't know which way is up."

Hunnicut and Bob Laverdiere had seemed to hit it off in the morning tour. Perhaps, Ken speculated, something had arisen during the afternoon.

"What makes you say that?"

Hunching over the table, Hunnicut lowered his voice. "You won't believe this, but he's convinced he's stepped into Doug Ecker's shoes and that he's going to stay there, no matter what."

"Even if there's a merger?" Ken asked.

"You've got it in one. He thinks he's set for life, and whoever takes over will automatically become Santa Claus. I'd be willing to bet he figures on going straight from being an Ecker vice-president to an ASI division manager. Believe me, that's not how it works."

Ken had seen this sort of difficulty resolved. "So he's in for a disappointment," he said. "It happens all the time. But Laverdiere's pretty good at production, isn't he? ASI might keep him on there."

Hunnicut reflected for a moment, then shook his head dubiously.

"I doubt it," he finally announced. "As near as I can make out, he got a lot of supervision from Doug Ecker. But now he's gotten used to being his own boss and he likes it."

"Then ASI gives him a golden handshake," said Ken, tiring of the subject. "That way he'll go quietly."

"Not with that wife of his," said Hunnicut knowingly.

Here he was overstepping the mark. Insights into Bob Laverdiere might be Hunnicut's province, but it was Ken Nicolls who had spent the afternoon with Tina.

"There's a lady with a good head on her shoulders," Ken said sharply. "*She's* not living in any dreamworld."

Hunnicut was all too ready to agree. "Exactly. That's what makes her part of the problem. She's too smart not to realize that she's married to a second-rater. So she'll try to protect him by going to work on his uncle."

Ken suspected that the young man sitting opposite him was making mountains out of molehills.

"Maybe Pepitone and Ecker covered all this over lunch," he said.

His bland comment was intended to end their discussion. But Hunnicut could discern flaws in his own company's performance.

"I'm beginning to think Phil didn't do enough homework on this one."

Suddenly Ken's suspicion took a new form. "Say, Vic, I never caught what you do at ASI."

Fishing out his wallet, Hunnicut produced a business card.

VICTOR M. HUNNICUT

Aqua Supplies, Inc.

Assistant Division Manager

Water Purification Division   609/256-7713

To the initiated, this modest legend was highly instructive. If ASI was going to need a new division manager, then Victor M. Hunnicut—like all ASI assistants—must itch to be that man. The kicker, however, was in the lower left-hand corner.

" 'Water Purification Division,' " Ken read aloud. "That means you're a chemical engineer. So Ecker really isn't in your line."

Hunnicut was prompt to reject what he interpreted as a reflection on his day's work. "Oh, I've had enough experience with these systems to do an evaluation. And I didn't see anything, anywhere, worth four stars."

"But then you didn't see Conrad Ecker, did you?" Nicolls reminded him.

Conrad, of course, was the company's main attraction, Hunnicut agreed warmly. ". . . but it's not as if he's into big technical breakthroughs. He just develops gadgets."

Ken shook his head at the hovering waitress. Hunnicut, however, wanted a refill and he was just raising his glass when Ken said, "Ecker's gadgets sell. And from what I hear, their product line does seem to mesh with ASI's expansion plans."

Hunnicut was unimpressed. "Sure, ideas are what

ASI needs," he said, "but what's wrong with going into the marketplace and buying them? It makes more sense than spending a mint to acquire a company—"

In the nick of time he recalled he was talking to Ecker's banker.

"—that may not be quite as good as it's cracked up to be."

Nicolls could be blunt, too. "Why doesn't ASI develop its own new products?"

As Hunnicut had already intimated, ASI, too, had its weaknesses, among them a research department that had losses and little else.

". . . I suppose that's why Phil got suckered into considering Ecker," he concluded moodily.

"He must like what he's seen. They tell me he's persuaded Conrad into another round of talks," said Ken. "But it's time for me to be hitting the road. You coming?"

Hunnicut shook his head.

"Not yet," he replied. "There are still a few things I've got to do in Bridgeport."

The following morning, when Nicolls presented himself at John Thatcher's office, he found Charlie Trinkham wrapping up his own conference.

"You just back from the boonies, Ken?" he asked the younger man.

"Connecticut is not Alaska, Charlie," Thatcher remarked.

Trinkham, a confirmed urbanite, confined his life to Manhattan whenever possible and persisted in treating Westchester as the beginning of the Frontier.

"They've got electricity and everything, Charlie," said Ken, absently producing a sheaf of notes.

"And how did your tour of Ecker go?" asked Thatcher, to signal the end of the preliminaries.

"Not bad," said Ken modestly. "In fact, I had a shot

at ASI, too. They sent up a scouting party and I got attached."

"Two for the price of one, eh?" said Thatcher, pleased. Without ASI in the wings, Ecker scarcely justified the special Sloan attention it was currently enjoying. Walter Bowman's massive research reports were excellent in their fashion, but personal impressions were always welcome.

Ken did not get to them until he had finished an exhaustive description of the Ecker system.

"Sounds more like a nonsystem to me," Charlie commented.

Nicolls demurred.

"It's deceptive, Charlie, because old man Ecker himself is so offbeat. But take him away, and you've got damned efficient manufacturing, both here and down in Texas. And I can tell you that Tina Laverdiere's running a tight ship with their financials. Everything's in apple-pie order."

"We already knew that," said Thatcher dampeningly. Sloan clients did not approach the bank with numbers jotted on cocktail napkins. But mention of Mrs. Laverdiere gave him a chance to broach the nonquantifiable. "How did they all survive the first round?"

"No sweat as far as I could see. Maybe ASI didn't realize how many relatives there are on the payroll, and maybe the Eckers didn't know how stratified places like ASI are, but that's about it."

"In other words, the standard misgivings," said Thatcher. "I suppose they'll get over them."

"They'll have to," Nicolls told him. "The brass is going full steam ahead. They've set up a meeting in Princeton to start on the real dog work."

Thatcher's head came up. "At which the Sloan will be represented," he said militantly. "Whether Ecker wants us or not."

This firmness was wasted. Both Ecker and ASI wanted and expected their financial advisers aboard.

"Splendid," said Thatcher.

Charlie added a cheerful coda. "So everybody's happy as a clam about merging?"

The question was designed to make bankers smile. Especially in family firms, there is always someone whose nose—or pocketbook—is put out of joint.

Ken painstakingly reviewed his gleanings in Connecticut. Then he said, "I honestly don't know how to answer that. It's obvious that the Laverdieres—and Alan Frayne, for that matter—are in a tricky position. There's always the chance that they'll lose their jobs, and cushy jobs at that. And naturally they won't make the big bucks that Conrad and his children will. On the other hand, none of them is clutching up, at least as far as I saw. The only one making noises against the merger is a kid from ASI named Vic Hunnicut. He bent my ear explaining why it's a major mistake. But then he's got his own reasons."

Charlie was the Sloan's student of humanity in all its guises.

"Doesn't fit in with his agenda?" he asked ironically.

"Put it this way," Ken responded. "If ASI decides to put their own man in at Ecker, logically it would be one of their assistant division managers, which is what Hunnicut is. But there are probably a whole slew of them with better qualifications than a chemical engineer, and it's eating him up."

An opportunity for someone else, Thatcher reflected, could be as bad as a defeat for one's self. "Terrible thing, too much ambition in the young," he pontificated.

Ken Nicolls prudently held his tongue, but Charlie advanced another alternative.

"Or else it was too much beer talking."

Thatcher pushed on to the details of that forthcoming meeting.

"Day after tomorrow," said Nicolls. "At ASI, this time."

"That's quite a pace they're setting," Thatcher mused.

But as he spoke, the phone in Nicolls's office was ringing to announce an unforeseen complication.

Chapter

A HOT PROSPECT

Earlier that morning, long before dawn, a solitary patrol car had been cruising the back streets of Bridgeport.

Sleet icing the windshield transformed the world into a gray murk. The only sound was the clanking of trucks already laying sand for the morning traffic. The car had passed most of the Ecker compound when the officer in the passenger seat spoke suddenly.

"Wait a minute. I think I see something."

The driver, simultaneously braking and scrubbing at the misted glass, brought them to a skidding halt.

"That's smoke!" he rapped out.

His companion was already busy on the radio.

Minutes later the first fire truck arrived and, thanks to a computer memory bank, a fire captain was able to allay some anxiety.

"You can relax, boys, Ecker's a clean operation. There won't be any toxic fumes."

"Thank God!"

The two policemen had not been looking forward to the evacuation of a ten-block area at 4 A.M. in below-freezing conditions.

"Besides," the captain continued, stepping aside to permit passage of several hoses, "that building contains offices. We're in luck. Do you know where they keep the sign with Doug Ecker's number?"

"Right by the main gate."

Like all such operations, the Ecker Company posted a number to be called in cases of emergency. But this one had undergone revisions. The original line was now a solid black bar with a new number embossed below.

"That's right," the captain reminded himself. "Doug Ecker's not here anymore."

When the phone roused the Laverdieres in Westport, they reacted differently. Bob, his pajama top cast aside, slowed to a standstill.

"Conrad's got to know about this. I'd better call him right away."

Tina, already snaking into blue jeans, froze.

"No," she said instinctively.

Now, if ever, was the time for Bob to display leadership. She could not, however, put it that way.

"We don't want to yank Conrad and Alice out of bed at this hour," she continued. "They're old, Bob, that's why our number is on the sign."

The Laverdieres, therefore, were the sole representatives of the Ecker Company on the scene a short time later. But they joined a large crowd. The same people who would have resented forcible evacuation had succumbed to the attraction that all fires exercise. These hardy bystanders, stamping their feet against the cold and muffling their ears, were gaping at a more dramatic spectacle than the thin plume of smoke spotted by the patrol car. Now there were spotlights trained on the building and ladders erected to the upper floor. Fountains of water gushing from every angle had created a widening lake of mud through which booted firemen squelched with their hoses. Even Bob Laverdiere paused in his progress to join the chorus of appreciative moans when tongues of flame burst through a window.

But he and his wife were all business when they succeeded in pressing their way to the fire captain.

"How bad is it?" Bob demanded anxiously. "Will it spread to the other buildings?"

"Is Gus all right?" cried Tina.

The captain was reassuring.

"You the Ecker people? It's not too bad. That fire isn't going anywhere else and we'll have it out pretty soon. We won't be able to tell the final score until things cool off. Of course, between the fire and the water, there'll be a hell of a lot of interior damage. As for Gus, he's okay. He was here a couple of minutes ago."

Gus, the night watchman shared by Ecker and several smaller companies, was already approaching.

"God, I'm sorry about this, Mr. Laverdiere. Everything was all right when I punched in there at two-thirty. But at four I was way over at Cummings & Tarboy. I didn't know anything was wrong until I heard the sirens."

This area of industrial Bridgeport was not a prime target for criminal activity, and Gus's duties covered a quarter-mile area.

Now that the human element was standing before him, Bob said the right thing.

"I'm just glad you're okay."

But Gus, conscientious to a fault, continued to justify himself. "There weren't any cigarettes or pipes smoldering when I was in there. I always check for that. And everybody had been gone a long time."

"Don't worry about it. There's just so much you can do."

"But how could it have happened?"

That was what Conrad Ecker wanted to know. As he was a notorious early riser, by six o'clock Tina had abandoned her qualms about descending on his household with the bad news.

"You'll have to ask Bob," she said wearily, cradling a mug of coffee to encourage the warmth seeping through her frozen fingers. "He's the one who talked to the fire people."

Bob was in the hall, calling Alan Frayne.

"It sounds as if it could have been a lot worse," Conrad muttered.

"I suppose so," she agreed, raising her hands to slick back her sodden hair. Relieved of that dramatic black frame, her stark features became almost nunlike over the high rolled collar of her fisherman's sweater. "Only the boiler house was involved. Bob says there won't be any shipping or production delays. It's the records that are a shambles."

That sounded almost too good to be true.

"How's he going to ship without purchase orders?"

"He has duplicates over at his end." Tina shrugged, impatient with nonproblem areas. "I'm worried about the financial data. Oh, I'm not saying we can't reconstitute the files. But it's going to be a monster job."

Conrad had never been one to cry over spilled milk.

"Can't be helped," he said before turning to the door. "Did you get Alan?"

"Yeah, he's coming right over," said Bob Laverdiere, sinking into a chair and wordlessly accepting a cup of coffee.

Conrad was considerate enough to delay his next question until Bob had taken several sips.

"What are they saying about the cause of the fire?"

"They can't tell yet. As soon as things cool down, they'll be looking into it. The sprinklers never went on, and the captain did ask me about our electrical wiring."

"We had a lot of rewiring done when I moved my computer operation there," Tina recalled. "I don't remember off the top of my head exactly how much we had done, but I can look it up . . . damn, I can't. Not now. But the Markham outfit did the job."

Conrad was shaking his head.

"There's no need for you to work on it. The insurance company should be getting back to me in a couple of hours. They'll be sending their own man for the appraisal. I guess we can leave the question of how it happened to the experts."

They were still debating how soon they could start the clean-up when Alan Frayne pulled into the driveway and thrust open the door from the screened porch. In suit and tie, he was a sharp contrast to those waiting for him.

Tina might at least have looked modish except for the grimy patches staining her clothes and the wild disarray of her hair. Bob's bespectacled pale face rose incongruously above a ski sweater in vivid colors intended to accent a glowing tan. Conrad had yet to get dressed. Unshaven, in an ancient bathrobe and scuffed slippers, he looked every inch his age. His wife had somehow found time to don slacks and a flannel shirt, but an old-fashioned hair net still confined the waves of her permanent.

The occupants were the only discordant elements in the kitchen. Everything else was clean and bright and orderly. Being the woman she was, Alice Ecker had met the emergency by not only filling the coffeepot, but by plucking from the freezer a tray already filled with the dough of cranberry muffins. Now the air was pervaded by the aroma of home-baking while a bowl of beaten eggs rested on the counter.

"Sit down, Alan. Breakfast will be ready in a minute," she invited, plunking a skillet on the stove.

Frayne barely heard her. "I drove past the plant," he said in a worried voice. "It looks like a disaster area."

"Nothing's affected but the boiler house," Laverdiere reassured him. "The line will be able to come in and get to work just as usual."

"That's a relief," Frayne breathed, finally acknowledging Alice's coffee. "From the car I couldn't get close enough to tell whether my test lab had gone up. I'm sorry about your operation, Tina."

Tina, usually a tigress when it came to protecting her domain, was making a determined effort to look on the bright side.

"It doesn't seem like the right time to complain," she replied with a wan smile. "Not with the plant, the warehouse and the lab all in go-condition. That means everything can run normally while I get my end straightened out."

Frayne was sympathetic.

"Is it a total loss over there?"

"It's too early to tell."

Bob had now imbibed enough coffee to show signs of life. "They wouldn't let Tina go any farther than the doorway," he volunteered. "She just got to peek inside."

Alice Ecker, now distributing laden plates, joined the conversation.

"Remember that fire at the Jardines, Conrad?" she said, referring to neighbors of the distant past. "They said it would have been easier to rebuild from scratch than to go through all that remodeling. Maybe you'll get a brand-new building out of this, Tina."

"I wouldn't object," Tina admitted, "but I'd rather have my records. And, Alan, it looked as if the files from the test lab went up in smoke, too. Is that going to be a problem?"

But Alan, large and genial, remained placid. Reaching for a second muffin, he said, "Don't worry. We've got the lab books for everything we're working on now. The stuff over in your building was historical. I would have liked to have it available, but it won't kill me to do without."

"There, now," said Alice comfortably. "Nobody likes a fire, but you all seem to be coming out of this one pretty well. No one was hurt, which is the main thing, and you can go on operating. You should be counting your blessings."

Frayne grinned at her. "Things aren't bad enough for that, Alice. Still, I agree that we've plenty to be thankful for. Poor Tina's the only one struck with a major headache. That is, always assuming our insurance is up-to-date."

Some aspects of business did engage Conrad Ecker.

"It sure is," he barked. "Doug insisted we upgrade at the last renewal."

Bob Laverdiere was rueful. "And I said you were overdoing."

"You said we were God's gift to the insurance company," Conrad riposted.

Swiftly Tina introduced another wrinkle: "I know we're all right about building damage, but what about the costs due to document destruction?"

"That's covered, too. You're going to be able to get yourself a team of temporary accountants and shell out for a pack of overtime," Conrad informed her, then added: "No thanks to your husband."

This time it was Alan Frayne deflecting them.

"Say, I spoke too soon when I said it was back to normal for everybody except Tina. What about your meeting with ASI, Conrad? Now that our financials are a pile of ashes, are you going to have to postpone?"

Scrambled eggs and cranberry muffins had restored Tina to her usual crisp dispatch.

"Absolutely," she said. "It will take more than a month to put together what we've lost, even with all the extra help Conrad says I can lay on."

"A month?" Conrad was dismayed. "That's too long."

"I'm afraid there's nothing we can do about it."

He was not prepared to accept this.

"The whole deal will be off the burner in a month. I don't say we're going to want it, but I sure as hell intend to find out."

Tina sighed. "Look, Conrad," she said, pushing aside her plate and leaning forward to explain. "This will be a complicated process of fitting together snippets of information from old invoices and tax returns and sales orders. It can't be done overnight."

She reduced him to silence, but not to acquiescence. For several moments Conrad brooded over his coffee. Then he looked up.

"I'm not talking about all that detail. It isn't as if we don't have other sources available. Hell, the outside auditors were in here two months ago for the quarterly report. And Bob's got sales summaries at the plant. ASI doesn't care that we shipped three hundred and fifty coffeepots to a buyer in Chicago on November eleventh. What we'll do is put together the major stuff, enough to go on with. You get busy on that and I'll postpone ASI for forty-eight hours."

Tina had her mouth open to protest but Conrad swept on authoritatively: "Right, Tina?"

"Right, Conrad," she echoed with reluctance.

It was Alice, curiously enough, who produced the next item to be addressed.

"And while all this is going on, Conrad, don't forget about finding out how this started. And see that it never happens again. Somebody could have been hurt."

There were some priorities Conrad did not argue with.

"Don't worry, honey, the insurance investigator will be telling me about that."

But the first person the insurance investigator spoke with was the fire marshal.

The marshal had learned that it paid to know the financial background before setting foot on burned-out business premises.

"No," the investigator reported. "The Ecker Company isn't in trouble. In fact, the opposite. They're coining money."

"I always ask when the sprinkler system doesn't work, but I didn't think that could be it," the marshal confessed. "Not with the kind of fire they had. If they'd needed cash, they would have burned down the plant."

The investigator nodded. "From what you tell me, they're not even going to be able to put in a claim for production stoppage."

"And the boys on the truck didn't see anything suspicious while they were in there. Of course, with a low-grade fire like this one, there wouldn't have to be anything out of the way. It could have been done with a kitchen match."

"Sure, but you need motive as well as means. If this boils down to simple document damage and minor reconstruction, the Ecker Company will just be left with a first-class pain in the ass."

The marshal had slumped down in his chair and was scrutinizing the ceiling. "The trouble is, you insurance companies only look at it from one angle."

"You mean our payout is affected only if the Eckers torched the place, while you've got to worry about the other possibilities? But we like to discourage this sort of thing, no matter who does it. Disgruntled employees, competitors, personal enemies . . ."

". . . hostile neighbors, ex-boyfriends," the marshal joined the chant. "God, the list goes on forever."

In spite of the extent of their combined experiences in the sordid world of arson, neither of them thought to include potential merger partners in their catalog.

Not yet.

Chapter

TRADING FLOORS

News of a delay in the summit meeting between ASI and Ecker was received by most of the participants with hardened resignation. In a world filled with grounded planes, twenty-four-hour viruses, and emergency root-canal work, everybody expects quirks in the timetable.

The only player seriously perturbed was Tom Robichaux, and when he and Thatcher finally embarked for their rescheduled trip to New Jersey, he whiled away the drive by sharing his misgivings.

"I don't like it," he grumbled. "This is no time to be losing momentum."

"They're not at a critical juncture," Thatcher pointed out. "This is just a preliminary get-together."

Robichaux shook his head. "It gives people time to think."

Thatcher fully appreciated that this was a process Tom had always viewed with suspicion.

"But it does tend to happen when companies are talking acquisition," he ventured on an apologetic note.

"You never know what they'll come up with," Robichaux said darkly. "The next thing we know, ASI could get edgy about this fire. Say it's too coincidental or something."

When Tom was well launched into the doomsday theme, there was only one practical expedient. Simply overleap him into even bleaker prophecy.

"You mean ASI will decide Ecker has deliberately burned down its record office?"

"Good God, no! Where would be the sense in that? ASI won't have any trouble finding out how profitable Ecker is."

"Then there's nothing to worry about."

But he was going too far.

"There's plenty to worry about," Tom retorted with a return to petulance. "You can always find objections to this kind of deal if you look hard enough. I say the thing to do is, get it over with and handle any problems later."

What he meant was, of course, get it over with and pay Robichaux & Devane their very hefty fees. Still, there was an echo of the old-fashioned matchmaker's contention that there was plenty of time after the wedding to discover any incompatibility. After all, this had been the guiding principle of Tom's hectic marital career. Thatcher did not presume to advise people about marriage but, as a banker, he held fast to the notion that would-be partners should acquire beforehand as much information as possible.

"Breaking up can be hard to do," he murmured. "I doubt if ASI wants to be quite that insouciant."

"Let me tell you, everything was going fine until now."

"No personality problems when they met face-to-face?" Thatcher asked, curious about the encounter that Ken Nicolls had missed.

"Oh, Pepitone and Ecker seemed to hit it off fine," Robichaux said perfunctorily.

In spite of the fact that Tom was one of the least perceptive men in the world, Thatcher listened with respect. As long as those precious fees hung in the balance, Robichaux would be alert to any potential threat.

And, undeniably, very few social lubricants rival the hope of mutual profit. It is this truth that makes international trade possible. With enough money at stake, business associates simply do not care about cultural differences. Which was just as well, because Thatcher suspected the chasm separating ASI and the Ecker clan might be wider than anything produced by a foreign language.

In the meantime, Robichaux's aberrant mind had switched to another grievance.

"And they call this Princeton!" he snorted as the limousine pulled into the last of a long row of industrial parks.

Technically his objection might have been at fault, but not spiritually. Apart from its mailing address, nothing at ASI suggested ivied halls or the storied past. The buildings were aggressively modern; the landscaping consisted of pachysandra and wood bark. But when Gardner Ives appeared to greet them, it was easy to visualize him residing on several gracious Princeton acres, complete with horses. He hailed Thatcher's presence as a sign of Ecker's seriousness of purpose.

"Delighted you could come," he began. "And once you send your people in, we'll cooperate with them completely."

If Ives embodied one familiar strain in corporate America, his executive vice-president represented another. Phil Pepitone had clearly risen from the bottom and was proud of it.

"It may not work out, Gardner," he cautioned. "Ecker's just coming to test the water."

Turning to Thatcher, Ives expanded, "Phil's the one who came up with Ecker. They never would have occurred to me, but the idea looks like a winner so far."

Pepitone produced a grin, but all he said was, "There's a long way to go."

Gardner Ives, however, continued to sing the praises of their choice. "I confess I was a little leery of Conrad Ecker at first. I'd heard so much about his being eccentric and all that. But I was very pleased with the way he sounded on the phone. He doesn't pretend to be much of a businessman. He says his son handled all that. He has, however, a very shrewd appreciation of the fundamentals. But then I don't have to tell you that. He's your client."

Any minute now, Ives would be describing Conrad Ecker as refreshingly down-to-earth.

"He's a client of the Sloan," Thatcher acknowledged. "But I only met him once several years ago. Of course a number of our people are familiar with him."

Thatcher did not feel it necessary to mention the intensive briefing from Milo Thompson.

"Well, they should be here any minute," Ives announced.

"They?" Thatcher wondered if the Ecker tribe moved en masse.

Pepitone explained that Mrs. Laverdiere was coming along. "She'll be huddling with some of our accountants."

"They tell me she's a very able person," Ives said ponderously.

"Yeah, she seems really on top of her job," Pepitone chimed in. "And a damn good thing, with this fire of theirs fouling things up."

Thatcher's ears were pricking. Was it simply imagination, or was the ASI contingent heaping praise on the wife to avoid talking about the husband? For that matter, was Ecker's choice of adjutant meaningful?

Apparently not, Thatcher soon learned. Conrad Ecker felt it necessary to explain why he needed any entourage at all.

"Don't see why we have to get a whole mob of people involved at this stage," he said, tactlessly ignoring the support personnel following Ives into the conference room. "But with this fire, Tina's the one who can tell your accountants what we've got right now, when the rest will be available, and what it will be."

According to a courtly Ives, Mrs. Laverdiere was more than welcome.

"And anybody else you'd like to have at our sessions."

"Sure," Ecker grunted, making it clear that went without saying.

But nothing could have been more obliging than his overview of the operations of the Ecker Company. He described the size and workings of his plant in Connecticut, the success of the enterprise started several years ago in Texas, and the current plans for its enlargement.

"I wasn't crazy about the idea when Doug suggested expanding outside our local area, but he was right as usual. We haven't had any problems with the manager he put in there."

Again Thatcher noticed that this casual encomium to the far-distant manager in Texas was not matched by a similar tribute to the nephew. Or perhaps Ecker felt that the success of the Connecticut plant was too well-established to require further comment?

Ecker was equally forthcoming about other experiments.

"Conrad, it says here that you've started importing some of your switches from Korea. Are you satisfied quality-wise?"

After due consideration Ecker said, "So far, everything's been first-class."

When everybody waited expectantly, he vouchsafed a little more. "But maybe they're making a special effort because it's early days. We keep watching."

Only on the subject of forthcoming innovations did he become evasive.

"I'm working on a couple of things," he admitted. "But it takes time to iron out the bugs."

Ives smiled benignly. "We're not asking for classified information, Conrad," he murmured. "We realize you have to be closemouthed about projects still in the design phase. And God knows, your product line is more than adequate for our needs. If there's anything more in the pipeline, we'd regard it as so much frosting on the cake."

A more polished man might have responded to the implied compliment, but Conrad simply stuck to the work at hand.

"The main thing, as I see it, is for Tina to get together with your bunch and explain the lay of the land."

"Of course, of course, I'll have them come in right now," Ives agreed.

But when the accounting team entered, Victor Hunnicut was trailing in its wake.

"I hope you don't mind, Phil," he said deferentially, "but I can't finish my report to you on the plant inspection without some answers. And when I asked Roy, he seemed to feel I'd better join you."

Roy, the senior accountant, added a slight emendation. "Well, I did say that Mrs. Laverdiere is the only person who can fill in the blanks."

"Fine, fine," said Pepitone largely. "Why don't we get that out of the way first?"

Brandishing a clipboard with extensive notes, Hunnicut began by asking the age of several major pieces of equipment.

Tina replied that she would not have specifics until the files had been completely redone.

Not surprisingly, Hunnicut's questions about service and replacement schedules produced the same rejoinder.

Evincing dismay, he exclaimed, "I didn't realize the fire had literally destroyed your basic documentation, Tina. They told me it was just minor damage. I hope we can make at least some progress on this."

When he doggedly pursued her into the realms of depreciation, Thatcher had to give Tina Laverdiere full marks for her conduct. Without the slightest loss of composure she turned to Roy and, soaring into the higher reaches of accounting, described her program for recovering this data. Thereafter, whenever Hunnicut spoke, she addressed her fellow accountants, sucking them into a discussion that was meaningful to them alone. As this systematic exclusion continued, Hunnicut leaned farther and farther across the table, while his voice became more and more hectoring.

The strange duel lasted a full fifteen minutes. Thatcher was unable to understand why. Even if Hunnicut was too myopic to see that Mrs. Laverdiere was gaining points on every exchange, he should have noticed the reactions of his own superiors. Phil Pepitone drummed his fingers on the table and Roy was openly restive.

"I think that does it for now," Pepitone said at last.

"If you say so, Phil," Hunnicut said grudgingly. "But, with the fire knocking out all the essential information, I don't see how I can come up with any conclusions."

"That doesn't matter," Roy snapped. "With Tina's guidelines, my boys won't have any problem. It may take a couple of weeks to get everything, but the major stuff is already available. Just leave it to us."

Pepitone was swift to follow his lead.

"Sounds like the right idea to me, so we'll let Roy handle it. Thanks for dropping by, Hunnicut," he concluded on an unmistakable note of dismissal.

And not a moment too soon, thought Thatcher, who disliked being forced to waste time. Hunnicut's entire performance struck him as self-defeating. Ken Nicolls would certainly have assumed it was designed to paint Ecker as incompetent. Instead it had given Tina the opportunity to flaunt one area of Ecker professionalism.

This made Thatcher's last glimpse of Victor Hunnicut all the more puzzling. In the stir caused by Roy's instructions to his team and their preparations to carry off Tina, the young man made his way to the door unnoticed. There he turned and Thatcher, shifting in his chair, saw the mask drop from those nondescript features to reveal a faint smile of satisfaction.

Chapter

AGGRESSIVE
DISCOUNTING

Whenever an enlightened CEO decides to emerge as a public benefactor, somebody else puts in the overtime. If, for example, ASI had sponsored a golf tournament, preparations would have consumed hundreds of man-hours before Gardner Ives could step forward to present the trophy.

But for five long years ASI's actual contribution to the enrichment of American life had been more cultural than athletic. This was the direct result of Ives's sister's third marriage. After husbands in the theater and the arts, Polly had rounded off the set with the managing director of a nearby public television station.

The wedding toasts were barely down when her lucky third seized on his new relative.

"Would ASI man the phones during your fund-raiser?" Gardner Ives echoed, liking the sound of it. "Why, of course. I'm sure we'll get an enthusiastic group to volunteer."

So orders had gone out, landing inevitably on someone who could neither dodge nor feint—in this case Wiley Quinn, one of Vic Hunnicut's fellow assistant division managers. Quinn knew from firsthand experience how precious time was to the average working couple. Without burdening Ives with any of the tedious details, he manfully performed prodigies of scheduling. He arranged for children to be picked up at day-care centers, he organized the reshuffling of car pools and, more than once, he ensured dinner for an ailing parent. He was rewarded every year by having Gardner Ives sweep into the studio and tell the world that it was a privilege for ASI to contribute its mite to the cause of quality programming.

Some things, however, were beyond Wiley Quinn's power to control. He could corral a respectable working party. He could commandeer food and drink to fuel their efforts. But he could not shanghai a TV audience.

This year the outlook was bleak. The New Jersey Nets, playing at home, were on a hot streak. ABC was airing a blockbuster movie. And, with Christmas looming, shoppers were deep into their frenzied countdown. It was hard to believe in viewers clamoring to write checks for the news in depth, for experts from stray fields of human endeavor, or for a mixed bag of BBC imports. About the only action Quinn expected that night was his own pep talk to the first-time volunteers.

"It seems simple enough," a young programmer said at the end of the instructions. "We just follow these guidelines."

An old-timer was cautionary.

"Oh, we'll follow them," she said. "But will they?"

Her forebodings were not put to an immediate test. Nonetheless Quinn, strolling around the room, was surprised to see his troops happily chatting in groups despite silence from the telephones. Curious, he approached more closely.

"Yes, but have you heard the latest?" a woman anxious to top her companions was whispering. "They're saying that Phil Pepitone may be on the take."

"Well, at least that would explain the Sparling business," a man said judiciously. "You know we're posting a colossal loss for them this quarter."

"But we picked them up years ago," someone objected.

"And we got taken."

Someone else pushed on to the inevitable corollary.

"You mean they were losing money at the very time Phil suggested the acquisition?"

The expert shook his head portentously. "It sure didn't look that way, which means they were pulling a fast one. But Phil pushed them down the board's throat. And he must have had a damn good reason."

There was a pleased intake of breath as the group gathered its forces for another onslaught on Phil Pepitone.

Wiley Quinn listened and wondered. He knew all about routine backbiting. But generally ASI was not a hotbed of malice. Partial enlightenment came from the back of the room, where he found another reputation being shredded.

". . . well, I agree with Vic," said a bespectacled youth from the controller's office. "Somebody should take a look at what Sam Bradley's been up to."

"Research isn't like production," retorted an engineer. "You can't guarantee results."

"Nobody expects R and D to meet any quota. But we've been pouring money into it, and Bradley's hired some good people. When that goes on for years, something should come out."

"But nothing has," a plump woman pointed out.

"Nothing for ASI. The question is, where's it gone?"

There were half-shocked gasps.

"You mean you think Bradley might have sold the worthwhile stuff from his lab?"

With a belated pretense of objectivity, the bespectacled youth shook his head. "I'm not saying that. But other people are. And it sure looks as if something fishy's going on."

Far from quarreling with this conclusion, everybody had an imaginative—and slanderous—variation of his own.

Wiley Quinn thought he was beginning to understand. He already knew that the potential Ecker acquisition was stirring up heat. He had not heard Victor Hunnicut sounding off about it, but he had heard him on plenty of other subjects. And it stood to reason that Hunnicut, having no chance himself, would be opposed.

"Nerd," he said to himself, with the automatic superiority of an ex-quarterback from Bates.

Furthermore, Quinn's common sense was affronted. Opinions might differ as to whether or not Victor Hunnicut was a loudmouth. But sneaky attacks on upper management could lead him into deep trouble.

The prospect did not cause Wiley Quinn any pain. But selfish pleasure had to yield to good works. The phone rang in front of a file clerk.

"Me first," she exclaimed, snatching up the receiver. "May I help you?"

Within seconds she was in difficulties.

Clamping a hand over the phone, she hissed to the room at large. "He's pledging ninety dollars, but he wants the sixty-dollar gift. Can we do that?"

The wayward public continued to make difficulties throughout the evening. Thanks to a recent Al Jolson retrospective, one of the lures was a Jolson album.

"But I don't want it unless it has 'You Made Me Love You, You Dog,' " an elderly male voice enunciated. "Otherwise I want the book on lions."

The volunteer was a young woman who knew all about the saccharine music of the older generation.

"Are you sure you have that right?" she asked indulgently.

The voice, becoming arctic, said the whole world knew that song.

Shaken, she agreed to check for him.

A cheerful young programmer thought he was equal to anything.

"Do the T-shirts run large?" he repeated. "Well, I don't know, but I do know my wife bought a small and she's . . ."

He listed his wife's dimensions, then fearlessly sailed onto the far more delicate ground of weight distribution.

His caller, equally uninhibited, responded in kind, taking him well beyond his depth.

"Maybe I'd better ask one of the women here," he said cautiously.

Only after muffling his receiver did he turn to the old-timer.

"She takes a 38-D bra and she wants a T-shirt, for Chrissake!"

"Tell her to order a large."

"Are you sure it shouldn't be an extra large?"

"Not in a man's size."

"But these are unisex," he protested.

Irene's scorn was crushing. "That's what unisex means."

"Oh."

Victor Hunnicut could have learned a lot about the unpredictability of human behavior simply by manning a phone that evening. It would have disabused him forever of the notion that he could expect his scandal-mongering to run in tidy, preordained channels.

The lower echelons at ASI, like their superiors, were

really interested in the place where they spend half
their waking lives, not some unknown outfit in Bridgeport. Hunnicut would have been disappointed to discover that the Ecker Company was barely mentioned.
For all practical purposes Bob Laverdiere and Alan
Frayne did not exist. Instead almost every conceivable
wrongdoing at ASI was being canvassed.

By ten o'clock only one possibility had been overlooked. Then a change in programming gave the assembled throng its final chance.

It was the manager's habit to discourse, for eleven
months of the year, on the failure of commercial broad-
casters to offer adequate entertainment to the literate
mind. In their insensate search for profit, the major
networks relied on infantile pap. But when the time for
fund-raising came, the manager confronted certain de-
pressing truths. People pledge only if they watch. They
watch only if there is something they wish to see. And
so, for one brief nonshining moment, Jove had to nod.
Two nights ago it had been Al Jolson. Tonight it was an
old Fred Astaire. On the principle that if you can't lick
them, you adopt them, Ginger Rogers was being presented as an exclusive discovery by the discerning intel-
ligences at public television.

Lending his own prestige to this fantasy, Gardner
Ives spent his annual ten minutes chatting with his
brother-in-law about the rare treat in store for those
astute enough to be watching.

Two responses followed, hard on each other's heels.
The tempo of incoming calls quadrupled, justifying the
program if not its introduction. And almost every volunteer suddenly realized that one figure had escaped
his fair share of defamation.

"You know," said someone during the first break in
phone activity, "when you come to think of it, Phil
Pepitone isn't the only one who's been touting Ecker."

"That's absolutely right. Phil just proposed it, but it's Mr. Ives who's been really gung ho."

Wiley Quinn could scarcely believe his ears when he heard what came next.

Chapter

TALK ON THE STREET

Things being what they are, Phil Pepitone heard rumors about Sam Bradley before he heard rumors about himself. At first he was inclined to dismiss them out-of-hand, although amused by the notion of Bradley running a scam.

Pepitone, however, was a veteran of many power struggles who instinctively distrusted coincidence. Allegations of misconduct within ASI's product-development staff could be attributed to Bradley's usual enemies. But coming just now, when ASI and Phil Pepitone were actively pursuing the Ecker Company, they made him uneasily consider linkage. Were all these brickbats really aimed at Sam Bradley?

As usual, when confronted by uncertainty, Pepitone sought counsel from his closest confidante. This did not entail leaving his own quarters. He had risen through the ASI ranks carrying his secretary with him. Pepitone and Irene had grown middle-aged and overweight together.

"I've always thought Sam was a washout," he began, "but I've never thought he was a crook. Still, I suppose anything's possible."

Irene's role was to let him ramble, then punch holes where necessary.

"Just how possible is it?" she asked. "They've got security over at the lab, don't they?"

ASI took all the usual precautions. Yet the question was not altogether rhetorical.

"It's a funny thing," Pepitone mused aloud. "But you don't do as much checking on a man when he claims to be a failure instead of a success. Security would tighten if Sam said that he was sitting on the biggest thing since the light bulb—not that that's likely. But I can see the whole system at the lab needs work."

"Do it very, very tactfully," she warned him.

He smiled, acknowledging an old joke. Irene had been softening Pepitone's rough edges for a long time.

"I'll figure out some kind of program, then you can figure out how we sell it," he promised.

"No problem," she said confidently. "I'll manage somehow. But, Phil, that won't take care of what's already happened."

He scratched his jaw reflectively. "We don't know that anything has happened. I'm just addressing a flaw in the system. But, for all I know, this talk may be a lot of garbage. Maybe Sam's clean as a whistle. I wouldn't prejudge anybody because of loose talk."

This attitude was reinforced at four o'clock, when Irene returned with her latest gleanings from the rest room.

"They're saying what?" he bellowed.

Without change of expression, she repeated the speculations that had startled Wiley Quinn.

"They're crazy," Pepitone muttered.

Irene always gave him a few minutes to adjust before offering advice.

"You'd better do something about this, Phil," she warned him. "And fast."

When Irene was worried, Pepitone knew he was in deep trouble.

"I will, believe me. And when I find out who's behind this talk, I'll kill him with my bare hands."

Sam Bradley was less combustible than Phil Pepitone. Furthermore, he was contemptuous of attacks on his ability. So long as he enjoyed Gardner Ives's confidence—and he took great pains to cultivate it—he remained untouched. Time, he was convinced, was on his side.

Yet the current spate of innuendo, repeated by a sanctimonious colleague who thought he should know, alarmed him. To be charged with mediocrity by people incompetent to judge was something he could dismiss. Accusations of criminal wrongdoing could not be shrugged off.

Unlike Pepitone, Bradley did not fly into a rage. Instead he withdrew to do some heavy thinking. Obviously one of his foes had decided this was the time to launch a covert attack. As he considered possible instigators and possible reasons, his hand unconsciously groped for a pen. Before he knew it, he was staring at a scratch pad with one bold black line: "The Ecker Company."

"Damn them to hell," he muttered, admitting to himself what he would deny aloud. Ecker was not only putting him into an invidious position, it was shadowing his future.

As a general rule Sam Bradley preferred to sit tight during crises, living to fight another day. Now he felt so threatened he prepared to abandon precedent.

First he dialed his home number.

"Eunice? Listen, something just came up. I'm going to be in the city until late. Don't keep dinner."

Questions were inevitable.

"No, it isn't anything important," he said, wishing this were true. "I'll be looking in on the Javits Center. We're exhibiting at the trade show this year and I want to make sure we're respectable."

But concern for the trade show was absent from his instructions to his assistant.

"Hugh, I'll be taking off now. Make sure Emerson finishes his report, will you?"

Urgent demands on Bradley's attention elsewhere were a commonplace to Hugh.

"It'll be on your desk by morning," he promised.

"Fine," said Bradley, already thinking ahead to routes north of the Javits Center.

There was no reason to conceal a trip to the Ecker Company, but instinct told him that there was nothing to be gained from broadcasting it, either.

Later in the day, after making recklessly good time to Bridgeport, Bradley found his forebodings justified. There were no vacancies in the modest strip of guest parking, so his final approach was on foot, through an industrial landscape light-years from Princeton.

Phil Pepitone and Victor Hunnicut, interested primarily in manufacturing capability, had taken their first exposure to the old mill in stride. But Sam Bradley found it unsettling in more ways than one. Harsh comparisons would inevitably be drawn between the track records of this nineteenth-century remnant and his own sleek facilities. Furthermore, he was used to maneuvering in the antiseptic gloss of ASI. Here, Bradley realized with dismay, he would not be dealing with a paper bureaucracy.

Within, however, Bradley was reassured to learn that

the distraction he had sensed in Tina Laverdiere's voice was due to the stress of housekeeping.

"As I told you on the phone, everything's still in a terrible mess," she lamented when he finally located her. "We're doing our best to pull together temporary quarters, but it isn't easy. Particularly when all the strong backs are loading our exhibits for the trade show."

Ready to seize on any occasion to establish fraternity, Bradley said, "I didn't realize Ecker was going to be at Javits. We'll see each other there. This is the first year ASI will have a display and we've been having problems, too."

"It's pretty much routine with us," she replied. "We've been there for fifteen years."

Bradley wanted no part of a situation in which ASI was cast as the novice. Fortunately, before he had to formulate a reply, a procession entered, burdened with yet more cardboard boxes. Supervising the parade was a stout, gray-haired woman.

"Just put them anywhere," she directed her helpers. "When Tina decides where she wants things, you can come back."

Tina introduced Marilyn Burrus, the office manager.

". . . but actually everybody's housemother here at Ecker. Marilyn, this is Sam Bradley, from ASI."

"Happy to meet you, Sam," said Mrs. Burrus casually. Then, after allowing him to shake her hand, she marched off.

Bradley, accustomed to rigid stratification at ASI, was taken aback. Seeing this, Tina explained the local hierarchy.

"Our job titles don't matter. The people who rank are the ones who were here at the beginning. And we've still got a lot of them."

Bradley thought he saw his opportunity. "That can be a strength—or a weakness," he said heavily.

Tina blinked and drew back.

"Now what can I do for you?" she said briskly. "When you called I didn't quite catch what you want. Is it the grand tour?"

"Oh, that would be too much of an imposition. What I'd really like to see is Ecker's test lab."

Before he could say another word, Tina cut in, "Fine. The man you want is Alan Frayne. I don't have phones yet, so I'll take you over."

Where Tina had been crisp, Frayne was blunt.

"Let's get one thing straight," he said after Tina introduced them and sped off. "I'll show you around the test lab. But there's not a chance in hell you're going to see our current projects. I know ASI's cozying up to Ecker, but until it's a done deal, I'm not handing over the keys to the safe."

Bradley recognized lines drawn in the sand.

"Good God, no!" he said reassuringly. "I know the rules of the game, and I'll tell you what I'm really interested in—how you develop Ecker's original concepts to the point where production is viable. With a one-man show, it's got to be different than what I'm used to. Any product that's already being marketed would do as an example. For that matter, I'd even be interested in the ones that were scrapped."

Relaxing, Frayne smiled. "Well, that's what my job is all about. Come to my shop and I'll show you the test-run material on the food processor. As for the no-shows, most of that stuff went up in smoke but we should be able to dig up something for you."

Happy to have banished the specter of industrial espionage, Bradley continued his questions as he was ushered down a corridor.

"No," Frayne corrected almost instantly. "Conrad takes things further than the drawing board. He has a rough working model by the time he comes to me. Then my crew gets busy mocking up a prototype, so we can get started on the gut work. We iron out the bugs, beef up the parts that will wear out, slim down the whole thing as much as possible, and design the casing. You could call that the first half of the operation."

"You mean you're still just dealing with a laboratory archetype?"

Pausing to stiff-arm a door that separated offices from utility space, Frayne nodded. "Then, if the thing has survived that far, I call in my pattern makers to design a production process. The final step is costing out the whole thing and making a decision. Often it would just be too expensive for the market. That's when I have to give Conrad the bad news."

Sam Bradley lived in a world where lines of authority were carefully demarcated. He was at a loss to imagine how you told the chief stockholder that his idea was no good.

"That can't be easy."

Frayne grinned. "I'm an old hand at it by now. Besides, years ago, we had a wonderful object lesson. I'd put the kibosh on his food smoker, and then someone else brought out almost the same thing. Damned if Conrad didn't take it to pieces. When he saw what they had to do to bring it in at the right price, he figured he'd had a lucky escape. Here we are."

They had arrived at Frayne's office, the most noticeable feature of which was a dazzling array of the entire Ecker line. In spite of himself Bradley was impressed.

"I've never seen them all together." His gaze swept from the famous coffeemaker to toasters, can openers, blenders, food processors. "My God, some of them have become real classics."

"People don't want everything to be trendy. Take this item, for instance," said Frayne, affectionately stroking the can opener with his finger. "People bought it because of those ratcheting jaws at the bottom of the housing. They really will open any jar in the kitchen. Of course a lot of clones came out in three or four years, but we'd already established a helluva reputation for durability. You could buy one of these things when you got married and never think about can openers again."

Bradley shook his head. "But what about the coffeepot? There are fancy European models that become popular all the time."

"Not really. They're all right to impress guests after dinner, but in the morning everybody wants something fast, easy and foolproof. Our only real competition is instant coffee. But come on into the lab and I'll show you the work we did on the food processor."

Fifteen minutes later Bradley was murmuring appreciatively as he laid down the last of the lab books.

". . . and the punch-button controls are more high-tech than what you did before."

"Just because Conrad's a rough diamond socially, people get the wrong idea. He took a first-class engineering degree and he keeps up-to-date. For instance, he had this great idea twenty-five years ago. You wanted to see something that didn't make it into production, didn't you?"

Frayne led the way to what looked like the standard Ecker blender. Then he produced a flexible power take-off that slipped into a small jack.

"There were a bunch of bits that you could use to grate nutmeg and squeeze garlic and shave chocolate. But it involved too much fussing. We never could simplify it enough. You're in luck on this one, I can show you the work we did. Normally our old lab books are over at the boiler house, but one of my people had pulled this file to take a look at it."

Bradley accepted this explanation blandly. Nonetheless he noticed that Alan Frayne was showing him a product made obsolete by the food processor.

"Very interesting," he said. Now might be the moment, he thought, to nudge Frayne into a discussion of the ASI inspection tour. "This must have been an eye-opener for Phil Pepitone. I know he considered a good many candidates for merger, but here at Ecker, he found a place that's ready to forgo short-term gains in order to concentrate on growth."

With a sardonic gleam in his eye, Frayne began to frame a reply. Then an internal censor clicked in and he bit down hard.

Sam Bradley dearly wished to know what that comment would have been, but Frayne, after briefly stating that Pepitone had been occupied with the production line, was making farewell noises.

"I'm glad you saw what you wanted," he said, rising. "Let me show you the way out."

This left Bradley with a haul that scarcely justified the effort of leaving Princeton. It did, however, reinforce his conviction that he had nothing to fear from the Ecker Company. Alan Frayne's chief value was his ability to handle a very old man. The threat came from ASI, as Bradley soon learned from the least-reserved member of the Ecker management.

Bob Laverdiere, taking the corner too fast, nearly cannoned into them.

"Oops!" he exclaimed breezily. "Sorry about that, Alan."

Before he could pass, Frayne detained him. "Have you met Sam Bradley, Bob? He's from ASI."

"Come to talk to Conrad?" Laverdiere guessed with cheerful nonchalance.

"Just taking a look around," Bradley replied.

"You guys are coming in waves," said Laverdiere. "Well, I've got to—"

But Frayne had clamped a heavy hand on his elbow, preventing movement. "Sam was just asking where Conrad does his work. Why don't you take a minute to show him? Meanwhile, I've got to get back to my desk. See you around, Sam."

As subtle as a herd of elephants, he handed off Sam Bradley, then disappeared down the hall.

Laverdiere was momentarily disconcerted, but he did his best to cover. "Glad to see anybody from ASI," he announced. "You know Phil Pepitone was here the other day?"

"Yes, and he was very impressed," Bradley replied automatically. He was busy being grateful that Alan Frayne, in his haste, had not identified Bradley's role at ASI.

"You'll laugh when you see what Conrad calls his shop," Laverdiere said. "It's down these stairs."

Sam Bradley had already seen enough of Ecker's ramshackle facilities. But Bob Laverdiere was the first talker he had encountered and, with any luck, an imprudent one.

However, conversation did not flourish as they stood in the doorway surveying Conrad Ecker's domain.

"Good God!" Bradley finally said, astonished. He was looking at working surfaces, tools and furniture that conjured up Thomas Alva Edison and Alexander Graham Bell. A thick layer of dust substituted for the sepia of ancient photographs.

"Conrad won't let anybody in to clean up," Laverdiere informed him. "Not that it really matters. He does most of his best work at home."

At ASI, the newest hire would walk out if asked to work in conditions like these.

"If I hadn't seen it with my own eyes, I'd never believe it," Bradley said with absolute sincerity.

"You and everybody else," said Bob Laverdiere. "People always say it's the kind of thing they've read about. Particularly if they come from big glitzy research operations like yours."

Bradley looked at him narrowly. Had Pepitone been discussing ASI's research division? "You haven't visited ASI, have you?" he asked.

"Nope," said Laverdiere. "But the way Vic Hunnicut described your equipment and staffing, it sounds like the twenty-first century compared to what we've got."

"I'm not surprised he bragged a little." Then Bradley added deliberately, "We're proud of our research facilities."

The dangling bait was successful. Innocently Bob Laverdiere continued his recollection.

"Of course it takes more than facilities. Vic was telling me that the main reason ASI is interested in Ecker is because they haven't come out with any winners themselves."

Victor Hunnicut! Bradley hastily readjusted his preconceptions.

"Did he now?"

Something in Bradley's tone made even Bob Laverdiere pause. "Of course Vic seems to be taking an interest in every aspect of Ecker, not just our production system," he said vaguely. "Tina told me he was even trying to get into some accounting problems that he really didn't understand. But then that's not so surprising. Phil told us he was one of your bright M.B.A. crowd."

This was intended as a tribute to ASI's management sophistication, but Bradley barely heard it.

"Hunnicut may not be as bright as he thinks," he was saying to himself.

"You mean you didn't know he was head of ASI research?" said Tina that evening when she and Bob were comparing notes over pot roast. It was a matter of pride to her that only true emergencies brought on Chinese takeout or pizzas. "I'll bet he was livid."

"Oh, I don't know," said Laverdiere, sponging up gravy. "He's pretty easygoing. But he was flabbergasted by Conrad's little cave. Not snooty, or anything, just surprised."

"Bradley can't afford to be snooty, from what they tell me."

Bob ducked the issue. "He seemed like a nice guy, though."

"You say that about everyone," she said with affectionate derision.

"Adolf Hitler? Saddam Hussein? That jerk Tom Herz, who stripped the pump this morning? I'm not the world's patsy, Tina."

He was, however, happy and contented enough to take kindly to his fellowman. He had already put Sam Bradley from his mind.

Not so Tina, visualizing Sam Bradley back in Princeton after learning that Victor Hunnicut had spilled the beans.

"He'll be mad enough to murder," she said with considerable relish. Then she corrected the exaggeration. "At least, he'll give Hunnicut a rough time."

"I don't know why you're so hard on Vic," her husband said mildly. "He's harmless."

Bob Laverdiere was just about to learn better.

Chapter

TO MARKET,
TO MARKET

The Jacob K. Javits Convention Center is enough to bring tears to Russian eyes. Located on the West Side, it is one vast marketplace where, depending on which trade show is in town, the visitor can wander through twenty-two acres of computers, dental equipment, shoes, or costume jewelry.

The National Association of Kitchen Suppliers brought out the usual hordes. Besides eighteen hundred exhibitors, the building teemed with salesmen, demonstrators, and buyers, all ready to deal. Since many audio-visual presentations were also vying for attention, the resultant din put a modern twist on Adam Smith. These days when men of the same trade gather, they make a tremendous racket.

Ken Nicolls entered this hive of esoteric activity with more confidence than he brought to most trade shows for the Sloan. He knew that his one-day exposure to the Ecker Company did not make him a match for a manufacturer's rep or a peddler of low-cost gadgets. But he had one ace up his sleeve. Three years earlier he and his wife had undertaken heavy research before remodeling their kitchen.

On the whole, he preferred to forget the subsequent ordeal. For months, chaos had engulfed the entire first floor. Men with jackhammers and circular saws arrived at dawn to pursue mysterious occupations. Every morning the Nicolls parents, bleary from lack of sleep, groveled on the living-room floor to plug in the coffeepot. Every evening they escorted their children to a restaurant. But grim and expensive as the entire process had been, it had left a useful legacy. Ken could approach his current task as a knowledgeable consumer.

Before an hour had passed, he realized he was deluding himself. Unbelievingly, he stared at a refrigerator equipped with a control panel worthy of the Concorde. Even microwave ovens had soared into complexity beyond his comprehension. Worst of all, however, was the display of kitchen cabinets. Here Nicolls discovered that there was some fatal, although unspecified, flaw in his own hinges.

In fact, Ken was as much at sea in the world of range hoods and dishwashers as he would have been in the midst of milling machines or smokestack scrubbers. The only familiar feature was the age-old interaction between buyer and seller. There was the usual electrical current when a major prospect appeared. There were the same smiles and offers of hospitality. And there was the nonstop chatter about warranties, credit terms, quality control.

Ken was two-thirds of the way through his tour before he recognized a face. ASI had gone whole hog, not only taking a row of stalls, but bringing out its big guns. Phil Pepitone was prominently to the fore, ready to beam at anyone, even a lowly junior from the Sloan.

"This is really something, isn't it?" he greeted Ken.

"Gardner's pleased as punch at the way things are going."

"You've certainly got an eye-catching display." Ken congratulated him.

"They're all interested in our water purifiers. The builders know that most new home buyers will be demanding them. A kitchen just won't be a kitchen without one."

Here was yet another shortcoming in the Nicolls establishment.

Unwisely Ken remarked that some people did not need a purifier. Before he knew it, he was inundated with a flood of statistics about the growing number of communities with water-contamination problems.

"Hunnicut did a good job on the background material, didn't he?" Pepitone concluded.

"Almost too good," Ken said unenthusiastically. "You make it sound as if we're all being poisoned."

Pepitone regarded this as a compliment. Nodding vigorously, he lowered his voice. "That's a buyer from National Hardware taking a look right now."

Ken could see Victor Hunnicut huddled with two men brandishing notepads, but the large crowd was around another ASI offering.

Pepitone had followed his glance.

"Our instant water heater," he explained. "Doesn't have the same market as the purifier but damned useful in certain situations."

Today, with everybody grist to his mill, Pepitone was treating Ken as an equal.

"Energy costs," he amplified. "If you've got a bathroom a long way from the main plumbing, you're wasting money. A source of hot water on the spot can bring down those bills."

Ken nodded sagely.

He had already abandoned his pretensions as home owner and decided to stick with his proven strength. A profit-and-loss statement would tell him far more about ASI than any amount of puffery from Phil Pepitone.

Phil Pepitone took to the trade show like a duck to water. Others in the ASI contingent had to get up to speed gradually. There is plenty of hard sell among private label suppliers, but it takes place a long way from the operating divisions.

To Wiley Quinn, what was going on around him looked a lot like hand-to-hand combat. He was one of many fleshing out the ASI presence, and to begin with, he was almost daunted by the pandemonium. But by the time lunch rolled around, he could see the joys of going head-to-head with customers. Furthermore, his tour of every rival garbage disposal convinced him that he—and ASI—could give them all a run for their money.

Gradually this satisfaction with the job he was currently doing led him to think about the future. That spelled the Ecker Company to everybody but Victor Hunnicut.

Wiley Quinn decided to take a look for himself.

But major shows are designed to discourage single-minded, straight-line courses. Quinn resisted the siren song of major appliances and dazzling countertops, only to fall prey to the gadgeteers. In spite of good intentions he joined a gray-haired man inspecting somebody's brainchild. It was a twenty-five-dollar attachment for a shop vacuum cleaner and the inventor was plying it over a mess of broken eggs.

"It'll never sell," Quinn's companion announced.

"But it seems to work," Quinn pointed out.

The gray head shook authoritatively.

"That doesn't make any difference. People don't bring shop vacs into the kitchen."

"Why not?"

"Don't know," the oracle replied briefly. "It's just so."

He considered the world at large before offering a generalization.

"People are funny, but there's no use fighting them. You've got to go along with the way they do things."

It was something that ASI should remember, Quinn reflected, now that it was leaving the safety of private labels to deal directly with a quirky, irrational public. And this was a talent that the Ecker Company had already mastered.

Five minutes later, when Wiley reached his goal, he was unashamedly eavesdropping on nearby conversations.

"Too bad Conrad hasn't come up with a new product this time around."

"Well, you can't expect one every year. God knows, when he does bring something out, it's a winner. We've been selling that food processor of his like hotcakes. And restocking isn't a problem because his delivery dates are reliable."

"The only thing we have against him is his advertising budget."

The first speaker almost snapped his reply. "Conrad doesn't have one."

In the ensuing exchange Wiley learned that the Ecker Company was notoriously frugal in this matter. Twice a year, during the houseware sales, they cut prices and contributed to newspaper supplements. That was it. Otherwise, the world was expected to trot forth and buy Ecker products without further inducement— and it did.

"As for that bottle warmer of his, people get one before the baby comes."

Quinn took due note of these opinions. Unlike little Victor, the people in closest association with Ecker didn't think it was a troubled company. Quite the contrary. Production, delivery, and quality control were all fine.

"Anything I can help you with?" said a large man who noticed Quinn's immobility. "Alan Frayne's my name."

Quinn introduced himself, then added, "They say your food processor's something special."

Frayne grinned. "Never seen one? Here, let me show you."

Guiding Quinn to the stack of boxes behind the stall, Frayne continued, "I'll bet they're disappointed that there's nothing new for the show this year. The thing is, Conrad's never short on ideas, but he's such a damned perfectionist, and you can't blame him. We've spent a lot of years building the Ecker name."

To illustrate, he produced the famous processor. "Look at this. Everybody else has a slew of separate cutters. Conrad built them all in, so they move in relationship to each other. You just punch in the configuration you want. Nothing to store, nothing to lose."

Quinn remembered a frustrated search for the tiny wrench that unjammed the disposal he himself produced.

"Of course, there's concern about Conrad's age," Frayne conceded, "and we all know he won't be around forever. But he's still got plenty of surprises for the trade up his sleeve."

Absently Quinn nodded. Taking shape in his mind was a new ASI division managed by someone with engineering skills just like his own. Contributions from Conrad Ecker would be gratefully accepted, but they would not be essential. This rosy picture evaporated at the sound of an all-too-familiar voice.

"Hello, Wiley. This is Ken Nicolls from the Sloan. We thought we'd like to see the Ecker exhibit."

As Victor Hunnicut nodded to Alan Frayne, Wiley braced himself.

"Nice display you've got here," Hunnicut commented. "ASI's got a lot to learn about this sort of thing."

Frayne sounded more wary than gratified. "Well, Ecker's been doing it a long time. It's not that hard."

"Oh, when you've licked a problem, it always looks easy."

Smoothly Frayne passed on to salesmanship. "Have you seen the Ecker toaster? This one went like clockwork from inception to production."

The toaster featured four normal slots that could be transformed into two extra-wide slots.

"It's amazing what people want to put into these things nowadays. Scones, muffins, croissants, you name it."

Ken, who harbored a passion for thick raisin muffins, momentarily forgot his vow to add nothing to the Nicolls kitchen for at least five years.

"We've been using a toaster oven," he said, leaning forward in interest.

Frayne smiled. "There's a war on for countertop space. Now that everybody has a microwave, Conrad says the toaster oven is on its way out. And speaking of Conrad, there he is and he's signaling. You'll have to excuse me."

Watching Frayne cross the hall's main concourse, Quinn saw with a shock that he was joining the elderly oracle about shop vac's.

"Boy, Ecker's really something," he said unguardedly.

"Are you crazy, Wiley?" Hunnicut said without bothering to lower his voice. "So they can mount a fancy display booth! What about the rest of it? Maybe ASI could make something of their operation, but is it worth the effort? Look at what we'd have to do just for starters—throw out that wimp of a production manager, make everybody else start to toe the line and keep a pretty sharp eye on that bitch who's in charge of the books. Don't be fooled by all the glitzy gimmicks you see here. The way you learn about Ecker is by hanging around Bridgeport like I did. And I found out plenty."

"Are you sure you didn't find out you're not up to the job?" Quinn retorted.

"Use your head. That isn't a company they've got up there, it's an old man's hobby. And ever since the son left, it's been ripe for the plucking. Ten to one, somebody's got their hand in the cookie jar. Why the hell do you think all their records were burned up?"

"Oh, for God's sake, so they had a fire. We've had a couple at ASI. These things just happen."

Hunnicut was openly contemptuous.

"Boy, are you living in a dreamworld. You don't even see that their great genius is past it, and Frayne's main job is holding his hand and covering up the fact that he hasn't brought out anything new. Apart from all the other troubles, ASI would have to mount a major R and D effort to take over from the old man. And Sam Bradley's already proved how good he is at that. We'd end up trying to use Conrad Ecker's rejects. Phil Pepitone is way off base on this one."

"I thought we'd get around to that." Over Hunnicut's head, Quinn shot Ken Nicolls a rueful smile. "Vic here's putting on a full court press to scuttle this deal. He's got everybody buzzing. Hell, the other night they were tearing Phil and Sam Bradley into little pieces. You'd better watch it, Vic. If the big boys find out what you're up to, they're not going to like it."

Hunnicut was stung. "Now wait a minute," he protested. "Everything I said was the absolute truth. I'm not responsible for what other people say."

But Wiley Quinn, almost without knowing it, had reached a decision. The Ecker Company represented a golden opportunity. There were better ways to fight for it than trading digs with a nothingball like Hunnicut.

"Do you think I don't know how you operate, Victor? Sure, you never accuse anybody outright. Instead you run around with a bunch of insinuations." Suddenly Quinn's voice lowered into a parody of Hunnicut's earnest tones. " 'Isn't it amazing how many great ideas have floated through that lab and how little has come out?' Then, inch by inch, you start zeroing in. 'Of course, all we know is what the company gets or, more accurately, what it doesn't get.' That way we can figure out for ourselves that those great ideas may have been sold on the open market so someone could line his own pockets. That's always been your style. Getting other people to put it into words for you."

Hunnicut was shaken by this assault, and by the corrosive dislike it revealed. Before he could collect his wits he was attacked from another quarter. While he and Quinn had been lobbing shots at each other behind the Ecker booth, the man demonstrating products had left by the front, to be replaced by a newcomer.

"Will you two shut up and get out of here," Bob Laverdiere snarled. "We don't need you sounding off in front of our buyers. And who the hell do you think you are, anyway? You talk big about turning Ecker upside down and throwing us all out. Where do you get off thinking you can do better? Look at your own record. You haven't established a name, you've never sold in the consumer market, you can't develop anything. In fact, you haven't done squat. From where I sit, you're a bunch of amateurs with big mouths."

Laverdiere's eyes were flaming with uncustomary pugnacity and his shoulders were hunched around his ears. This bellicose posture was wildly at odds with the barbecue apron that he was wearing and the skewer—already embellished with one perfect mushroom—that he clutched.

"You're absolutely right, Ecker's a great operation," said Wiley, hastily distancing himself from his colleague. "This bastard's poor-mouthing you because he's jealous."

Bob Laverdiere was not placated.

"And you can keep your filthy tongue off my wife! She's already told me how she flattened you in Princeton. I'll see you in hell before you get one foot in my plant. As for our fire—"

He might have gone on forever but he was interrupted.

"I've been looking for you two," said Sam Bradley, peering around a stack of boxes. "You've got some people from True Value at your place, Wiley, and there's a crowd looking at the purifier. We're trying to make an impact here today."

Hunnicut was only too happy to seize on this excuse and even Quinn preferred not to bandy words with Laverdiere in his present mood. When the two had hurried away, Ken Nicolls tried to pacify Laverdiere.

"Don't take this too seriously, Bob," he said. "The two of them are competing with each other, and they say more than they mean."

He received no help from Sam Bradley.

"It sounded like more than that to me," he drawled.

Laverdiere was not even willing to listen. "I don't give a damn what games they play over at ASI," he snapped, coming down the steps. "But it's time someone told Conrad what's going on over there, before the trouble spreads to us."

Bradley grimaced as he watched Laverdiere stamp off.

"Oh, that's just great. Now the old man'll be on the warpath, too."

"What's all the fuss about anyway?" Ken replied. "Hunnicut isn't important and Conrad must know it."

"Everybody knows it except Victor himself."

Mindful of his duties to the Sloan, Nicolls shook off his curiosity about the steel edge to Bradley's remark.

"Well, Ecker is our client. I'd better get over there and find out what the damage is. But I still don't see what Hunnicut is up to."

"I don't know and I don't give a damn." Bradley's gaze drifted across the hall in the direction of the ASI display. "But I do know that he's playing way out of his league. Victor doesn't have a clue how rough things can get."

Chapter

WORKING STIFF

Blundering across the main aisle, Bob Laverdiere scattered everybody unlucky enough to be in his path. All he could see with any clarity was the whole structure of his life crashing down in ruins.

Before overhearing Victor Hunnicut, Bob had tepidly accepted the ASI merger as a necessary evil. There would be inconvenient summonses to New Jersey. There would be directives over unknown signatures. But basically Ecker would continue unchanged—safe, reassuring, comfortable.

Victor Hunnicut had just given Laverdiere a glimpse of hell—a hell with Hunnicut installed in Bridgeport, exercising absolute authority over everything and everyone.

By the time Laverdiere broke in on Conrad and Alan Frayne, he was incoherent with rage.

"What's going on?" Frayne demanded of Ken

Nicolls five minutes later. "I've never seen Bob worked up like this."

After one look at Laverdiere's face, Ken sank Hunnicut's remarks about Tina and the plans for her husband's future.

"Hunnicut was shooting his mouth off about how Ecker would have to be reorganized," he said vaguely.

Mild as this rendition was, it made Conrad stiffen and sent Laverdiere into orbit.

"Reorganized!" he choked. "He's going to toss me out and make everyone else toe the line. Not to mention that Tina doesn't measure up to his high standards."

"Look, Bob," Alan Frayne urged, trying to stem the tide, "we don't even know that Hunnicut is going to have anything to do with us."

"He sure as hell thinks he will. And that other one who was with him—the big one—he was—"

"You mean Wiley Quinn?" Frayne interrupted with a puzzled frown. "But he liked what he saw."

"He didn't agree with everything Hunnicut said, but he was taking it seriously. And they both know more about their company's plans than we do. Why should ASI tell us a damn thing? They're not interested in Ecker. They just want to buy Conrad's ideas. Hell, they're so hard up they'll even use his rejects. But the rest of the package is expendable."

"Now wait a minute. Maybe—"

But the more Frayne tried to act the peacemaker, the more he activated Bob's memory.

"You haven't heard the half of it. We're all has-beens as far as that little shit is concerned. Conrad, you're already on the shelf, and Alan's no good for anything except being your nursemaid."

Conrad Ecker emitted a slow hiss that reminded Ken of a kettle coming to the boil.

"Oh, is that so?"

"Hell, he didn't stop there. He was even taking pot-shots at his own people." As Laverdiere continued to ride the waves of his fury, he brandished his skewer as if he were beating time. "Phil Pepitone has rocks in his head for choosing Ecker and, oh, you'll love this one. As soon as ASI was going to inspect our books, we burned them to the ground."

"We did what?" Conrad growled menacingly.

But for once Bob was paying no attention to his uncle's reaction. He swept on:

"You wouldn't believe the things Hunnicut came up with. According to him, he saw plenty of dirt hanging around Bridgeport after that inspection trip."

"You mean he didn't go back with Pepitone?" Frayne demanded. "He wasn't anywhere in the compound. What the hell was he doing?"

Ken felt bound to make his contribution.

"Well, he was having a drink with me, for one thing."

Three accusing glares instantly fastened on him.

"He was the one who did all the talking," Ken added hastily. "I admit he was poor-mouthing Ecker, but I thought he was just sour because he saw his ASI competition would have the edge."

"Then where did he find all this so-called dirt?" Ecker rumbled.

"I don't know. He was still in the bar when I left. Maybe he was meeting someone else."

Ignoring this side issue, Bob rolled on. "And he's got a humdinger about the lab, too. Not enough is coming out to justify what's going in. I tell you, nothing's beyond him. Hunnicut wasn't at our display for ten minutes, and by the end of that time we're a bunch of morons, Phil Pepitone has got something going on the side, lab developments are being sold on the outside market, and there's a firebug running loose. I tell you—"

"You mean all this was going on at our booth?"

Frayne cried incredulously. "Where anyone could hear it?"

"That's right," Bob rejoined. "In fact, it was some big shot from ASI who broke it up. For all I know, he got an earful."

Territorial considerations had never occurred to Ken as factors likely to heighten this audience's reaction. But as he saw Conrad Ecker's neck engulfed by a rising tide of purple, he remembered the pride that everyone at Ecker took in their display, the weeks of work that went into its creation, the crowd of important prospects that it attracted. Cudgeling his brains, Ken could dimly remember several figures in the background as Hunnicut and Laverdiere exchanged salvos. One of them had probably been Sam Bradley. If the others represented major Ecker accounts, there was justification for the muted bellow that caused surrounding heads to swivel.

"We'll settle this right now," Conrad Ecker roared, rolling up his sleeves for combat. "I'm going over there and lay down the law."

When Laverdiere moved forward, too, Frayne held out a detaining hand.

"Not you, Bob," he urged. "From what you say, we've had enough publicity. We don't want to turn this thing into a donnybrook. I'll go with Conrad."

He ended by casting a plea for support at Ken, who immediately obliged.

"You know I think he's right, Bob," he said. "About having any more fights in public, I mean."

"And you can see for yourself that Conrad's steaming. He'll settle their hash," Frayne pointed out. "I just hope he doesn't overdo. What we need over there is someone who'll calm things down, not get everybody worked up."

But Laverdiere, still seething, was not easy to dissuade. Like many men rarely stirred to belligerence, he persisted in hugging his grievances. So Alan Frayne, obviously champing at the bit, stayed put. In the end, however, it was a lucky reference by Ken as to Conrad's probable quarry that did the trick.

"Who the hell cares about Pepitone and Gardner Ives? It's Hunnicut who has to be settled," Bob snarled. "Oh, all right, all right. You go, Alan. I'll stay away."

Then, shaking himself free from Frayne's grasp, he stood there glowering.

By the time Conrad Ecker, magnificent in his wrath, stormed up to the ASI stalls, the only senior representative present was Gardner Ives. Sam Bradley had already done his work and done it with a skill that Victor Hunnicut might well have emulated.

Ten minutes earlier Bradley had plucked at Phil Pepitone's elbow, saying quietly, "We've got to talk, Phil."

Pepitone had made no rejoinder, simply allowing himself to be drawn aside.

"You've probably heard the talk that's going around about me," Bradley began.

Pepitone nodded, committing himself to absolutely nothing.

"I thought you probably had, and it's just as well. It makes the next part easier. Do you know that there's talk about you, too?"

This time the half-hooded eyes detached themselves from the water heater on which they were fixed to slide sideways toward Bradley.

"Yes."

The single monosyllable was devoid of inflection.

Patiently Bradley continued. He had not expected to be welcomed with open arms when he raised this subject.

"I figured I'd better find out how this all got started."

"We've both got enemies," Pepitone said evenly. "We both know who's out to get us."

"Sure we do, Phil. But we've had those enemies a long time. And they've never been slow to say that we're doing a bum job. But have you ever before heard anything like this?" Bradley was still not sure how much Phil Pepitone really had heard. Shrewdly, he began with the charges against himself. "When have they ever claimed that I was stealing from ASI, that I was taking R and D's best work to sell on my own? When have they claimed you were taking payments under the table?"

The calm with which Pepitone listened told its own story. He was not reacting to something new. Instead he was examining Bradley thoughtfully.

"Get to the point, Sam," he suggested.

Over the years, whenever they had taken each other's measure, each had recognized a fellow survivor. They had never become friends but their interests did not conflict.

"You're not going to believe this, but the trouble-maker is Victor Hunnicut, that little punk from purifiers."

Pepitone was openly skeptical.

"An assistant division manager? Are you sure?"

"I just heard him at work myself. The way I figure it, the twerp wants to pour cold water on the whole Ecker idea. There's no way it's going to do him any good. So he got the bright idea of claiming that there's something fishy going on. By the time he'd run that past the right people, some of our friends were only too happy to take the bit in their teeth."

Sam Bradley had no difficulty interpreting the expressions that chased across Pepitone's face. A major recalculation was in process. If each of the two men had been under separate siege, an alliance was out of the question. In their world, you did not clutch a man going down for the third time. But an attack by a conniving assistant manager was an entirely different matter. There was no danger of adding to one's enemies or upsetting the balance between factions. With the two of them acting in concert, the outcome was foreordained.

"My God, it's just possible, it could be the way you say. For Chrissake, I let him muscle his way up to Bridgeport," Pepitone muttered.

As Pepitone became convinced, Bradley could afford to relax.

"Kind of like taking a shotgun to a mosquito in the living room, isn't it?" he asked lightly. "And blowing out all the windows in the process."

If he saw the incongruous results of Victor Hunnicut's efforts, Phil Pepitone fastened on the element of presumption.

"That little slimeball. He's got some nerve, when he wasn't even aiming at us."

"How could he? He doesn't know anything about us."

"There isn't anything to know," Pepitone said emphatically.

"Of course not."

Their eyes met briefly in perfect communication.

"I'll have his hide for this," Pepitone promised.

Bradley's sober tone gave no hint to his satisfaction.

"Well, don't be surprised if he plays dumb. I just heard Wiley Quinn explain little Victor's tactics. He doesn't say anything outright. He just says things like: 'Isn't it surprising that Phil turned down all the better prospects in favor of Ecker? Makes you wonder, doesn't it?' He had the gall to tell Quinn he never went beyond the truth."

This had been a deliberate gamble and it paid off.

"He won't try that with me, he won't get the chance."

Pepitone's chunky figure and incipient *embonpoint*

normally suggested the middle-aged flab of the desk-bound executive. But now, without changing dimensions, that entire body had tightened into a menacing hulk.

"Well, you can't tackle him now," said Bradley, his height allowing him to glance over intervening heads toward the purifier stall. "He's not at his station."

"Then I'll track him down," said Pepitone, preparing to leave. "As far as I'm concerned, Javits has just become a boxing ring. Hunnicut can run, but he can't hide."

Arriving late, Alan Frayne missed the brisk one-two punch with which Conrad Ecker had scored a victory.

"I quite agree with you, Conrad," Gardner Ives was saying. "It should certainly not have happened."

He sounded as if he had been saying it for some time.

"And either you control your people, or you keep them away from mine," Ecker sailed on, unappeased.

"Of course, and I'll send Hunnicut over to apologize as soon as he turns up."

Conrad Ecker instinctively recognized a good curtain line.

"See that you do!" he barked, turning on his heel to march off into the crowd.

Alan Frayne took a deep breath. From his point of view, the situation was unsatisfactory. Establishing dominance was all very well and good, but had Conrad addressed any of the real problems? Was Hunnicut going to play a substantial role in Bridgeport if the merger became a fait accompli? Was he speaking for a significant party at ASI? What future was planned for Ecker's current management? Bob Laverdiere would certainly demand an answer to every one of these questions.

"You'll have to excuse Conrad for being so brusque, but you have to understand the provocation," he began, hitting a nice balance between conciliation and justification. "I'm sure he'll regret speaking with so much heat once he's had time to cool off."

"Naturally he was angry. Hunnicut had no right to upset your people."

"I wasn't there, but he certainly got Bob Laverdiere going."

Ives wagged his head regretfully. "I noticed that Hunnicut and Mrs. Laverdiere didn't seem to hit it off when she came to Princeton."

If that was all that Ives had noticed, someone would have to straighten him out.

"Conrad doesn't blow up like this because of a simple personality conflict. Hunnicut put the fat in the fire with what he was saying—"

"And where he said it," Ives added grimly. "It's outrageous that he should go over to your place and create a scene."

Now it was Alan Frayne's turn to be surprised at the insistence on territorial violation. But Ives was speaking as a fellow sufferer. ASI was also proud of its first-time-ever display, and Conrad Ecker's fury had been voiced without regard to bystanders.

"It's a shame we had this incident," Frayne said before they could again be sidetracked. "But all you have to do is explain things to Conrad. He'll always listen to reason when he's himself."

"The first thing he'll listen to is an apology. Hunnicut will get down on his knees if that's what it takes."

Once more Frayne tried to take them beyond gestures and on to substance. "That's fine, and Conrad will appreciate it. Then, perhaps, we could—"

But even though Alan's voice was decently lowered, Ives was still sensitive to the possibility of an audience. Casting an agonized glance around the ASI area, he spied a means of escape.

"Ha! There's Hunnicut back in his booth. I'll read him the riot act right now."

He bustled off with the air of a man about to resolve all difficulties, leaving Alan Frayne plunged in thought. It could scarcely be an accident that Ives had avoided answering a single one of Bob Laverdiere's questions.

Ken Nicolls had already given the trade show more time than it deserved and, in the process, considerably delayed his lunch hour. Encountering a colleague from the Chase in the same plight, he welcomed the suggestion of departure.

"I just have one thing to tidy up and it won't take a minute," he said as he spotted Conrad Ecker leaving a refreshment stand.

Ken knew that John Thatcher would wish to hear the result of the Ecker-Ives confrontation.

"Oh, it went all right," Conrad said moodily. "Ives is making that kid apologize."

Now that the heat of battle was over, Ecker seemed to have lost interest.

"And you'll be going on with the talks?"

Ecker shrugged. "Why not?"

That was all Ken needed. Happy at his release, he joined his friend.

"Not that way," said Ken's companion, redirecting their path to turn a corner. "One of our clients let me park my car with his trucks, so we take the freight elevator."

He then wiled away their passage by describing that client's latest breakthrough. It was a cooking top presenting an unbroken surface with the surrounding counter space.

By now Ken was openly hostile to space-age technology in the home. Punching the button, he said, "It sounds like a rotten idea to me. How do you know where to put a pot?"

The elevator doors opened and the question was

never answered. There, exposed to full view, was a human body, its knees drawn up and its arms flung wide.

Stunned, they stood motionless as a woman passing behind them began to scream . . . and scream . . . and scream. With her eldritch screeches ringing in his ears, Ken dazedly realized that it was Victor Hunnicut lying in that pool of blood, his features distorted and his eyes sightless.

And, as a final macabre note, protruding from his chest was a common kitchen skewer.

Chapter

QUALIFIED OPINIONS

For Ken Nicolls, the nightmare was just beginning. The security guards acted with speed and discretion. Within moments the hysterical woman was swept off to the first aid station. The immediate area was closed to traffic and rumors of an accident were circulating.

"You two will have to wait for the cops," a guard said, hustling Ken and his companion into a small office. "It may take a while. They'll want to identify the body first."

Still stupid with shock, Ken replied like an automaton. "His name was Victor Hunnicut."

The older guard paused at the door. "You knew him?"

Ken hastily rejected the suggestion of intimacy. "I met him once before today. On business."

"Then they really will want to talk to you."

Under other circumstances this conclusion might have seemed ominous. Now, however, Ken was engulfed by one overwhelming desire. He wanted to eradicate forever the image of what he had seen behind those elevator doors.

But as the minutes accumulated first into a half hour and then into an hour, different preoccupations emerged. Huddled wretchedly over a cooling cup of coffee and exchanging aimless remarks with his friend from the Chase, Ken began to examine his professional plight. Someone was going to have to tell the police about those top-secret merger talks, about the quarrel at the Ecker booth and, worst of all, about Bob Laverdiere brandishing that skewer with its ridiculous mushroom. But the longer the detectives spent on the floor, the more likely they were to discover these facts from other sources. With luck Ken Nicolls would not be the one who had to rat on a longtime Sloan client.

Luck had very little to do with it. Detective Inspector Leonard Giorni was skilled at isolating essentials. He inspected the gory scene inside the elevator, listened to the bare recital of a subordinate, and fastened on one feature.

"You say his wallet and watch weren't touched?"

"That's right."

"Then I'll start with the head honcho at ASI."

The head honcho, also known as Gardner Ives, reflexively produced organ notes when informed of Victor Hunnicut's demise. It was a tragedy, he declaimed, such a promising young man cut down in his prime. When Giorni asked about the last encounter with the victim, Ives mistakenly continued in the same vein.

"It must have been about an hour ago. I regret to say it was necessary to reprimand him for his conduct. Now I wish it had been otherwise, but that's so often the case after a death, isn't it?"

"Reprimand him about what?"

His eyebrows raised in astonishment, Ives became

evasive, but he was no match for the detective. Within short order Giorni was master of the basic situation.

"But I must impress on you, Inspector, that our preliminary talks were confidential. If any word of this leaks out, I'll hold you directly responsible."

Giorni looked at him pityingly. Didn't this pompous fool realize that a murder inside Javits was going to raise merry hell? The Mayor's office was already in convulsions. The Convention Bureau was demanding that the culprit be drawn and quartered. It was only a matter of time before the press appeared, ready for a carnival.

"Anybody else from your outfit hear this quarrel over at Ecker?" he demanded.

By now Gardner Ives was only too happy to direct the inspector to Wiley Quinn and Sam Bradley.

The stories they told were almost identical. Victor Hunnicut had regarded the proposed acquisition as a disaster. Unaware that he could be overheard by Bob Laverdiere, he had freely accused Ecker personnel of everything from rank incompetence to felonious conduct. He had been particularly nasty about Laverdiere's wife because a recent fire had destroyed her financial records.

Sam Bradley, however, added one further observation as he concluded his narrative.

"You could tell that Laverdiere was damn near out of his mind. Otherwise he never would have stamped across the hall looking that way."

"Looking how?"

"Oh, he'd been giving a demo of their rotisserie. He was wearing one of those silly barbecue aprons and waving a skewer with a mushroom on it." Catching sight of the inspector's face, Bradley hesitated. "I guess you had to be there to see how comic it was."

"I guess so," Giorni agreed.

* * *

Conrad Ecker did not look like a promising candidate for the role of murderer. Giorni found him sitting in a folding chair, his face lined with the strain of what was turning into a very demanding day. His management was ranged behind him in a protective semicircle, but he took charge immediately.

"I just found out the stretcher case was Hunnicut from ASI. What happened?"

"He was stabbed to death," Giorni said baldly.

"Christ!"

Ecker seemed to feel that this stark comment was sufficient. When Giorni asked him to confirm Ives's account of their exchange, he nodded.

"That's right. The kid was supposed to apologize."

"Weren't you surprised when he didn't show?"

"Not particularly. Ives was going to send him over when he turned up. Nobody seemed to know when that would be."

Giorni transferred his gaze to Alan Frayne. "That how you remember it?"

Scrupulously Frayne confirmed that was how things stood when Conrad had left.

"But by the time I was through, Hunnicut was back in his stall and Ives was about to tackle him."

When Giorni switched to Tina Laverdiere, she was no help.

"I did my stint at the display this morning," she explained. "Since then I've been looking at the other exhibits, so I missed all the excitement. Bob was just telling me about this little dust-up with Victor Hunnicut."

Giorni accepted this statement with reservations. A wife might wish to minimize her husband's hostile encounter with a murder victim. But it was also possible that it was the husband doing the minimizing.

"And now suppose you tell me about it, Mr. Laverdiere," he invited.

Apparently Bob Laverdiere asked nothing better.

"I tell you, Hunnicut must have been crazy," he said eagerly. "After taking a bunch of swipes at us, he went on to his own people. Wiley Quinn had obviously had a bellyful of his snide remarks about Pepitone and Sam Bradley. He said they all knew how Victor spread dirt. And Ken Nicolls told me afterward that Bradley was planning to do something about it. They were just as steamed with his dirty tricks as I was."

"So you admit you were steamed," Giorni asked placidly.

"Sure I was. He was sounding off in front of a bunch of customers. That's why I complained to Conrad."

"And I told Ives to put a leash on the kid," Conrad growled. "I don't know what he was up to at ASI. I just didn't want him around us."

Thus far the honors were even. ASI claimed that Hunnicut was harassing Ecker. Laverdiere claimed that Hunnicut was harassing ASI. There remained, however, a piece of material evidence.

"Mr. Laverdiere," said the inspector, "I want you to come and look at something for me."

Leading his unwilling witness toward the office he was using as a command post, Giorni maintained a flow of distracting questions. Had Hunnicut advanced any instances of Laverdiere's supposed incompetence? What form was Conrad's senility supposed to take? How precise was the accusation of arson?

He did not relent until they were standing beside a large desk. Then, with the smoothness of a conjurer, he whipped away a towel to reveal a skewer still thick with a dark-red deposit along its shaft.

"Oh, God, is that how it was done?" groaned Laverdiere, looking white and sick.

Giorni nodded. "They tell me you were carrying a skewer when you left your booth to find Ecker."

Bob swallowed several times, as if his throat were suddenly dry.

"That's right. I told you I was starting a demo. I'd already begun filling the skewer."

"Is this the same one?"

"How the hell should I know?" Laverdiere snapped with a sudden flash of defiance. "This is a kitchenware trade show. The place is stiff with barbecues. There must be skewers at twenty displays."

For the first time Giorni relaxed the pace of his questions. "Let's stick with the one you were carrying. What did you do with it after you had your session with Conrad Ecker?"

"I took it back to the booth."

"To give your demonstration?"

"No. I was just filling in while the regular man took his lunch break. He was due back in a couple of minutes anyway, so I dumped the skewer and went off to look at the show."

Bob Laverdiere was no longer mounting a show of resistance. His voice had become a thin thread and his final statement, instead of ringing with conviction, was lackluster.

"But I never used that skewer to stab Victor Hunnicut. It never crossed my mind."

Giorni sounded almost sympathetic. "We're going to want your fingerprints, Mr. Laverdiere."

On the principle of tidying up as he went along, the inspector did not wait for the fingerprint results. Instead he proceeded to the Ecker booth, where he found the regular demonstrator still hard at work.

"There wasn't anybody here when I got back from lunch," he replied to the first question. "But the skewers are all right. See, there they are."

Giorni looked at the tangled heap.

"Do you know how many you start with?"

"Of course. I get them myself, and I always bring two eight-packs. That's more than enough."

"Suppose you count them."

The demonstrator had to begin by unsnarling the tangle. Then he ticked each one off with his finger.

"One . . . two . . . three . . ."

But when he came to the end, he gave a cluck of dismay and began again to make double sure.

"Say, that's funny. There are only fifteen here."

Inspector Giorni had long since completed his own tally and his attention was now elsewhere. The unused foodstuffs were still in containers. The discards were presumably in the garbage can. Only one item was out of place. Lying on the counter was a single mushroom, its pristine white surface marred by a small brown puncture.

The demonstrator hastened to explain the disarray.

"That was here when I got back. It hasn't been cooked, so I was going to use it the next round with the rotisserie. So far I've just done the food processor and the coffeepot."

Giorni was still considering the possibilities of that mushroom when his subordinate arrived with preliminary fingerprint results.

"The top of the skewer was wiped clean. There is one print further down but it's in the upside-down position. We'll get the final lab results later, but Mahoney is sure it's Laverdiere's."

"So it could go either way," Giorni mused.

"That's right. Either Laverdiere stabbed Hunnicut and, when he was wiping the skewer, forgot he'd handled it differently at the booth. Or someone else killed Hunnicut and he *knew* he hadn't handled the skewer down there."

"There's another thing," said Giorni, going on to explain the solitary mushroom. "I'd give a lot to know whether that was still on the skewer when Laverdiere was complaining to Ecker."

The subordinate's voice was tinged with doubt.

"I suppose you could ask Frayne or the old man."

"Somehow I think I'll do better with someone more impartial. It's about time I talked with that banker they're keeping on ice."

When the door at long last opened to admit a figure of authority, Ken Nicolls hoped for the best. The inspector did not sit down, he had the air of a man going through the motions and his questions were all directed toward the discovery of the bodies. Had they noticed anyone near the elevator, did they know if the elevator had come from downstairs, had they any sense of how long the elevator had been in motion?

After a steady stream of negatives, Giorni turned to Ken's companion.

"Thank you very much for waiting. I know it's been a nuisance, but there's no need to keep you any longer."

With a sinking heart Ken felt the atmospherics change even as his friend was leaving. Giorni picked up the recently vacated chair, reversed its position and sat down with his elbows along the upper rail.

"Now, Mr. Nicolls, I've been hearing a lot about this merger and the fight between Hunnicut and Laverdiere," he began cozily. "Make yourself comfortable, because I think we're going to be here a while."

By the following morning, the NYPD was still not ready to bring charges. The newspaper coverage was regrettable, as well as uninformative.

" 'Bank Biggies Find Body,' " read Ian Nourse, who masterminded public relations for the Sloan. "I've put in a call to Ed already."

"Nicolls did find a body," said the general counsel.

Before agitation could lead Nourse to point out that Ken Nicolls was not a biggy, Thatcher intervened:

"This is simply a tempest in a teapot. The Sloan will

drop out of the picture once the police start releasing information."

"That," said the general counsel with a predatory look at Nicolls, "is what we want to be absolutely one hundred percent sure of."

Since Denton had already exhaustively reviewed Nicoll's treatment by the police, Thatcher considered this entire ad hoc gathering unnecessary.

"It was just Ken's misfortune to be in the wrong place at the wrong time," he observed.

Nicolls was too tired to be grateful for this vote of confidence. When he staggered home from the Javits Center, he had found a family demanding all the grim details and telephones ringing off the hook. This morning he had not taken off his coat before PR and the law department clapped him into custody and began grilling. Furthermore, he suspected the kindly John Thatcher really envied him for getting in on all the action.

". . . no, I was not at the trade show," Thatcher was saying. "As a result, I didn't learn what happened until I got home and Ken called."

"Well, thank God it was Nicolls, and not you," said Nourse.

"Yes, yes," said Thatcher somewhat testily. If Denton and Nourse insisted on making mountains out of molehills, he wanted them to do so in their own offices. "I'm sure that both of you are keeping on top of the situation."

Denton took the hint and rose to depart. "Why don't you come along with me, Nicolls?" he said from the doorway. "There are a few more things we might talk about."

Nourse, just behind him, indicated that he, too, would like another crack at Ken.

As Thatcher knew, loyalty is a two-way street. "I'm afraid I'm going to need him," he said, speeding his zealous subordinates out. When they were off the premises, he continued, "Don't worry, they'll simmer down. But just to be on the safe side—Miss Corsa, will you hold my calls for the next hour?"

When one of his proxies returned from a sensational murder, he felt that some curiosity was defensible.

"You know I met Hunnicut myself in Princeton," he said, plunging in without false shame. "He seemed to be playing some obscure game, and playing it rather badly. In his attempt to make Mrs. Laverdiere look incompetent, he succeeded in irritating his own superiors."

"I suppose you could say the same thing happened yesterday, except that Hunnicut managed to turn the heat up."

Before Ken could proceed further, Charlie Trinkham bounced in. Having brazened his way past Miss Corsa in order to hear the juicy details, he wasted no time.

"You look pretty good for someone coming off a third degree. Are you home free, or are the cops just giving you enough rope?"

Under Charlie's masterful touch, Ken produced his first grin in almost twenty-four hours.

"Skewers aren't my weapon, Charlie. I'm into guns," he said. "But seriously, I don't see how the police can waste much time on me. They've already got a bagful of prime suspects. Almost anybody who had much contact with Vic Hunnicut probably had a motive."

"Come now," Thatcher protested. "You're not implying that he was killed because of the ASI-Ecker negotiations, are you? He wasn't even a principal figure."

Ken replied by describing the hostilities at the Ecker booth in as much detail as he could recall.

"Of course at the beginning Vic was aiming his shots at this other assistant manager, Wiley Quinn," he amplified. "He had no idea that Bob Laverdiere could overhear, so he was really letting himself go. If you ask me, Vic thought Quinn had a good chance of getting that promotion if the merger went through."

It was a situation, Thatcher reflected, in which two young men might easily say more than was prudent.

"And Quinn would be resentful if the gold ring were snatched from his grasp," he murmured. "So I suppose he defended the Ecker acquisition."

"Actually he launched an all-out attack on Vic's methods. Apparently there are a bunch of rumors flying around ASI, thanks to Hunnicut. Of course I'm not familiar with the setup there," Ken cautioned with suitable modesty, "and I couldn't follow it all. In fact, when they began talking about suspicious no-shows from the lab, at first I thought they meant Ecker. But then it turned out that the main targets of the smear campaign at ASI are Phil Pepitone and a guy named Bradley who heads up their research. And he's the one who barged in at the end of the slugfest."

Thatcher shook his head at this further example of Victor Hunnicut's ability to antagonize the wrong people.

"And Bradley heard all this?"

"He sure heard enough. The last I saw of him, Bradley was saying Hunnicut didn't know how rough things could get."

From Charlie's point of view, things were looking more and more promising.

"Well, Hunnicut learned the hard way, didn't he?" he commented as he began toting up a list. "Now that makes Quinn and Pepitone and Bradley, for starters. And God knows how many more at ASI. You may be right, Ken. Maybe to know Hunnicut was to have a motive."

"But," Thatcher remarked, "none of them was waving a skewer around. I assume this point has not eluded the police."

"Hell, no. They kept digging at me about it," Ken remembered grimly. "That inspector wanted to know if the mushroom was still on it when Bob was squawking to Conrad."

This was a detail Ken had overlooked in his previous account and he was forced to expand.

"That makes sense," Charlie argued. "If that mushroom was still there when Laverdiere left the booth, then he's got some proof that he returned the skewer to the display. So what did you say?"

Ken looked unhappy. "That I couldn't remember. And I still can't."

"Another eyewitness who didn't notice a thing," Charlie said censoriously.

But Thatcher was interested in motive as well as means.

"A good deal would depend on the depth of Laverdiere's reaction to what Hunnicut was saying," he commented, turning receptively to Nicolls.

"I think he was in shock. You haven't met Bob, have you?"

When Thatcher shook his head, Ken continued: "He's an easygoing, sort of innocent guy who takes people at face value. He and Vic spent a lot of time together on the inspection tour. Bob thought they got along like a house afire. He was stunned when he found out how Hunnicut really felt about the Ecker operation—or at least what he was saying about it."

"But surely when his wife told him about her bout with Hunnicut in Princeton, Laverdiere would have been alerted," Thatcher objected.

"I'm not so certain." Slowly Ken dredged up his impressions of the husband-and-wife team. "Tina's a little protective about Bob and this was bound to upset him. If she told him anything, I'll bet she softened it up. Anyway, whatever she said didn't prepare Bob for hearing that his bitch of a wife burned her financial records because she had her fingers in the till."

Charlie whistled softly. "Oh, that's a good one," he said with the appreciation of a connoisseur.

Even Thatcher was blinking. "Hunnicut certainly had a gift, didn't he? I think you can add both Laverdieres to your list, Charlie."

"And I've already put the famous Conrad down," Charlie said, proving that he was no respecter of Sloan clients. "From what everybody says he's got a unique approach to life's little problems. Maybe he reacts to charges of senility with a display of homicidal vigor."

"Frayne didn't like that senility bit, either," Ken reported. "And it didn't help that Vic was talking as if he'd be the one in charge. The Eckers were already confused about him during the inspection. He made it sound as if he was doing more than an equipment report. And then Pepitone went out of his way to parade Vic's credentials. I could see Tina having second thoughts right then and there. And by the time Bob was shouting at them yesterday, Conrad and Frayne began to wonder, too."

"Did Ives straighten any of this out?" Thatcher asked curiously.

"I don't think so. From what Conrad said, they agreed to this formal apology, that's all."

To Charlie it sounded too rich to be real.

"What does it all boil down to? A kid who likes to spread mud, and the dirtier the better. We've all met that kind. But nine chances out of ten," he said regretfully, "it'll turn out that Hunnicut was sleeping with someone's wife. Are the cops putting any muscle into that?"

Ken's recollection of Detective Inspector Giorni did not suggest a man who overlooked the obvious.

"I'll bet they're working on his personal life right now."

Chapter

THE INFORMED
CONSUMER

"**G**od, it's hard to get a handle on this guy," remarked Leonard Giorni, standing in the middle of Victor Hunnicut's condominium in New Jersey.

The victim's next of kin had been identified as a widowed mother living in Salt Lake City and a married sister in Seattle. Neither had seen Hunnicut for over a year. To make things more difficult, Hunnicut had been living alone for two months.

"That was when Peggy Summers left," said a helpful neighbor. "I'd had them over for a couple of parties and she said good-bye to me when she was moving out."

"Had there been a big blow-up?"

"Hell, no. They were both damn cheerful. Peggy got a better job in Alanta and was moving south."

Looking around the living room, Giorni decided that Peggy must have taken the humanizing touches with her. There was not a single decorative object anywhere, not a house plant or a bowl of goldfish. For the most part this home could have been furnished by a motel keeper.

Even worse, Victor Hunnicut had clearly been a neatness freak. Every book, every compact disc, every video cassette occupied its appointed place. The same military order prevailed in the bedroom, where the only signs of the departed Peggy were several empty drawers. Hunnicut's system for organizing his socks and shirts was too efficient to spill over into extra space. His financial papers were so well filed it took only ten minutes to establish the basic facts. He lived well within his means, paid his bills regularly on the first of the month, and possessed a slowly accreting portfolio of conservative investments.

A large address book that bristled with extensive notes held out some hope. But these entries simply represented the painstaking care Victor Hunnicut lavished on his professional connections.

"He must have the location and employment history of everybody he was at school with, everybody he worked with, everybody he ever met," Giorni concluded.

Space had already been reserved for Ken Nicolls. When the inspector reached the S's, he found the same soulless detail about Peggy Summers. There was her past employment, her present employment, her field of expertise. If Victor Hunnicut ever wanted to know about computer engineering firms in Atlanta, he had the number to dial.

Personal entries were relatively few and, for the most part, restricted to services—a dentist, an auto mechanic, an oculist, a dry cleaner. The few women entered for social purposes were labeled with suitable restaurants and activities. If Hunnicut wanted to go to a concert, he called Marcia; if he wanted to go to a hockey game, he called Cynthia.

"The guy must have seen somebody on a regular basis," Giorni said despairingly. If he himself had lived in this place, he would have been out as much as possible.

His sergeant was examining a checkbook.

"Well, there are regular checks to the Zichy Salle des Armes and annual dues to something called the Foil and Saber Club."

Giorni flipped to the Z's and reached for the phone. "Anything's worth a try."

At eight o'clock that evening Inspector Giorni examined his surroundings with interest. He was on the sidelines of a large wood-floored room, watching several dozen masked figures jab swords at each other. The air vibrated with the sounds of thudding feet and scraping blades. This beehive of activity occupied the second floor of a shabby building that housed a dance studio below.

The Hungarian couple in charge had not only admitted knowledge of Victor Hunnicut but had also advised an evening visit to meet other acquaintances. Giorni had been greeted by Mrs. Zichy, a slim, wiry figure who had pulled off her mask to talk to him. The Salle, she explained, was the proprietor of the premises, which were usually used for group classes and private lessons. But on Wednesday and Friday nights the facility was rented to the Foil and Saber Club so that its members could work out with each other and compete with other clubs.

"Victor tried to get here twice a week," she concluded. "He had a regular lesson scheduled with Laslo on Saturday afternoon, and he practiced with the club on Wednesday night."

When asked about intimates, Mrs. Zichy revealed that it was here that Peggy had entered Hunnicut's life.

"We were sorry to lose her. Peggy is very good on the foils. Victor was primarily an epee man."

This was a revealing formulation. Under the circumstances Mrs. Zichy might have been expected to express sorrow for the loss of Hunnicut, rather than Peggy. But Giorni began to understand when he spoke with Mr. Zichy and several of the club members.

"He came to us as soon as he moved to Princeton," Laslo said. "Before that he had been studying the epee in St. Louis. He was not bad. He had the right build, he had quick feet and a strong wrist, he practiced diligently. But he had no dash on the attack, no inspired transformation of a retreat into an advance. His problem, *au fond,* was that he required absolute safety at all times. So he never would have made a first-class fencer."

And this seemed to be the sum of what Laslo had to offer. He had been giving the man private lessons for over two years, and all he had noticed was second-class potential.

"Did you ever talk to him about anything but fencing?"

A sardonic smile flickered over the tight features.

"Victor would have felt cheated if I had not directed every moment of my attention to a critique of his performance."

"What about when you weren't on the floor?"

Laslo shrugged. "Victor's lesson was scheduled for three. I have other regulars at two and at four. Saturday afternoon, you understand, is a busy time for me."

He did, however, point out several people who had interacted with Hunnicut in the Foil and Saber Club.

"Sure, I'll tell you what I know," gasped the first. "But let me get some juice. That was a real workout."

By the time they were settled on a bench, he had recovered his breath.

"Say, wasn't that something about Victor being murdered? I couldn't believe it when I caught it on the news."

So far he was doing better than Mrs. Zichy but it was still not a grief-stricken reaction.

"Vic and I worked together on the club's calendar committee last year. That means scheduling when and where we'll compete. Vic was an okay guy."

This lukewarm assessment was as far as anybody cared to go. Two of those present were part of the regular Wednesday crowd and they dispelled the notion that Victor Hunnicut was a loner.

"Oh, he'd join us afterward for a beer or a hamburger, but he was pretty quiet," the first recalled. "He did liven up a little when he was with Peggy."

"Mostly he talked about the events of the day," the second added. "Like, if there'd been some big political news or if the Nets had played. Hell, even though I knew he was an engineer, I didn't know he worked for ASI until I read it in the papers."

In other words, Hunnicut had carefully kept his worlds apart. At the Salle he did not speak about ASI. And, now that Giorni came to think of it, there had been no sign of his fencing at the condo. It was a sure bet that many of these enthusiasts had crossed foils over their mantel or a mask on a wall. But Victor compartmentalized his life as well as his underwear.

Without high hopes Giorni followed Mrs. Zichy to the locker room. The key chain that had given him access to the condo made short work of the padlock. Hanging inside were the accoutrements of fencing. On the shelf a small dobb kit contained toilet supplies. The only extraneous object was a bright red bandanna, creased and stained, tossed on top.

"What's that for?" Giorni asked.

"He kept it in his sleeve so he'd have something to wipe the sweat with."

It was a relief to discover one area over which Victor Hunnicut did not have complete control.

"This is the only place we'll find out anything about him," Giorni said the next morning, pulling into the ASI parking lot.

"If they have any sense, they'll claim that they loved him, that he was a grand guy to work with and he never caused any trouble," one of the sergeants predicted.

Gardner Ives went even further.

"I didn't know him at all. In fact I wouldn't have recognized him before the trade show."

Phil Pepitone, who had already been questioned about his angry search for Victor Hunnicut, could not disavow all acquaintance. He did his best.

"You get a couple of jerks like him in every big company. They like dreaming up wild melodramatic ideas and feeding them into the rumor mill. That's what Hunnicut had been doing and I was about to straighten him out. That's all there was to it."

"Exactly how were you going to straighten him out?" Giorni asked politely.

Unspoken was the suggestion that it might have been with a kitchen skewer.

Pepitone flushed darkly. "I was going to ream him out. For Chrissake, Gardner had to do the same thing. We certainly weren't going to have Conrad Ecker upset by some two-bit assistant manager."

In other words, Hunnicut was far too lowly to be a serious problem to his betters.

Sam Bradley was the one who struck out for new ground. "Hunnicut made a big mistake, shooting off his mouth in front of Bob Laverdiere. The people at Ecker didn't realize how unimportant he was. After all, we could just fire him. They didn't have that option."

Bradley was not pretending to be above the battle; he was trying to divert the big guns.

Even Wiley Quinn watched his words.

"Look, you have to understand. This was the only job at the manager level likely to open up for a long time. Victor was hoping that, if the Ecker deal fell through, something better for him might come along."

"And you'd lose out. That must have made you sore."

"I wasn't worried about a thing once he tipped his hand to Laverdiere. Victor was only a menace when people didn't know what he was up to. As soon as the brass found out he was antagonizing people, he wasn't a threat anymore."

Giorni leapt into the opening. "But the brass found out more than that, didn't they? What exactly was Hunnicut saying about Pepitone and Bradley?"

Quinn was a loyalist all the way. Victor had targeted the Eckers. In passing, he may have hinted at Pepitone's questionable judgment or Bradley's poor record. That was all.

"I'll bet," said Giorni to himself.

An hour later, however, he finally located someone who had nothing to fear. Fred Uhlrich, Hunnicut's immediate superior, had returned from California. His alibi was impregnable.

"So what can I tell you? I've been three thousand miles away ever since this Ecker business started," he began, laying his cards on the table. "It's barely forty-eight hours since I got back and I've been tied here ever since. Didn't even make it to New York for the show."

There, he seemed to be saying. Cross me off your little list.

"You can still be a big help."

"Not if you want to know exactly what dirt Vic was spreading," Uhlrich shot back. "I don't know, and I intend to keep it that way."

Giorni nodded pacifically. "Oh, we'll find out, never fear. But the thing that's really weird is the trouble Hunnicut was causing. What made him think he could get away with it?"

Reflecting, Uhlrich rasped a finger down a jaw already showing signs of dark shadow. "Basically he was an ambitious kid too impressed by his own credentials. Naturally we've got the usual batch of bright M.B.A.'s over at headquarters, but out here in the divisions, Victor was the first. He figured that meant he'd make division manager right away."

"I'm surprised he didn't go after the obvious job."

"You mean mine?" Uhlrich grinned. "He could never have filled my shoes."

Deliberately provocative, Giorni continued to probe.

"They say he was damn good at his job."

"He was, but only because I had him do the things he was good at. Being a division manager calls for a lot of talents and most people don't have the whole packet. For instance, Vic wouldn't have been half as good at running a production line as Wiley Quinn because he really didn't know the first thing about people."

Giorni was not entirely convinced.

"Wait a minute," he objected. "He sure knew how to get people talking, didn't he?"

Uhlrich shook his head impatiently. "Hell, anybody can get things going. Trouble was, Vic never knew in what direction they'd take off. You know, he was scared to death of direct confrontations—that's why he tried being so damn cute. When he started pulling tricks here, I called him on it and he backed down damn fast."

Giorni recalled an earlier expert appraisal.

"No dash on the attack, eh?" he murmured.

Uhlrich blinked. "I suppose you could put it that way," he said dubiously. "The point is, that if there's been talk about Phil or Sam Bradley, that wasn't what Vic intended. The poor dope thought that if he got everybody suspecting something fishy about the Ecker deal, it would be dropped like a hot potato."

"That's dumb all right. What's more, it's dangerous."

Uhlrich abandoned the pipe he was tamping.

"How so?"

"Your boy was in the same position as someone who calls a bunch of people and says, 'Give me ten thousand dollars or I talk.' Of course the slob may get his money, but then he can also get a skewer in the chest."

Uhlrich disliked where they were heading.

"Before you get any funny ideas, just remember that Victor did most of his talking about Ecker."

"I realize that. All I'm saying is that, when you scatter shots the way he did, there's always the chance you'll hit a real target. That may be what your boy did."

"Christ, what a mess. You know Vic wasn't all bad. He might even have straightened out. All he needed was to do some growing up." Uhlrich sighed heavily. "When you get down to it, he was just a kid. It's a real shame."

Giorni was content. He not only had a handle on his victim, he had finally heard someone, admittedly not a Hunnicut fan, indicate some sorrow at the death of a young man.

The second sergeant accompanying the police contingent was a woman in plainclothes. She flourished her credentials and held formal interviews with members of the clerical staff. But she also lunched in the cafeteria, visited every ladies' room in headquarters, listened sympathetically to personal problems, and even helped a beginner with her computer.

By two-thirty, Sergeant Gwendolyn Belliers was sharing her catch with Giorni.

"The scuttlebut is that Pepitone gets an under-the-counter payment from Ecker, and that Bradley is developing new products to sell on his own," she announced triumphantly.

"Well, if Hunnicut hit the bull's-eye with either of those, it's no wonder he's in the morgue," said Giorni, completing his earlier line of thought.

"And that's just the ASI end," she grinned. "There are some honeys on the Ecker end, too. According to Hunnicut, their production manager was falsifying records to cover his tail, their test-lab man was hiding Conrad Ecker's senility, and the Laverdiere wife was skimming the profits."

Giorni groaned. "Jesus Christ!"

Sergeant Belliers was proud of her day's work. "Actually he wasn't that successful at the beginning. He wouldn't have gotten anywhere if it hadn't been for the godsend of the Ecker fire. When he said that they'd torched the place, people began to pay attention."

"Did you get anything on movements at the trade show?" Giorni asked.

"Not really. You already know that Bradley fingered Victor Hunnicut as the source of the rumors. Then he overheard the row at the Ecker booth and was mad enough to light a fire under Pepitone. By the time he succeeded, everybody was shooting off on his own."

"For guys who were supposed to be running displays, they were all over the place," Giorni said disapprovingly. "Wasn't anybody minding the store?"

Fair-mindedly she reported that most of the commercial action had been through by then. "The only person who was in his booth during the critical time was Gardner Ives. He was glad-handing some people from Sears. Everybody else admits being on his own. But there is one thing."

"Yeah?"

Gwendolyn's eyes were snapping with interest. "That was a real uproar the Ecker people had. Laverdiere was repeating Hunnicut's threats, they were yelling at each other, they were swearing to do something. The three of them were real upfront about all of this after the murder. But in all the talk, there's not one word about the Laverdiere wife. She might just as well not have been in New York. And that makes me wonder what the hell she was up to."

Unbidden, the image of Tina Laverdiere rose before Giorni. He could see the bold, handsome features, the air of decision, the obvious dominance over her husband.

"One thing's for sure," he said. "That lady wasn't watching someone mix up a batch of biscuit dough."

Chapter

A PANEL OF EXPERTS

But the Ecker fire had not been a gift from God to Victor Hunnicut.

"It was set," the fire marshal announced. "No doubt about it. The sprinkler system didn't work because it was deactivated. After that, the job was simple. The financial discs were tumbled out of their cabinet and the kindling was paper soaked in an accelerant. Then somebody stood back and tossed a match. Considering the way plastic burns, it was overkill. I could have done it without gutting the whole building."

The Winstead Insurance Group trained its adjusters to proceed in an orderly fashion. "Then we can scrub the idea of a professional torch. What was the layout there? Would an outsider know on sight where the financial records were?"

"The way Tina Laverdiere had the place organized, a six-year-old could have figured it out."

"So we're right back where we were. Anybody could have done it."

But this was more of a question than a statement.

"Not exactly. We've got a little more information now."

With the preliminaries over, the adjuster crumpled the wrapping from his Danish pastry and shot it into the wastebasket. "Yeah, I've been reading the papers, too. I didn't realize that Ecker was on the brink of a merger until that murder. We could have a whole new ball game now."

"I don't know if you could say they were on the brink, because nothing had been settled. There were people at Ecker who weren't crazy about the idea, and there was at least one guy at the other place trying to derail things. He's the one who got himself killed."

"Just because he was against the merger?" the adjuster protested.

"That's the problem. Apparently he was an all-purpose troublemaker. It could have been because he nosed out some scam at ASI. From what I hear about this Hunnicut, it's surprising he made it to thirty-two."

The adjuster grunted in dissatisfaction. "Wonderful. So we've got a fire that anyone could have set and a victim everybody wanted to waste. It looks like a great big blank to me."

But the marshal shook his head gently, showing the beginning of a smile.

"No, some interesting items are popping up. That's really why I called you. Hunnicut was part of an ASI inspection team that came up here two weeks ago. But he didn't go back with his boss. Some banker who was along says that he stayed on to have a drink with Hunnicut. When he left, Hunnicut was still sitting in the lounge of the Holiday Inn. Well, that got the New York police thinking. They asked our boys to check around in case Hunnicut ran into somebody from Ecker and had an argument or something. After all, the Laverdieres or Frayne could easily have dropped by. But what came out was a lot more unexpected than that."

"Go on."

"At first they got zilch because they were concentrating on the Holiday Inn. Then they came up with the bright idea that he might have had dinner someplace else, so they circulated the restaurants. And what do you know? At the Thai place over on the east end of town they remembered him clearly. He was the last customer there when they closed up—at eleven o'clock."

The adjuster knew the basics of Bridgeport geography.

"You mean he was near the Ecker plant at eleven?"

"That's right." The thin smile had blossomed into a broad grin. "And when they got busy on that part of town they were able to backtrack Hunnicut. He spent the interval before dinner having a few beers in the tavern where the Ecker line drops by after work. Some of them hang around to eat and watch the game on TV."

For a moment the two men were silent, visualizing a solitary stranger quietly lingering in a crowded bar filled with regulars.

"He must have been trying to pick up ammunition for his fight. Just eavesdropping in the hope of hearing something he could use."

"That's the way I see it," the marshal agreed.

The adjuster's forehead was knotted in thought. "Okay, so we come to the home question. Do the New York police know what time Hunnicut finally got back to New Jersey?"

"Not yet. The guy lived alone in one of those big condo complexes and the nearest neighbor was out of town. All anybody knows so far is that he showed up for work the next day. He could have been anywhere between eleven o'clock that night and nine o'clock the next morning."

"No wonder you're looking like a cat with a mouse. This means we've opened up two possibilities and both of them are beauts."

Belatedly the marshal introduced a caveat. "Only if we assume that Hunnicut hung around Bridgeport until the wee hours. In that case the first scenario is that he set the fire himself."

"Right. And that brings us to the really tricky one."

The fire marshal was with him every step of the way.

"If Hunnicut was hanging around the Ecker plant at the right time, he could have seen someone else sneaking in."

Again they were faced with a compelling picture—a deserted factory obscured by icy sleet, a furtive figure at the gate, a hidden observer in the shadows.

"God, it all sounds so unnatural," complained the adjuster, who had no taste for melodrama. "But then, so does trying to play detective in a saloon, and we know he did that."

"He was a weirdo trying to get an edge."

"Okay. So how many people did Hunnicut meet on this inspection tour?"

"All of the family. He would have recognized the Laverdieres, or Frayne. And he'd probably seen photos of old Conrad."

This was going too far.

"Oh, come on. A seventy-year-old slinking around, waiting for the night watchman to clear the area? I don't believe it. Besides, the Ecker people would have had a right to be there; but somebody from ASI? Hunnicut would have known right off the bat they were up to no good. Now what about access to the compound?"

"Easy enough. That fence is designed to prevent people backing in a truck and stealing a load of expensive equipment. Someone jimmied the pedestrian gate, either because it was an outside job or to make it look like one."

"And getting into the boiler house?"

The marshal spread his hands. "Hell, half the windows in the place were broken by the time the first truck got there."

With the general outlines established, the adjuster was prepared to zero in on the technical details in which they both specialized.

"Okay, suppose you tell me about the sprinkler system. If somebody tries to turn off the individual heads, an alarm sounds at the fire station. So there are only two ways to go. Either you beef up the fusible links so they don't melt when the temperature rises or—"

"Hell, no. I told you this was a simple job. The guy jimmied open the fire-alarm box and threw the master switch."

The adjuster pounced. "So he had to know where the box was."

"And it's sitting right in Tina Laverdiere's operation, plainly marked. Both the visitors from ASI spent time there. And all these systems are identical. They're bound to have the same setup at ASI."

The adjuster already knew from the marshal's tone that the facts would be of no help in isolating the arsonist. Nonetheless he persisted to the bitter end.

"And the accelerant?"

"Acetone. The stuff is so damn water-soluble, we had a hell of a time getting a spectrometer reading."

Busily counting the industrial uses of acetone, the adjuster was silent for several moments. Then he snapped his fingers.

"Of course. They use it to clean up electrical connections after a manufacturing process. There'd be a ton of it over on Bob Laverdiere's side." His enthusiasm abated as his thoughts raced to the inevitable conclusion. "And I'll bet you're going to tell me that they have it at ASI, too."

The marshal was smug. "They sure do!"

"Oh, all right. But I tell you, there's one thing that still bothers me. Both the Laverdieres were at the fire and they were allowed to look at the damage. If Tina Laverdiere had locked her records in that cabinet and they were all over the floor, how come she didn't know it was a torch job right away?"

"Give the lady a break. I told you this was a case of overkill. There were wooden shelves holding all the stuff from before computerization—ledgers, sales books, invoices, auditors' reports, lab books. When that went up, the shelving collapsed over the cabinet. Then the ceiling came down, with the plaster and laths burning away. Finally a couple of tons of water were dumped on the whole mess. She just saw a war zone. After all, we couldn't tell what happened until we sifted through the debris."

Abandoning his attempt to play devil's advocate, the adjuster now produced his own pitiful contribution.

"You know we've been doing some work at Winstead, too. All the standard arson suspects have been checked out. We ran down the list of disgruntled employees, competitors and so forth, and there just wasn't a strong enough grievance anywhere. But this merger business opens up a new can of worms. We're practically forced to assume somebody felt desperate enough about that to roast the Ecker records."

As the marshal rose to his feet, he was jovial.

"And what's so hard about that? After all, someone felt strongly enough to commit murder."

The police had launched an all-out effort to pinpoint Victor Hunnicut's return from Connecticut. Their inquiries inevitably filtered back to ASI, carrying the news that the Ecker fire was of suspicious origin.

Gardner Ives lost no time in disseminating his version of events.

"This explains everything," he told Tom Robichaux. "Poor Hunnicut, in an excess of zeal, remained behind in Bridgeport to develop further background about the Eckers. Unfortunately he saw one of them surreptitiously enter the plant and had to be silenced. Naturally we'll be holding off on any decision about the merger."

Reluctant to see healthy profits disappearing over the horizon, Robichaux roused himself to say, "If somebody's been skimming the profits, it could be an even better buy."

"Very true. But until we know what's going on over there, it would be folly to get involved."

Gardner Ives, with a solid alibi, could afford to take a lofty view. Phil Pepitone and Sam Bradley had even better reasons for hailing the latest news. Neither of them, however, felt obliged to include a eulogy to the late Victor Hunnicut.

"That little shit was so busy trying to dig up something that he finally hit pay dirt," Pepitone told his entourage.

"What in God's name made him think he'd find out anything in the middle of the night?"

"Who can tell? If he hadn't taken shots at every single person at Ecker, we might have some idea."

It went without saying that, from now on, the only Hunnicut accusations worth recalling were those against the Ecker Company.

Sam Bradley's approach was less abrasive, but it carried the same message.

"Folks tell me young Hunnicut was nosing around the Ecker place at just the wrong time. The way he was flailing around with charges, I suppose he was desperate to come up with something solid."

"Well, he certainly chose the wrong guy to tangle

with," said one of the expensive scientists employed by R and D.

Bradley shook his head, becoming more avuncular by the moment. "Hunnicut knew people would be sore if they caught him blackening their names for no good reason. I'll bet it never occurred to him things could get a lot more serious if he turned out to be right."

"You'd think by now the police would know what's going on at Ecker."

"That's not a normal company up there in Connecticut," Bradley intoned, making Bridgeport sound like an outpost of Hudson's Bay. "The Eckers are all kin, so they'll cover for each other."

Scientists can be cynics, too. "Don't bet on it! They've all been feeding from the same trough. If one of them has been stealing from the others, they'll turn on him."

Sam Bradley was not demanding impossible standards of accuracy. As long as the brand of culprit was firmly affixed elsewhere, he was content.

"Then we'll just have to wait and see, won't we?" he said lazily.

Given the drastic results of loose talk at ASI, Wiley Quinn waited until he reached the safety of his home to voice his own suspicions.

"I'll bet that bastard set the fire himself," he told his wife. "That way he could put some meat on his jabs at Ecker."

"Then why was he murdered?"

"How do I know? But I'll tell you one thing. When I left the Ecker booth, Bob Laverdiere was already boiling. If, on top of that, he realized Vic set the fire, it would have been enough to send him over the edge."

Mrs. Quinn had been watching her husband age with every fresh round of police interrogation, and she had her own priorities. Theories about Hunnicut setting the fire could lead anywhere. Casting him as an innocent onlooker led straight into the Ecker camp.

"No," she said, shaking her head, "it doesn't make sense, Wiley. I know you think Victor would have done anything to stop you from getting the promotion. But he'd have to be crazy to set that fire."

"I'm beginning to think he was," Quinn said stubbornly.

Actually the person spending the most time with the police was no longer a suspect. Instead, Ken Nicolls had become their most promising witness. A disinterested spectator at both Bridgeport and the Javits Center, he had also produced a bonanza with his drink at the Holiday Inn. In return he picked up considerable information to be relayed back to the Sloan.

"They say the fire at Ecker was set," he reported, "and there's a possibility that Victor Hunnicut saw it done."

Ken would have lurked modestly in the outer office until his superiors had finished their conference but Miss Corsa said philosophically, "They'll all want to hear about this."

As usual she was right. Charlie Trinkham welcomed him cheerfully and Thatcher waved to a chair. Even Everett Gabler, the most single-minded member of the staff, raised no objection.

"So Tom Robichaux tells us," Thatcher said. "I gather the people at ASI are pretending that this explains everything."

"The police aren't," Ken rejoined. "Ives is trying to sell them on Hunnicut as so dedicated to his job that he was simply working overtime."

"And you don't agree?"

Ken snorted. "He was trying to torpedo the deal for his own purposes. Which leaves one great big question."

"It sure does," agreed Trinkham, nodding happily. "If this dedicated employee saw somebody firing the place, why didn't he tell them at ASI? Why keep it up his sleeve?"

Everett Gabler never had any difficulty espying human depravity. "And just what was Hunnicut's ultimate purpose?"

"To get the next opening for division manager."

Meticulously placing the tips of his fingers together, Gabler advanced into the realm of hypothesis. "Is it possible that with his knowledge about the fire he could blackmail one of his superiors into helping him achieve that end?"

"One of them wouldn't do him much good," Charlie objected. "It isn't that easy. At places like ASI they work by committee."

Thatcher waved aside this comment.

"Surely the important thing is whether Hunnicut thought so. From what you say and from my brief exposure, I doubt if he was very perceptive at reading people's responses."

"And there's another side to the coin," offered Charlie, swift to see interesting possibilities. "One of the rumors was about Pepitone taking a handout to arrange the merger. And didn't somebody say there haven't been any outside accountants at Ecker for a couple of months?"

These two seemingly unrelated points inspired Gabler to add a third. "Ecker is a closely held company."

"I like the script," caroled Charlie, who had no qualms about putting it all into words. "Let's say there was a big stock transfer to a Pepitone nominee. Then the rumors start and he gets nervous enough to want to erase that transaction. While they're reconstructing the files, they could use a better straw man. But Hunnicut sees him strike the match."

Ken was swept along by this imaginative flight. "And I picked up something else from the police. Pepitone, after he talked with Bradley, was searching all over Javits for Victor Hunnicut. So look what could have happened. Hunnicut is publicly humiliated by Gardner Ives and plenty mad about it. Then, out of the blue, Pepitone catches up with him and gives him hell about the rumors at ASI. Hunnicut shoots back that at least he hasn't been torching places."

"Or," said Gabler, who tended to ascribe his own fixity of purpose to everyone, "he immediately tried to blackmail Pepitone for the position he wanted."

"Either way it makes a hell of a good motive," Charlie announced.

Trying to keep his feet in this surging tide of speculation, John Thatcher brought them all to a halt.

"And Pepitone just happened to be carrying a skewer from the Ecker booth?"

There was a moment of silence.

"You're saying that it must have been premeditated?" Gabler asked thoughtfully.

"Unless you can think of a good reason for someone to be carrying it. I admit that's not beyond the bounds of possibility for one of the Eckers. But not for Pepitone."

This disheartening realism was pursued by Ken Nicolls. "Or even Sam Bradley. I was right there when he left the booth and his hands were empty."

"Bradley? Is that the R and D man?" queried Everett Gabler. "I thought the rumors about him were unrelated to the Ecker Company."

"As far as I know he doesn't have any connection with them," Ken confessed. "Except that he went tearing up there right after the fire."

Charlie Trinkham's capricious fancy could always weave a connection. "What would make things perfect," he suggested, "is to find that one of ASI's still-born projects had slid from their R and D to Ecker's test lab."

"Very neat," applauded Thatcher.

But Everett Gabler was still searching for input. "I understand that Robichaux has been in the midst of ASI for some time. Doesn't he have any idea about Hunnicut's activities?"

Robichaux's views on this subject had been brief and unalterable.

"Unfortunately," Thatcher replied, "Tom is taking the position right now that all M.B.A.'s are certifiable lunatics."

"I suppose they've got one over at his shop who's giving poor old Tom a hard time," said Trinkham with ready comprehension.

"He wants Tom to use a computer."

A murmur of understanding greeted this announcement. Everyone present had, in his own way, survived the great computer revolution at the Sloan. Only Charlie Trinkham had succumbed to the lure of the monitor and could be found, at odd moments, pecking his way to knowledge.

"You learn to love it," he said, trying to convert the heathen. "All you do is put in absolutely everything and then, whenever you want, there's nothing you can't find out."

Ken Nicolls was another virtuoso of the keyboard.

"That's the system Doug Ecker was following," he chimed in.

John Thatcher surveyed the two enthusiasts.

"Then I think we can safely say that Doug Ecker is the cause of all this trouble," he pointed out. "Those all-embracing files of his must contain an unexploded bomb."

Chapter

BANK HOLIDAY

The Winstead Insurance Group sent its Christmas card by special messenger. It arrived a week before December 25.

" '. . . cooperating with state and local authorities,' " Tina Laverdiere read aloud. " 'But, as is usual practice, Winstead will initiate a complete review of all Ecker coverage.' And they want to start with an interview with us as soon as possible. Oh, Lord!"

With the flick of a wrist, she tossed the letter onto her desk and sat down. That rat-a-tat of long fingernails on metal was the only further personal comment she allowed herself.

Tina knew that in this context "interview" meant grueling hours of preparation, protracted disputes about every detail and, very likely, steep new charges to the Ecker Company. Marilyn Burrus, who had delivered the unwelcome communication, saw other negatives.

"We're going to have to tell Conrad," she said with a sigh. So often things went better without him.

"And he'll hit the roof," Tina predicted.

But on this particular subject, Mrs. Burrus knew more than she did.

"No, he'll get stubborn. Nobody's going to tell him what to do."

"This time," said Tina, "I'm afraid even Conrad can't dig in his heels."

But, of course, Conrad found a way. Before the day was out he had dictated a stiff letter to the Winstead Insurance Group and had taken special pains to have it delivered by courier.

In the sunshine of Fort Lauderdale, Conrad relived the episode.

"I told them we'd cooperate up to the hilt," he was declaring a few days later. "What else could I do? They'll tie up poor Tina with more paperwork—as if she isn't swamped already. But, by God, I told them they were going to have to wait until after Christmas. Whoever set that fire did enough damage. I'm not letting them wreck our holidays."

Conrad liked to go native in Florida, so a violent Hawaiian shirt and a fraying straw hat lent color to his vehemence.

"Good for you, Dad," said Doug Ecker. His major concession to the tropics was a deep tan. In well-cut slacks and a polo shirt, he lounged in the deck chair, looking trim and healthy enough to warm a mother's heart.

But Alice Ecker, having schooled herself to avoid sentimentality, reverted to the Winstead Insurance Group.

"Well, I should hope so!" she exclaimed. "Christmas is the time for families to get together."

Earlier in their married life, she had sometimes

found it impossible to lever Conrad out of the shop. Now the December visit to Doug and Gloria had become a high point of his year.

And with Doug looking so well this time, Alice felt particularly pleased. Despite palm trees, sparkling water, and a temperature in the eighties, she was humming a Christmas carol when she bustled off to help Gloria in the kitchen.

Conspiratorial silence descended on the patio, while father and son waited until the coast cleared. Then their eyes met.

"Of course, once it turned out to be arson, Winstead had no choice," Doug commented, watching for reaction.

"Sure," said Conrad snappily. "But it's going to be another damn nuisance and Tina's still knee-deep in reconstructing the records. Winstead will want to go over every policy, down to the last panel truck in Texas. And if they don't grab the excuse to raise our rates, I don't know insurance companies."

Doug Ecker was privileged to press a little further than most people. "And this stuff about cooperating with state and local authorities doesn't bother you?"

Conrad snorted. "Why should it? We've got nothing to hide. There's no sane reason for anybody at Ecker to have set that fire."

This was said so defiantly that Doug Ecker stiffened.

"We can't be absolutely sure of that, can we, Dad?" he suggested.

Stirring uneasily, Conrad said, "All right, all right. But that's no reason to let an insurance company push me around. They come when *I* say so—not them."

Doug had already tried exploring this topic in telephone calls that neither Alice nor Gloria knew about. So he moved on.

"Let's talk about the ASI merger," he began cautiously. "It sounded great at first, but lately it's looking like a jinx. Tell me how you're feeling about it now."

Family calls to the Eckers in Florida were supposed to be scrupulously nonstressful. Nevertheless, like static, small crackles of concern had been accompanying the small talk recently. And his investments in a string of miniature golf courses did not keep Doug Ecker too busy to read the New York papers.

To his surprise, Conrad did not accept the invitation to air his opinions.

"Jinx or not, I think the merger's probably off," said his father indifferently. "We're just treading water these days. I suppose it's only to be expected."

Since Doug knew how much the initial decision had cost Conrad, he frowned.

"There's nothing to worry about, Doug," Conrad said hastily. "This glitch doesn't change the fundamentals. Our best bet is still a merger. If it isn't ASI, it will be someone else. Ecker's in fine shape, so it will be a great buy for whoever turns up. And believe me, it's going to be a good deal for us, too."

With the feeling that they were at cross-purposes, Doug was about to explain how unnecessary all this reassurance was. He was forestalled.

"What are you two talking about?" cried Alice gaily, advancing with a tray. Behind her, Gloria carried a large pitcher.

Conrad and his only son had forged a smooth working partnership.

"I was just telling Dad how early we have to pick up Doug Junior."

"Can't see why these kids don't pick planes that arrive at a decent hour," Conrad grumbled.

"Economy fares," said Gloria in defense of her young.

"And you of all people should appreciate that, Conrad," said Alice tartly. Then, looking from husband to son, she added, "And what are you two grinning about?"

Alan Frayne was on the phone to another one of Alice's grandchildren.

". . . so your grandpa got on his high horse and said we were all going to take our usual Christmas break. That's why I could come up to Stowe."

"Neat," said Frayne's twelve-year-old son.

"The skiing's great," said Frayne.

That was neat, too.

Like many men before him, Frayne had discovered that divorce suited him. There was, for example, a very attractive lady friend enjoying Stowe with him. And while he occasionally regretted the lost comforts of domesticity, he did very well without Broadway openings, chi-chi restaurants, and every good cause in eastern Connecticut. Now that the original unhappiness of Conrad and Alice had faded into acceptance, Frayne's separation from Betty could be described as a success—except where the children were concerned. Despite many long-distance calls and school vacations, he never knew what to expect.

"He's just going through a phase," said Betty when she came on the line for a few civilized words. "How are you, Alan?"

He replied, then asked about Betty and the new family. This exhausted what they had to say to each other, but holidays demand more.

"Mom and Dad went down to Florida to be with Doug," said Betty, who often forgot that Alan was in closer touch than she was. "And Aunt Virginia just called. Bob and Tina are out with her for Christmas. She says everybody's having a lovely time. I'm so glad all of you could get away from Bridgeport."

In the spirit of the season, Frayne did not respond

that getting away from Bridgeport had always ranked a little too high on Betty's wish list.

Bob Laverdiere was trying to exercise similar restraint.

"If only you weren't so far away," said Virginia Ecker Laverdiere plaintively. "I'd like to see my grandchildren growing up."

A deep sigh measured every mile between the Ecker Company and Lake Shore Drive, in Chicago. The condominium overlooking Lake Michigan was a suitable successor to the handsome suburban home in which Bob had been raised. The senior Mrs. Laverdiere, who enjoyed excellent health and a very respectable income, had furnished it to her heart's desire. When she tired of shopping, she played cutthroat bridge and traveled, logging thousands of miles each year, including many trips to Bridgeport, where she had every opportunity to spoil her grandchildren. Most of the time she was as brisk as her brother Conrad. But Christmas, Easter, and some birthdays reminded her that she was A Widow.

In these heavily decorated surroundings, Bob felt like a bull in a china shop. Shifting uncomfortably, he mumbled something.

"What was that, dear?"

"I said," he repeated with an attempt at a smile, "that considering how you twisted Conrad's arm to give me a chance there, it's pretty late to discover how far Bridgeport is."

Hurt, she reproached him: "Why, Bob, you make it sound as if I drove you away."

Tina, shepherding two snow-suited toddlers into the room for approval, saw that it was desirable to shoo them and their father out as quickly as possible.

"Santa Claus at Marshall Field's," she said brightly. "But no candy! I don't want anybody's appetite spoiled for dinner tonight."

Two angel heads nodded, and Bob shot her a look of heartfelt gratitude. Then, grabbing his daughter with one hand and his son with the other, he fled.

Tina had not overheard the exchange between him and his mother, but Virginia's saintly expression told all.

"Have you finished wrapping all your gifts?" Tina asked, introducing a diversion. "I did ours before we left home, so I could help you if you'd like."

But it was not to be that easy.

"Bob's tired, isn't he?" said Mrs. Laverdiere, gazing pensively at the Christmas tree in the corner.

"He's been working hard," said Tina, amused despite herself. She understood her mother-in-law better than Bob did. As a result, she knew his decision to shield Virginia from the unpleasantnesses back east would be put to the test.

"For that matter, you're not looking your best either, Tina."

When Tina did not reply, Virginia Laverdiere straightened.

"Is everything all right between the two of you?" she demanded sharply.

"Everything's fine," said Tina, with all the sincerity she could summon.

Openly unconvinced, Virginia studied her before saying, "Then it must be the business. Is it this foolish idea of Conrad's to sell out?"

Tina felt quite unable to describe the changing currents at Ecker to a woman who could not balance a checkbook.

"The merger is making everything complicated—for all of us," she said vaguely.

"Conrad!" Virginia sniffed. "And Alice, too! All they can think about is Douglas, Douglas, Douglas. Oh, of course I'm sick about the heart attack, too. It's a terrible thing, for somebody so young. But it isn't as if

Doug is the only one who could take over. You know I'm tempted to give Conrad a piece of my mind. After all, Mike did help him get his start."

No good deed goes unpunished. By repaying his debt generously, Conrad had increased the Laverdiere family prosperity and sowed ineradicable seeds of envy. Virginia, whose innocence about money was legendary, knew she was well off. But Conrad—and Alice and Douglas and Betty—were rich.

"And it isn't as if Betty ever lifted a finger to help her father or her mother. Not like Bob has," she complained. "When she divorced Alan—not that I ever liked him—I warned Alice . . ."

The shortcomings of our relatives are an inexhaustible subject, so Tina relaxed prematurely. She was caught off guard when Virginia, like a homing pigeon, lit on Bob again.

". . . but at least this will give Bob his chance to show them all," Virginia was saying with complacency.

Tina blinked at this unlikely knowledgeability.

"What do you mean?" she inquired.

"Bob explained it all to me," Virginia boasted. "Obviously, if these people take over Ecker, they'll have to put him in charge. After all, who could they find as good as he is? And that way he'll get to show Conrad— and Alan Frayne, for that matter—and all the rest of them, what he can do. You know, I've never thought they appreciated Bob's value. No, it's always Douglas this, and Douglas that . . ."

Tina was tempted to ask exactly when Bob had made his disclosure. But doing so would suggest disloyalty or, even worse, jealousy of his mother.

Without bothering to listen to what Virginia was saying, she concentrated on how Virginia looked. The elaborate toilette was as elegant as ever. Virginia's eyes were bright with zest as she excoriated her nearest and dearest. There were no visible signs of ravage, pain, or anxiety.

Tina sagged with sudden relief. For one insane moment she had wondered if Bob was bottling up other confidences that could only be poured into an all-forgiving ear.

Chapter

BLACK TUESDAY

Christmas travel is a two-way street. While the management of the Ecker Company had been packing its bags for a long weekend, others were hastening from afar to enjoy the holiday at home. Among them was the only man whose name had not yet been crossed off the police list of those entering the Javits basement during the trade show.

The detective dispatched to the Long Island City offices of Xavier Trucking was not hopeful. He had already spent twelve interminable days on unproductive interviews. He had talked to security guards and maintenance men, to exhibitors and buyers, to electricians and PR men. Bruno Sclafani had simply proved harder to reach.

Nor was Sclafani please by the interruption to his first day back on the job.

"This will just take a minute," Detective Heidt promised.

"Then let's get on with it," grumbled Bruno. "I've got a schedule to meet."

"Your time slip for December tenth puts you at Javits sometime in the early afternoon. Do you remember that?"

Bruno nodded impatiently. "Sure, it was my last day before taking off. There was a big show there."

"Good, now I'd like to get that time a little firmer if you can manage it."

From a rear pocket, Bruno produced a much-thumbed logbook. Thereafter he conducted a monologue with himself.

". . . holdup at the tunnel before my first delivery on the East Side . . . Markham Novelties at twelve forty-five . . . loading dock at Apollo Passementeries blocked—God, why don't they do something about these out-of-towners?—finally dropped off at one thirty-five . . . Javits two twenty-five . . . That's when I managed to get the signature in the middle of all that action. I must have parked around two-ten. Afterward, in my cab, I put my flimsies in order before crossing over to Jersey. It would have been five or ten minutes before three when I left."

With the fluency that comes from frequent repetition, the detective outlined the geography of the basement with particular reference to the scene of the murder.

"How far were you parked from there?" he continued.

"The spots around all the freight elevators were filled. I could have been around a hundred and fifty feet from that one."

Naturally, Heidt thought to himself. If there was a witness present at the right time, he would be too far away to see anything.

Nonetheless he plodded on. "Now, we're interested

in anyone getting into or out of that elevator. Try to re-create the scene in your mind and—"

"Oh, him," Bruno said casually.

The detective tensed.

"Him?"

"Sure. I heard the elevator doors close, and when I looked up, there was this guy running away. He beat it right across the floor to the stairs and skedaddled up them."

This was no time to startle a sitting bird. Trying to match Sclafani's nonchalance, the detective said, "I realize you could only get a general impression. You were a long way off, so—"

Once again Bruno interrupted.

"I was a long way from the elevator," he corrected, "but I was only two slots from the stairs and there's a light over them. I saw him plain as day."

"Then suppose you describe him."

But Bruno's stellar performance seemed to have peaked.

"What's to describe? He was just a normal guy. Middle height, middle weight. Wasn't really dark or really blond."

All policemen are experienced at trying to put flesh on bare bones of this kind. After arduous efforts, Bruno declared that the man could not have been much over forty.

"Not with that kind of sprint. He ran pretty good for a desk type."

"What makes you say he was a desk type?"

For the first time Bruno was forced to ponder his own words. "Must have been those round glasses," he finally decided.

At the end of another five minutes, Heidt was sweating and Bruno was openly rebellious.

"That's it. The guy was one of hundreds like that. I

can't remember any more about him." Bruno shrugged irritably. "Not unless you count the barbecue apron."

Resisting the impulse to throttle his witness, Heidt said very slowly, "You're telling me he was wearing an apron?"

"Yeah, it flapped when he ran, just like a woman's skirt."

"And what else did you notice about it?"

Suddenly a clothes critic, Bruno cocked his head. "Well, at least it didn't have any of those rinky-dink jokes on it. It was solid, like a shop apron, except for the picture of a grill—that was in white."

"Do you remember the color?"

This provoked a spasm of annoyance.

"For Chrissake! I told you it was a shop apron, didn't I? Haven't you ever seen one? It was blue denim, of course."

When he finally exited from Xavier Trucking, Heidt congratulated himself on getting out of there without having laid a finger on Bruno Sclafani.

"You say this guy hasn't seen any television or newspapers?" Inspector Giorni asked unbelievingly.

"That's right. He's some kind of cold-weather-survival specialist with the Army Reserve. They do their hitch in the winter, instead of the summer like the rest of us. He's been trekking through the Rockies, building snow igloos. That's why I didn't show him any pictures."

A witness absolutely unsullied by media coverage is a minor miracle and treated with due respect.

"You were right. As soon as Laverdiere's back home, we'll have an identification parade."

By Monday night the District Attorney's office was a major player in the conference at police headquarters.

"Sclafani picked out Laverdiere without batting an

eye," Giorni reported. "He says he's sure and the apron pins it down."

"Then that's it," the prosecutor said triumphantly. "We've got everything we need—means, motive, and opportunity."

"Now wait a minute," Giorni's captain cautioned. "A lot of this can be explained away."

The lawyer snorted. "So Laverdiere claims that he was never in the basement and this trucker is mistaken. You call that an explanation? What else can he say when we produce an eyewitness who never even heard about the murder?"

Now that Giorni was clued in on the department's position, he felt free to make his own comment.

"We don't really know we've got a motive."

"Like hell we don't. Laverdiere had some kind of scam going at Ecker that he tried to cover by burning down the records office. But Hunnicut cottoned on to his little game and kept yapping about it. Then Laverdiere shut him up."

"But it would be nice to know what that scam was," Giorni said temperately. "The insurance people are going to be extra tough about the Ecker audit. If we wait a week or so, we'll have something solid."

"A week!" This protest emerged as an involuntary squeak. The prosecutor readjusted his voice to a lower pitch. "Do you know the kind of heat we're taking? We'll have the financial stuff in time for the trial. All we have to do now is arraign the guy and the pressure will be off."

The captain tried another approach.

"Look, Laverdiere isn't going anywhere."

"And he came right back from Chicago. There's no danger of his skipping."

"That's not what we're worried about. We just want everybody off our backs."

* * *

In later days John Thatcher was always to maintain that Robichaux had nobody to blame but himself. If Tom had been on time, they would have been safely out of range before the thunderbolt hit. Instead, he had been a fateful twenty minutes late.

The last item on the Princeton agenda had concerned the two financial advisers. It was agreed that, after Christmas, Ken Nicolls would be let loose in ASI so that the Sloan would be better able to offer guidance to its client. Likewise, an underling from Robichaux & Devane would be ensconced at the Ecker Company. Theoretically Thatcher was accompanying the rival team in order to introduce them to the Eckers. In reality, he assumed that Conrad Ecker might welcome a chance to discuss merger strategy in the wake of Victor Hunnicut's murder.

At first all went well in Bridgeport. Everybody expressed gratification at meeting everybody else and the underling was dispatched with a guide for a tour of the premises. Conrad Ecker was midway through a proposal to sweep his more distinguished guests off to lunch when the door suddenly opened.

"I didn't know what to do," babbled a secretary, still clinging to the knob. "It's the police."

Before she could continue, the two large patrolmen followed on her heels.

"Hello, Jerry, what's this all about?" demanded Conrad Ecker, frowning. "And can't it wait?"

"I'm awfully sorry, Conrad," the older invader replied. "But they told us Bob Laverdiere was here."

Tina Laverdiere barely waited for him to finish. "Well, it will have to wait," she announced coldly. "We've decided that Bob isn't answering any more questions without his lawyer."

"That's right," Bob corroborated.

Looking profoundly embarrassed, Jerry shook his head. "The lawyer will have to come down to the station. We're not here to question Bob, we're here to arrest him."

"Arrest him!" Alan Frayne echoed incredulously.

As proof of purpose, the younger patrolman began to read Laverdiere his Miranda rights while most of his audience gaped. The Laverdieres, however, simply ignored the familiar recitation.

"Now, honey, keep a grip on yourself," Bob urged. "We knew this might happen."

"But they're going to take you to jail!"

"It was always in the cards—especially since yesterday. You concentrate on getting hold of Macomber for me."

"I never really thought it would go this far," she whispered back fiercely.

The two police officers shuffled their feet sheepishly but showed no inclination to terminate this colloquy. Either they had faith in the ultimate cooperation of their prey, or they expected someone else to take charge.

Amazingly, it was Bob Laverdiere who did so.

Engulfing his wife in an embrace, he spoke to Jerry over her shoulder. "I think the sooner we leave, the easier it will be on Tina."

Then he firmly set her aside, nodded to the patrolmen and, with uncharacteristic dignity, marched out between his escorts.

Tina stood rigid, her gaze fixed on Laverdiere's retreating form until the closing door masked him from view. Uncertainly she took two hesitant steps forward before her control collapsed and a shudder racked her body.

"Bob!" she screamed in anguish as her eyes went alarmingly blank.

Then, in a paroxysm of sobbing, she hurled herself straight onto Tom Robichaux's chest.

For what seemed an eternity the other three men were transfixed while Robichaux, stiff with indignation, broadcast a silent appeal for rescue over a mass of tumbled black hair. Alan Frayne, after one impulsive movement, thought better of interference. Conrad Ecker gnawed his underlip as he scowled darkly at what he could see of his niece. John Thatcher sent up thanks that it was Tom, not he, who had been in Tina's path.

Finally Conrad broke free from his trance. Without changing his position he opened his mouth and bellowed at the top of his lungs:

"MARILYN!"

The office manager, arriving at a trot, drank in the scene.

"Oh, for heaven's sake," she clucked.

By this time Tom, still turned to stone, had flexed one hand sufficiently to essay a tentative pat on the heaving form pressed to his bosom.

"Poor Tina," Marilyn continued. "We'd better take her over to Alice."

Conrad hailed this suggestion with a great gust of relief. "That's right. Alice will know what to do."

Frayne, gazing with horrified fascination at Tina's limpetlike clutch on Robichaux, said unenthusiastically, "Do you want me to help?"

With a glance of withering scorn, Marilyn rejected the offer. "Get me one of the girls. We can manage."

"I'll get Janet," said Conrad, proceeding to brush past his guests. "Then I'll go downtown and find out what the hell those two have been up to."

The scene began to dislimn upon the arrival of the unknown Janet. Throughout the detachment process Robichaux remained superbly immobile, but somehow the women succeeded. By then Tina was exhausted and had to be half-carried from the room.

"Sorry about that," Alan Frayne said fatuously.

Robichaux ignored the apology. For the first time since the onset of his ordeal, he spoke.

"I want a drink, and I intend to have one."

". . . don't even know the damn woman," he was saying bitterly as he grounded his glass twenty minutes later.

"She didn't pick you out deliberately," Thatcher assured him. "You were just in the wrong place at the wrong time."

Robichaux was not feeling kindly toward anybody.

"And you certainly weren't much help."

"What did you expect me to do? I would have needed a crowbar to get her off you," Thatcher defended himself.

"This is some client you've got."

"Just remember you're drinking their Scotch. Besides, we knew there was a murder investigation going on. An arrest was at least a possibility."

"They can arrest anyone they want as long as I'm not around," Tom retorted.

With Thatcher's wily encouragement, Robichaux had managed to vent most of his spleen by the time Alan Frayne returned from his bout in the restaurant's phone booth.

"Alice says she's got things under control," he reported when he sank into his seat. "And I left word where Conrad can find us."

"You don't think he'll go home?" Thatcher asked.

"Not on your life. Conrad'll avoid it like the plague until the smoke settles. He hates scenes."

"Who doesn't?" Robichaux demanded vigorously.

Thatcher intervened. "Did you find out why they've arrested Laverdiere?"

"No, Bridgeport must just be executing the warrant."

"Well, this lawyer will no doubt acquire some information when he turns up."

"We may not have to wait that long. That's why Conrad went chasing off downtown," Frayne explained. "Half the force here either worked for Ecker once, or their fathers still do. He's got plenty of buddies at the station."

Remembering Jerry's novel approach to the arrest, Thatcher could well believe that Conrad would be on matey terms with the Bridgeport police.

"God, what a mess," Frayne groaned. "I can't imagine why this has happened. The cops in New York had Bob's fingerprints on that damned skewer, but there was a reasonable explanation and they've known about it since the trade show."

Their unprofitable speculation was brought to a halt fifteen minutes later, when Conrad Ecker joined them. Without wasting time on social niceties, he beckoned a waitress and waived aside the proffered menu.

"Rye and Seven-Up," he barked with a determination that matched Tom Robichaux's.

Everybody had the sense to wait until he had taken his first sip.

"Well?" Frayne then demanded.

"Bob lied about being in the basement at Javits," Ecker replied baldly.

"Christ!"

Ecker was pursuing his own thoughts. "I knew those two had been up to something. When Bob left early yesterday, it was because the police asked him to come into the city. They put him in a lineup and somebody identified him. Tina and he have been sitting on this since five o'clock yesterday."

Well, thought Thatcher, that explained the strained dialogue between the Laverdieres. They had been waiting for the ax to fall all day.

The implications of the police action were too wide-ranging to sink in immediately, but Alan Frayne was already afraid of them.

"Wait a minute. They've been interviewing everybody at Javits for days without finding anything like this. How come somebody pops up out of the blue and claims to have been there?"

Unmoved, Conrad shot down this objection. "It's some truck driver who's been on the police list all along. He saw Bob running away from that freight elevator."

Frayne was still counterpunching. "Then why didn't he say so sooner?"

On that Conrad drew a blank. Encouraged by his shrug, Frayne continued, "And we're talking about a brief glimpse over a week ago. How good is that?"

Drearily Ecker replied, "He described Bob's barbecue apron before they had the lineup."

Gloom settled like a heavy pall and Alan Frayne's attempt to shake it off backfired.

"What does Bob say about this?"

"He swears he wasn't in the basement." Ecker paused, then added judiciously, "Bob's a damn fool."

In view of the cold realities, Thatcher was not inclined to dispute this assessment. His own roundtable at the Sloan had been quick to supply Laverdiere with a motive to murder Victor Hunnicut. Throw in being placed at the scene of the crime and things looked bleak—even without useless and misguided lies.

"And, of course, they already had him with that skewer in his hand," said Ecker, determined to lay it all out.

This drum roll of bad news was giving Thatcher insights into the Ecker Company. Tough old Conrad was a problem solver and strategist, flourishing every unpalatable detail before devising his battle plan. Alan Frayne was the scrapper, improvising as they went.

"So what does it all come down to?" Frayne asked

rhetorically. "A fingerprint on a skewer that he had every right to be handling, and a little panic about having been down to the basement. That's all they've got, and it doesn't amount to a hill of beans."

"We already have two fools around here, we don't need a third," snapped Conrad, beetling his scraggy eyebrows. "Face facts, Alan. You can't get around the fire marshal's report. That's what's got everybody targeting Bob. They can't figure out what's going on. And, for that matter, neither can I."

Forced to the wall, Frayne now put up another kind of fight. Shaking off the unexplainable, he said stubbornly, "This is circumstantial garbage. You're right, Conrad. Bob isn't the brainiest guy in the world. But he's not a murderer. You and I know that!"

John Thatcher held his tongue. Bob Laverdiere might not be lying to save his own skin, but someone else's.

Chapter

A HOSTILE TAKEOVER

Both the Sloan Guaranty Trust and the Javits Center resented figuring in the lurid coverage of Victor Hunnicut's murder. But the conventional wisdom of their experts on the subject was comforting. Beyond the wide Missouri, other banks and other exposition halls were the local fixtures, so sensationalism was geographically contained. In New York itself, another outrage would switch the spotlight elsewhere sooner rather than later.

The experts forgot that all over the nation there were kitchens with Ecker can openers on the wall and Ecker food processors in the cabinet. Since Madison Avenue had lusted in vain for an Ecker account, the trade was decidedly miffed.

"Jeez, talk about name recognition!" muttered the specialist in disposable diapers.

The night before, network news had featured Bob Laverdiere's arrival at court for his bail hearing. The mob of frenzied reporters, the chorus of howled absurdities, the Camcorders aimed like rifles had been worthy of a rock star. But when Laverdiere was hustled indoors, the chaos did not subside. With undiminished hysteria, the pack flung itself on the grimy sedan disgorging Conrad Ecker at curbside.

"And the old man couldn't have played it better," said a colleague, putting Conrad up there with Ronald McDonald, the Marlboro Man, and other immortals.

Icy rain had turned the streets into skating rinks where unsteady pedestrians were buffeted by stinging pellets. By sheer fluke, Conrad Ecker's Christmas gifts had included a deerstalker hat (from his grandson) and a wondrously gnarled Irish walking stick (from Alan Frayne). Thus equipped, he emerged to do battle with the press. Beetling his eyebrows under the checked brim, brandishing his stick, flinging pithy Americanisms at his tormentors, he had within three short minutes stomped his way into legend. Every reporter closed his coverage with a commentary on the colorful career and personality of Conrad Ecker. The hero of these potted biographies was more than life-size—successful beyond the dreams of man, remorselessly inventive, a national treasure. It was the stuff of which feature stories are made, and everyone in the media knew it.

As a result, after posting bail, the Eckers returned to Connecticut to take up life under siege.

Alan Frayne fully expected to man the fort alone, while his more vulnerable associates hid behind locked doors and drawn curtains. He was startled, when he turned from hanging up his coat the next morning, to find Tina Laverdiere striding into the office.

"My God, Tina," he protested. "You didn't have to come in today."

"There's a fence here," she replied shortly, conveying a vivid picture of conditions in Westport. "Bob's gone over to the plant."

Alan opened his mouth, took another look at her, and refrained from further comment.

At the plant they faced an even more embarrassing situation. What do you say to the boss when he's out on bail for first-degree murder? While the sales manager, the freight dispatcher, the warehouseman struggled with this question—and reached the cowardly decision not to mention the subject unless Laverdiere introduced it—the union representative took the bull by the horns.

"Glad to see you out, Bob," he grunted. "I suppose they're giving you hell over at the house."

"You wouldn't believe what it's like. We had to fight our way to the garage," said Laverdiere, more open than his wife.

"Tough."

It would have surprised Laverdiere's many detractors to learn that he was a shining star at employee relations. On the plant floor he was a reasonable man with just the right touch.

"Look, if there's going to be any trouble with the line about this, Russ, I'd appreciate a word in advance."

"Not to worry," Russ said stolidly. "I've got everything under control. After all, the guy who was killed wasn't one of ours."

Tina Laverdiere's co-workers had an easier row to hoe. No doubt existed about the proper approach here. Tina refused to utter one word about her husband's plight and conversation was confined to the business at hand.

If the Laverdiere house resembled a war zone, the Ecker home had become a carnival site. The press was incredulous and delighted to discover Conrad's modest habits. All the revealing contrasts that had fueled mild jokes at the Ecker plant for years burst on the reporters with dazzling force. Other reserved parking slots were occupied by Mercedes and BMWs while Conrad trundled around in an elderly Oldsmobile. On the long daylit evenings of summer, others left early enough to get in a round of golf. When Doug had suggested the country club to his father, Conrad had simply replied: "What would I do there?" The same disparity surfaced when management helped itself to extra holidays. The Laverdieres took ten days to ski at Chamonix, Alan Frayne disappeared into the Caribbean for two weeks, but Conrad's chosen moment came in the fall with his ritual hunting trip to New Hampshire.

Alan had seen the photographs in the newspapers and the footage on television. Now he learned from Marilyn that *People* magazine wanted to do a feature on Conrad.

"What in the world for?" he protested in spite of himself.

"They'll probably put him on the cover and push him as the sexiest old man in America," she snapped, tired from fending off too many ridiculous suppliants. "Thank God Conrad's coming in today. He can handle some of this himself."

Frayne assumed that Conrad, too, was fleeing to a secured location, but he soon learned otherwise.

"It's the insurance company," Ecker explained on arrival. "We've got a meeting today."

"Christ, I'd forgotten about them."

"Pack of vultures, that's what they are," Conrad snarled.

Automatically Frayne adopted his usual role of peacemaker.

"I suppose you can't blame them for being uneasy," he offered.

This well-intentioned attempt was shot down immediately.

"The hell I can't!"

Conrad was still fuming when Bernard Stillman of the Winstead Insurance Group was announced. Stillman, an old hand at this sort of situation, had come prepared with an opening statement designed to cast a gloss over his company's position. He was barely allowed to finish before Conrad went on the attack.

"What's the big deal? It's not as if there's a major loss here."

"Not a major loss, but a major crime."

Conrad's hackles rose.

"That charge against Bob is a lot of bullshit."

"I'm not talking about murder," Stillman said patiently. "I'm talking about arson."

Before Conrad could deliver the remark quivering on his lips, Alan Frayne intervened.

"Winstead isn't involved in investigating Hunnicut's killing, Conrad. But you can't deny they have a legitimate interest in the fire."

The mulish cast to Conrad's face suggested that he was capable of denying that two plus two equals four. Furthermore he was unwilling to admit any connection between the two crimes.

"So investigate the fire," he growled. "Nobody's stopping you."

But Bernard Stillman had not traveled to Bridgeport to avoid facing facts.

"Our legitimate interest goes well beyond the fire loss," he said evenly. "We carry a lot of your other insurance. Your product-liability coverage, for starters."

As this was one of the areas in which the police hoped to find Bob Laverdiere's motive, they were now on thin ice.

"You've never had a single claim for us on that policy," Conrad retorted.

"I am well aware of that, but your financials went up in smoke as well. Under the circumstances, Winstead would like to be assured that the reconstruction is disinterested."

"You're saying we're liars."

Stillman was neither surprised nor perturbed by his

reception. In his experience, hostility signaled only a troubled mind. And Conrad Ecker had more justification for anxiety than most. Family loyalty might dictate a posture of complete confidence, but behind that facade, Ecker must be desperately uncertain. No wonder the man sounded like a bear at stake.

Unfortunately Stillman tried to indicate understanding.

"Look, I'm saying that it's to the best interests of everybody to get this thing straightened out so we know where we stand. Ultimately we have the same goal."

Sympathy was the last thing Conrad wanted.

"You come in here calling us a bunch of crooks and then say we've got the same interests?"

"Cool down, Conrad," Frayne urged. "He's just saying Winstead wants our bank or our accountants to participate. Tina could probably use the help. We don't want to make a federal case out of this."

But Conrad Ecker was past making fine distinctions. Heaving himself to his feet, he glared defiantly across the desk.

"There's not a damn thing crooked about my company."

"No one would be happier to be assured of that than Winstead."

"Crap! What you really mean is that you think we're up to our elbows in some kind of dirt."

Looking into the red face hovering over him, Stillman tried to lower the temperature. "Not at all. We merely want to clear away some of the doubts that have been caused by these crimes."

"Oh, yeah!" Conrad shot back, drawing himself up to his full height. "Then I'll tell you what. Bring in your own accountants and do the job by yourself. You won't find a single thing wrong."

Frayne sighed. "You don't mean that, Conrad. There's no reason this can't be a joint undertaking."

"Like hell I don't mean it." Already circling his desk, Ecker swiveled toward Stillman. "You heard me. Winstead can reconstruct the files. Be my guest, have yourself a ball."

Swift to capitalize on this rash invitation, Stillman nodded.

"We can have our people in here tomorrow."

Conrad was already at the door.

"Go ahead. Just don't give me any of this horsewater about common interests."

The slamming door supplied the punctuation.

It was Alan Frayne who had the unenviable task of breaking the news to Tina.

Taut as a whip, she repeated his statement in tones of stark disbelief.

"Winstead takes over completely? I'm totally out of the picture?"

"That's what Conrad agreed to."

Tina's fingers were flexing and unflexing like claws. "Conrad might as well have come out and said I'm not to be trusted. How could he do that?"

"Conrad got himself into one of his states," Alan said wearily. "He was accusing and denying and this was just his way of throwing down a challenge to Winstead. He didn't think how it would look."

"Then why didn't you make him understand?"

"You know what Conrad's like when he gets going. Nobody could have stopped him. And maybe it's not such a bad idea anyway."

Tina's level glance flicked across Frayne.

"You, too, Alan?"

"Oh, for Chrissake! You know better than that, Tina. But the pressure is going to stay on until this is cleared up. What difference does it make who does the job? It'll be a relief to have it over and done with."

"The rest of you don't know what pressure is. Bob's

the one who's under arrest for murder. And how in God's name do I explain this to him?''

Frayne shifted uncomfortably. "This doesn't have anything to do with Bob," he mumbled.

"Says who?"

". . . so the Winstead boys will be going in there tomorrow," Tom Robichaux concluded his report.

"Very satisfactory from everybody's point of view," Thatcher commented. "And this came about because Conrad Ecker lost his head and challenged them to do their damnedest?"

"That's what Winstead claims." Robichaux paused to take the first critical sip of his vodka martini. "Don't believe it for a second myself."

As usual, Tom Robichaux's utterance could stand clarification.

"You think Winstead's lying?"

"No, I don't believe the old man lost his head."

It was rare indeed for Tom to cast himself as a percipient analyst of human motivation.

"Go on," said Thatcher, enthralled.

Robichaux, after glancing around for enemy ears, lowered his voice. "Fact of the matter is, same thing happened over at our shop years ago. My father told me about it. They began to suspect one of the youngsters was diddling his accounts but it was awkward, his being family. They didn't want to start anything themselves, so they goaded the outsiders into demanding an investigation. Back at the turn of the century, that was."

Nobody likes scandal in their organization but Thatcher felt that after a hundred years it was no longer necessary to whisper.

"So the Robichauxs have a skeleton in their closet," he said bracingly. "What difference does it make by now?"

But Tom was waggling his head solemnly.

"Wasn't a Robichaux," he intoned. "It was a Devane."

"Ah!"

Some things remain constant. For four generations Robichaux sprigs had sowed wild oats with wine, women, and song. The Devanes, Quaker to a man, had been cut from different cloth. They dissipated their youthful high spirits by driving ambulances for the American Friends Service Committee. The shots from Sarajevo had barely died away before they were speeding around the trenches. Subsequent decades had given them more continents to play with. At this very moment, Thatcher recalled, Francis Devane had a grandson in Ethiopia.

"That's interesting," he said, tactfully turning to less sensitive areas. "So you think Conrad Ecker did this deliberately? It makes sense, of course. He has more reason than anyone to want to know what's happening."

But now that Robichaux had remembered that even a Devane could go wrong, nobody was above suspicion.

"Unless he already has a damn good idea."

Although Conrad Ecker dispensed with fancy cars and country clubs, he was the beneficiary of at least some perquisites of power. Regularly, if unconsciously, he drove his companions wild—and they never retaliated. Today was to prove a gold-star exception.

Having shoveled his difficulties onto other backs, Conrad carefully removed himself from the fall-out area. Arriving home flushed with success, he incautiously answered the phone. The voice that pierced his eardrum resembled a whistling teakettle.

"Dear Lord, what is going on there? They've arrested Bob and Tina won't talk to me, I don't know what—"

"Virginia? Will you calm down? I can't understand you."

"Calm down? I saw it all on TV. They have my son in

jail, where anything could happen to him. It must be some terrible mistake and . . ."

It was typical of his sister, thought Conrad, that she had seen the coverage of Bob in custody and failed to catch the footage of his release.

"Bob's not in jail anymore," he bawled over the nonstop flow.

"What's that?"

Alice had now been attracted by the bull-like roars emanating from her husband. Wildly Conrad semaphored toward the kitchen.

"He's out on bail," he continued. "So you can relax."

"If he's home, why doesn't he answer my call? All I ever get is the answering machine. There's something you're not telling me," the dental drill said accusingly.

With profound relief, Conrad had heard the click of an extension.

"Virginia, it's me, Alice. There's nothing we're not telling you. But Bob and Tina are being hounded by the press, so they're probably not listening to their messages."

"My poor baby, going through this all alone," moaned Virginia, erasing wife and uncle in one sweep. "I'll fly out as soon as I've packed."

Conrad, who had carried the phone to the limit of its cord, was shaking his head furiously at the kitchen doorway.

"You mustn't do that."

"How can you say that, Alice? My place is at my son's side. If it were Doug, you wouldn't hesitate for a second."

It is difficult to tell someone that her mere presence may be the straw that breaks the camel's back. But Alice, more concerned for Bob and Tina than for her husband, knew she had to come up with something.

Infusing her voice with grave anxiety, she said: "It's the children, Virginia. That house is no place for them. If there's no improvement, the best thing would be to send them to you."

Virginia's neutral murmur suggested that she was torn between the roles of tigress mother and savior grandmother.

"I know Tina's at her wit's end," Alice continued slyly. "But I suppose the children could go to *her* family."

That did the trick. Unfortunately, Virginia was now free to turn to other matters.

"How could anyone think of Bob as a murderer? It's just so absurd. And why isn't Conrad doing something? You'd think that after fifteen years . . ."

Alice was able to run interference with Conrad's sister, but she was out when his daughter called. The ensuing conversation was alarming enough to make Betty take the unusual step of speaking to her ex-husband twice within the same week.

"Alan, I'm worried about Daddy."

It had been a long, hard day for Frayne.

"And I'm worried about everyone. Bob and Tina are just about at the breaking point."

"Oh, so little Miss Efficiency can't handle this one," purred his ex-wife with malicious satisfaction.

Frayne sighed. Tina had always been a problem for Betty. On the one hand, as she became more and more captive to the Westport way of life, Betty found employment at the Ecker mill unspeakably plebeian. On the other hand, she had never warmed to the sight of her father and her husband and her brother including Tina in their business discussions. To be absolutely fair, Tina had not helped the situation any with her open boredom at the long recitals of Betty's cultural triumphs.

"God, can't you lay off for a minute? We've got enough on our plates. The last thing any of us needs— and that includes Conrad—is a lot of sniping from some-one on the other side of the country."

Affronted, she retreated into dignity. "I am naturally concerned about my family."

"Crap! You want to be part of the action in Bridgeport when it suits you, and forget about us the rest of the time. You're the one who decided to take off. So now, why don't you just butt out?"

One of the underrated joys of divorce is the glorious freedom from previous inhibition. When Alan Frayne finally hung up, he reflected with pleasure that some other man was going to have to cope with the inevitable sulks.

Taking a leaf from the Laverdieres' book, Conrad Ecker had resorted to the answering machine himself. But this was no protection when trouble loomed right in his own precious workshop.

"I don't see what you're bellyaching about," he told a white-faced Bob Laverdiere.

"Like hell you don't!"

After two irritating exchanges with his female relatives, Conrad was ripe for blood.

"Don't blame me for your problems," he thundered. Then, with considerable satisfaction, he reviewed his nephew's blunders. Bob had started a fight with Victor Hunnicut, waved a skewer around, and told a bunch of stupid lies. "Naturally you're in hot water. It's all your own silly fault."

Over the years Conrad had become accustomed to dismissing his nephew without a second thought. But this time he sparked a fierce counterattack.

"Oh, sure! Who got the wonderful idea of selling in the first place? Who decided that ASI was the way to go? Who brought that little shit Hunnicut up here? You set the whole stage for big trouble, and then you act as if forcing Ives into an apology solved everything. Like hell it did. All it did was save your face."

Genuinely outraged at the suggestion of flaws in his

own performance, Conrad took his stand on what he regarded as unassailable ground.

"Don't forget you'll make a mint out of the sale."

"Listen, you're not talking to Mother now," Bob flashed back as if he possessed second sight. "Tina and I have given you fifteen years of hard work and loyalty. And as soon as the insurance company uses a little muscle, what do you do? You throw Tina to the wolves."

"That's not what it means—"

"You might just as well have accused her of fraud."

Alice, fluttering around the belligerents like a moth, tried to mediate.

"Now, you're both saying more than you mean."

Her husband, striving to regain his usual dominance, paid no attention. "That's crazy," he blustered. "I'm just letting them do the dogwork. It isn't as if—"

"In fact," Bob broke in, "anybody would think you know there's something wrong."

He was overriding Conrad with an ease that stung his uncle.

"It's my company. I can do what I like."

"Not when it comes to railroading Tina."

"Who the hell do you think you are? I'll do any damn thing I like to protect my son's interests."

Bob was piling on the scorn.

"Your company, your son. What it all boils down to is *you.*"

"Oh, Lord, now we're in for it," Alice half-whispered.

Both men were on their feet, facing each other in bristling anger. Their legs were splayed, their shoulders hunched, their jaws thrust forward. To Alice the most alarming feature was their resemblance to each other. With Conrad so sensitive about Doug and Bob so sensitive about Tina, there would be no holding them.

"How dare you say that!" Conrad roared.

But Bob was going from strength to strength.

"You're selling out so Doug will never have to worry about money. You don't give a damn about anything else. That's all this company is to you—a chance to play God any way you want to. And you're ready to shaft everybody else—me, Tina, Alan. Sure, you've put a lot of sweat into this, but so have we. Well, play with your toys, but keep your mitts off Tina."

"So you're taking care of Tina now. Well, that's a switch," Conrad sneered. "For years she's had to play mother to you."

Shaking his head as if he had received a blow, Bob sucked in his breath and then went straight for the jugular.

"You know what your trouble is? We all felt sorry for Doug when he had his heart attack. But you felt sorry for yourself," he snarled, deliberately trampling over sacred ground. "That's the way it's always been. All you can see is that something's upset your apple cart. You've been sour as hell ever since. You're just jealous that the rest of us are here and Doug isn't. While you're running around telling everybody that Tina's responsible for the company's finances, why don't you go further? Why don't you tell them Doug set up our little systems and Doug is now in Florida managing God knows what investments."

With eyes bulging, Conrad slammed a meaty palm on the bench so hard he involuntarily winced.

"Get out of my house!" he yelled. "Get out right now!"

For the first time in many a year it was Conrad Ecker who broke off hostilities.

Chapter

RED INK

W hat goes up, comes down—although usually not at the same time. Nevertheless, just as the Ecker Company catapulted into nationwide notoriety, it dropped off the radar screen at ASI. Some buzzing about Victor Hunnicut's murder continued throughout the tabloid-reading work force, but headquarters was suddenly overtaken by something far more ominous.

". . . according to my sources, here's what they're taking to the grand jury," said the bearer of bad news. With lawyerly exhaustiveness, he read out a list of criminal and civil charges that turned his audience pale.

". . . and finally, two shipments of bored pipes— that's gun barrels in everyday language—to Gubelhaas GmbH, a front for Libya. Sparling will be charged with violating II Commerce 48–50. That carries jail time as well as a hefty fine. In other words, gentlemen, Sparling's about to raise an almighty stink."

With a bleak look at Phil Pepitone, Wade Sullivan, ASI's internal auditor, dismissed counsel's opinion. "We already knew that Sparling is a disaster area."

Since everybody else grasped the difference between a financial disappointment and a public catastrophe, Sullivan's ill-advised comment was met with silence. Around Gardner Ives's big desk, the men charting ASI's immediate future rubbed their jaws, fiddled with their glasses, and thought darkly about Sparling Castings, of Muncie, Indiana.

Sparling had been ASI's first timid venture in acquisition. It had been promoted, by Phil Pepitone, among others, as a modest expansion of ASI's core business. Tubing, pipes, and well-digging equipment, when available at the right price, had looked like a safe and solid bet.

But, as Sullivan had just reminded them, Sparling never really panned out. Plagued by inexplicable breakdowns, output rarely met monthly quotas. Accounting slovenliness surfaced with alarming regularity. Within two years, opinion at ASI was sharply divided along party lines. Sparling was either a bad joke, or a criminal mistake.

The more vocal faction insisted that it was all Phil Pepitone's fault. Their carping had never weighed heavily on him. Since Sparling, a minor specialty operation, was too small to merit top-echelon attention, he dismissed lower-level criticism as petty backbiting. Privately, Pepitone remained confident that, in the fullness of time, he could take care of both Sparling and his detractors.

The shattering news from Muncie had just wrecked this game plan. Sparling was no longer a troublesome thorn in Pepitone's side; it was an ASI emergency.

"Thank God, we've got the policy in place," Gardner Ives congratulated himself.

The working party nodded dutifully, although damage control was not a popular assignment. But too many oil spills, chemical explosions, and doctored cough drops have encouraged companies like ASI to brace for any contingency.

"You all know the drill," Ives continued, impersonating a squadron leader.

The team's practical experience was limited. Nonetheless, preparations promptly got under way. The strategists pondered how and when to launch overtures to the governmental agencies pursuing Sparling. To neutralize adverse public reaction, press releases were stockpiled, describing ASI as a tower of integrity, a victim of misplaced trust or—in the worst-case scenario—a penitent sinner. Finally, an elite unit was readied for a rescue mission to Muncie. These operations were conducted on a need-to-know basis.

"They're trying to play it close to the chest," said Ken Nicolls, phoning the Sloan from his cubbyhole at ASI. "Of course everybody knows."

"Of course," Thatcher repeated with some asperity. Earlier in the morning he had digested situation reports from the Ecker Company that included, above and beyond the arrest of Bob Laverdiere, serious internecine fighting and a no-holds-barred insurance inquisition. Even without unsavory developments at the ASI end, Tom Robichaux's golden merger was beginning to look like Sloan time and money wasted.

And, as Ken Nicolls assured him, there was more to come.

"Nobody's admitting anything," said Ken, conjuring up tight-lipped men who knew all and said nothing, "but it's the girls who do the typing. Everybody in the place is waiting for Sparling to explode like a bomb."

The impossibility of keeping secrets is a recurring shock to some minds. Thatcher simply accepted Ken Nicolls's hearsay at face value. Even when the boys do the typing, there will be leaks.

"They may be overreacting," he observed, looking without much success for a rosy lining. "It isn't as if ASI is a titan of American industry."

From his ringside seat Nicolls respectfully disagreed.

"Maybe," he said, "but even if there aren't major convulsions when the news breaks, ASI's already all steamed up. They're pretty close to panic here."

"That," said Thatcher grimly, "is all we need. One merger partner is in the thick of a murder and the other is semi-hysterical. Remind me to avoid Robichaux for a while."

Apart from the imminence of pyrotechnics, Nicolls had little to add about ASI. His own research into ASI's pension funding, as it would impact Ecker, was proceeding. The police, who had been omnipresent for a few days, had disappeared since Laverdiere's arrest. All was calm, except for the tom-toms beating up in Gardner Ives's neck of the woods.

"They're locking the barn door after the horse has been stolen," Thatcher reflected aloud.

Nicolls was not sure that he followed.

"If a little of this effort you describe had been expended on supervising Sparling," Thatcher explained, "these dramatics might have been avoided."

"Well, they're scurrying now," Nicolls told him.

"I'm sure that will be a great comfort for Robichaux and Devane."

The Sloan Guaranty Trust, it went without saying, was reserving judgment.

The activity level at ASI was high, and rising. Ad-hoc conferences cluttered the hallways while last-minute typing kept the Princeton lights burning late. People rushed in and out of Ives's office at all hours, with adrenaline pumping.

Conspicuously absent from the loop was Phil Pepitone. His opinion was not solicited and progress reports bypassed his desk.

"Hell, you'd think I was the only one responsible for picking up Sparling," he grumbled. "People want to forget that the board went along, just like Ives. Now, you'd think I was contagious."

Pepitone's allies recognized his wisdom in downplaying a pivotal role in the Sparling purchase. Less comprehensible was his current placidity. Apart from complaints to his closer associates—and to Irene—Pepitone endured his internal exile stoically. Necessity distanced him from Gardner Ives and the Sparling salvage mission. Otherwise he remained as vigorous as usual, and even somewhat more genial. His behavior prompted some misguided allusions to grace under pressure, but Phil Pepitone could not play nature's nobleman if he tried.

He did, however, expect to emerge from this flap with a whole skin.

"I can sit this one out, if I have to wait until hell freezes over."

Long before that, fatigue began taking its toll on Gardner Ives.

"Is that the best you can do?" he demanded.

Through pleas, threats, and cajolery, his hard-pressed staff was making perceptible progress. Legal proceedings remained inescapable, as did severe financial penalties. But the burden of delinquency was firmly attached to Sparling, with barely a mention of ASI. The much-feared PR bloodbath was fizzling. Few Americans are mesmerized by industrial piping, and really juicy scandals need the human touch that both ASI and Sparling lacked.

For Ives, anything short of perfection left a bad taste.

"It's giving me some second thoughts," he said, after most of his lieutenants had filed back to the treadmill.

The man sitting where Phil Pepitone usually sat read him perfectly.

"About Phil?" he suggested.

"About Phil—and about Ecker, too," said Ives repressively. Like everybody else, he had convinced himself that Pepitone was the sole author of the Sparling troubles. Beyond that, he did not care to comment aloud.

"Look, Gardner, give the guy a break. So, Sparling was a bummer. Everybody makes mistakes. What's past is past. We should put Sparling behind us as soon as we can—and let Phil off the hook right now."

Ives sighed, reminded once more that quarantining Pepitone had cost him the sharpest intelligence at ASI. Any dolt could sermonize about forgiving nasty revelations from the past. As Phil Pepitone would have been first to point out, it was the future, and the Ecker Company, that counted now.

In most corners of ASI, Sparling was somebody else's problem. One of these remote outposts was Sam Bradley's lab. There, sublime ignorance about infractions of the law was balanced by vast authority about mankind.

"Somebody's head will have to roll," predicted one owlish researcher. "My guess is that Pepitone's days are numbered. Oh, he could tough it out when people were just talking about Sparling. Now that it's blown up in his face, he doesn't have a future here."

A colleague quarreled with this analysis.

"You're oversimplifying, Stanley. Sure, people would like to give Pepitone the shove, wrap him and Sparling up in the same package. But don't forget Ecker. Because canning Phil would mean that Ives is ready to scratch Ecker. And I don't see him doing that. In fact, Sparling actually helps Phil's position. It shows how ASI really has to broaden into the consumer field.

Diversification is the only insurance against risks like these."

Sam Bradley, without openly encouraging idle speculation, helped it along.

"What makes you think Phil's in trouble?" he asked, as if he did not already know.

"God, Sam. They're treating him like an untouchable already," said the expert.

"People always have their ups and downs here at ASI," said Bradley, tolerant of human frailty. Few of them, he did not add, were as resilient as Pepitone. "I wouldn't count Phil out too soon."

However, once the possibility was raised, it proved difficult to dislodge. Deep in calculation, Bradley retreated to his office where, quite coolly, he contemplated an ASI without Phil Pepitone. Then he moved on to an ASI without the Ecker Company, and his detachment began to falter.

"Who cares if Pepitone comes or goes!" Fred Uhlrich fulminated. "I'd trade the whole front office to get Vic Hunnicut back."

This was not his eulogy to the departed. The murder had left Uhlrich's Water Purification Division shorthanded during a hiring freeze. So he was sedulously cultivating every assistant division manager he could collar, seeking a replacement. His current catch was finishing lunch in the cafeteria.

"One of you guys should put in for it," Uhlrich said, reverting to his main theme. By transferring into Water Purification, some assistant would be making a smart career move. Familiarity with one of ASI's most profitable divisions would look good when the time came for promotion. And, to sweeten the pot, Uhlrich thought he could wangle a tidy little raise.

For a variety of reasons, his arguments fell on deaf ears. Technical qualifications are not as easily interchanged as Uhlrich wanted to pretend. Water Purification was too blue-collar for some tastes. And while Uhlrich was appealing to prudence, the young men he was exhorting had bigger ideas.

"Good old Fred," said one of them when Uhlrich left to pursue his quest elsewhere. "Solid as the Rock of Gibraltar."

"Particularly between the ears."

"Oh, come on," Wiley Quinn protested. "Fred's the best damned division manager at ASI, and you know it."

"So why don't you take him up?" replied his companion. "Transfer into Purification, work your tail off for ten years, and chalk up enough brownie points to get promoted before you retire. Who're you kidding, Wiley? That's Fred's style—not yours and mine."

Quinn had to agree. He was less disrespectful than some of his contemporaries, but he was of their generation. And the new wave at ASI, like new waves everywhere, had a lot to teach its elders.

"Poor Fred doesn't realize that if Pepitone's really riding for a fall, the whole equation here gets rewritten," said Wiley's tablemate, resuming the discussion Uhlrich had interrupted.

Exchanging generalizations came naturally to Quinn and his friends, but Phil Pepitone brought them to a subject that caused more constraint.

Quinn finally broke the ice. "If Pepitone's on the way out, where do you think that leaves the Ecker merger?"

"Oh, I think Ecker would still be on," said his colleague airily. Like Quinn and every other assistant, he viewed Ecker through a private prism. It was the only fast track in sight. "That's always supposing that the Laverdiere arrest doesn't sour things. I suppose you're real relieved that they're off your case, Wiley."

Wiley Quinn ignored the jibe. Luck had given him an

advantage over his rivals. Being present at Javits when Hunnicut was cut down had singled him out of the crowd. Gardner Ives and Sam Bradley and Phil Pepitone all knew who he was, which was more than most assistants could claim.

Unfortunately, the police did, too. Quinn told himself that this no longer posed any threat. But, since it always pays to be prepared, he began thinking of ways to deflect a threat, should the need arise.

NOTICE OF REDEMPTION

While ASI was still waiting for attacks from outside, the enemy was already within the gates at Ecker. The Winstead Insurance Group had descended like a wolf on the fold. They had been received with arctic civility by Tina Laverdiere. She introduced them to her assistants, delivered a short lecture on the location of key documents, and then, her back like a ramrod, stalked to her car and swept out of the compound.

She was not the only one lying low. For several days there was not a peep from Conrad himself. Immersed in his workshop at home, he simply ignored the occupying forces. He was not hiding from Winstead; he was trying to avoid the Laverdieres.

Alan Frayne, therefore, was the only member of Ecker's top management who remained at his post during the invasion. Whenever he emerged from his test laboratory, he saw accountants in every nook and cranny of the company, file clerks stacking invoices, and strangers monopolizing the phones. On the third day they even penetrated his own domain.

"Examine anything you want," he invited gruffly.

"We won't disturb you long," the leader promised. "Just a quick look at your current records."

"Sure," Frayne grunted with a jaundiced smile.

He was no longer the calm reassuring presence to which his co-workers had become accustomed. When he encountered Marilyn, carrying a pile of ledgers, he could not restrain a grimace.

"More fodder for their mill?"

She shrugged. "Conrad said to show them everything."

"I know. He's even letting them see the results on stuff that isn't patented yet. God knows I don't blame him for being out of his mind with worry, but I don't see how we'll ever get back to normal."

"One of them told me they'll be gone by the end of the week."

Frayne rejected this offering.

"I'm not talking about them, Marilyn. I'm talking about us. Bob and Conrad still aren't talking to each other. I went over to Bob's place last night but it was a waste of time. There's no reasoning with him."

"At least he's got some excuse. He's been arrested for murder. But Conrad is such a stubborn old fool!" she said tartly. "When he called this morning he just refused to discuss it with me."

"Well, we've got a great future," Frayne sighed. "The chairman of the board and the president are both holed up, hiding from each other, and an insurance company is putting us through the wringer."

Alan Frayne saw only the immediate convulsions, but the ripples spread far beyond the confines of the Ecker compound. There is, after all, a basic arithmetic to all manufacturing operations. The production of goods entails certain costs. The sale of those goods generates income. The difference is profit. Of course there are niceties, such as deciding whether inventory will be valued on a FIFO basis: first in, first out; or a LIFO basis: last in, first out. These and other subtleties offer opportunities for the enterprising felon. But the basic simplicity remains.

Once the Winstead team had assembled the numbers available in Bridgeport, they turned their attention to corroborative sources of information. But wherever they went, the story was the same. Suppliers confirmed Ecker's purchases, customers confirmed its sales, the union confirmed its payroll. And very few of those contacted could resist praising Conrad Ecker and all his works.

In New York the buyer for a major chain of department stores produced his records, then scoffed at the suggestion of manufacturing defects.

"Are you crazy? That is one company that stands behind its products. Why, I remember once about five years ago," he said, waxing nostalgic, "some idiot woman returned a can opener saying it didn't work. She must have had it for twenty years because it was gummed up with the filth of ages. But I asked Conrad how he wanted to handle it, and do you know what he did? He had the damned thing steam-cleaned and returned it with a polite note suggesting that if she brushed out the dirt every couple of years, it would work forever."

In California the representative of a federation of independently owned hardware stores was more interested in extracting information than furnishing it.

"Say, do you actually know Conrad Ecker? What's he like? I've just seen him on TV," he said chattily to the phone. "Doug Ecker used to come out here once a year, but I've never met the old man. I'm real sorry I didn't make it to the New York trade show this year."

Upon being pressed for any negative experience with Ecker goods, he simply snorted.

"Hell, I've had one of their coffeepots myself for ten years and it's still got the original glass bubble."

A supplier in Chicago produced a backhanded compliment.

"The only thing wrong with Ecker is that they're so damned picky. If our stuff isn't well within specs, they ship it right back to me. Of course," he continued reflectively, "I don't put up a fight. Somebody else'll take it."

As an afterthought he admitted that Ecker was otherwise irreproachable. They ordered with sufficient lead time and they paid on the dot.

At the union office in Hartford they chortled at the notion that Ecker might be shortchanging the pension fund.

"You've got to be kidding. That's the kind of thing we notice. Every penny is paid when due." With some difficulty the muscular speaker rose above his parochial concerns. "At least that's the way it is with our fund. I wouldn't know about the management fund. But who cares about that? If you ask me, the old man is overpaying them anyway."

But nowhere were they more indignant at the possibility of irregularity than at Bridgeport City Hall. In an ancient mill town with a crumbling industrial economy, a local son had fathered a flourishing enterprise and become a major employer. The Ecker Company contributed to municipal coffers in many guises. Conrad had always been regarded with respect in the city treasurer's office. Since his emergence as a national personality, they were inclined to be reverential.

"It's more than that," they said after assuring Winstead that all taxes were up-to-date. "They do a lot for this town. They gave us the land for the East End Park, the company sponsors a Little League team, and Mrs. Ecker was vice-chairman of the Heart Fund this year."

And the many professionals employed to assist Ecker merely swelled the chorus. The auditors reported that all was sweetness and light with the Internal Revenue Service. The lawyers saw no problems on any distant horizon. The bankers affirmed that all accounts were in order.

". . . what's more," Thatcher informed Winstead's New York representative, "Milo Thompson always rated Ecker as one of our most creditworthy clients. We've had no reason to change that evaluation."

After ten days of sustained effort, Winstead's chief investigator took a deep breath and prepared to confront his superior.

"What the hell have you been doing?" demanded Bernard Stillman.

"Tearing the place apart. And we haven't come up with one damned thing."

When he unleashed the dogs of war, Stillman had become a general ordering the saturation bombing of an enemy city. Now he was being presented with aerial photos of an unscathed target. Like most generals, he assumed his troops had been attacking the wrong town.

But not according to his subordinate.

"We've checked purchases and sales, taxes and payroll. My God, I had boxes and crates opened so we could actually count inventory. The boys have talked to everybody who does business with the company, and they're all happy. Ecker is so clean it squeaks."

Conveniently forgetting that he himself had initiated this draconic probe, Stillman said swiftly, "Well, Dan, we already knew they'd been vetted a couple of months ago. So it has to be a recent scam."

Dan looked at him more in sorrow than in anger. "If

you're thinking somebody looted a couple of million, forget it, Bernie. The Sloan showed us all the records. Nothing's gone missing."

"What about an enormous liability of their manufacturer's warranty?"

Dan shook his head. "No way. We've talked to most of their major customers. The story's the same everywhere. Ecker products don't have defects."

"You haven't talked to all of them."

"Be reasonable, Bernie. Maybe one Ecker food processor did turn into a grenade. If so, the victim's been damn quiet about it."

"Pollution!" Stillman cried desperately. "They're sitting on a giant toxic waste dump."

"Ecker isn't into chemicals. And neither was the outfit that was on the site before them. All their waste is accounted for, and it isn't the lethal stuff anyway."

"Who knows what's lethal these days?"

Even to his own ears, Stillman sounded as if he were flailing. But he stubbornly persisted.

"Half these poisons they didn't know about years ago. Maybe everybody at Ecker has some rare form of cancer."

"OSHA inspects regularly. It would have to be so rare the government doesn't know about it, the union medical people don't know about it, and the victims don't know about it. In which case, how come the Eckers know about it?"

Stillman's jaw suggested that he was silenced but not convinced.

"Look, Bernie, it's not impossible that there's a cute wrinkle somewhere," Dan conceded. "For all I know, a supplier could be playing a straw man for one of the Eckers. But then the company is even stronger than it looks, if it's absorbing that kind of cost and still doing so well."

Stillman thought he saw an opening.

"You think somebody might be afraid Hunnicut tumbled to this scam?"

"Not a chance. If we can't find it, he sure didn't," said Dan, on his professional mettle.

"But if there's nothing wrong there, why are they setting fires and killing people?"

"Maybe they aren't. Maybe someone else is."

At the Sloan Guaranty Trust they were pleased to learn that their client had been given a clean bill of health, but they reserved their professional appreciation for one particular aspect of the final report.

"Good heavens! Have you seen this summary on their credit union?" Everett Gabler exclaimed.

Two negative grunts were his only reply as Thatcher and Charlie Trinkam continued to study different items.

"Fiscal responsibility of the highest order!"

Bursts of commendation from this quarter were so rare that both of the others abandoned their own documents to move behind Gabler and read over his shoulder.

After a cursory examination, Trinkam went further. "They could sure teach a lot to some of those bozos up in Rhode Island," he remarked, referring to some spectacular failures.

John Thatcher delayed responding to complete his mathematical calculations.

"Don't be so niggardly, Charlie. Proportionately speaking, you could say they're doing better than most New York banks."

A moment later he regretted his impetuous remark. On this subject Gabler could go on forever. Charlie and Thatcher, both instinctively moving to avert the familiar lecture, collided in mid-air.

"Their real estate valuations are so conservative that . . ."

"Ecker's been booming. Instead of laying off, they've actually been hiring, so the credit union . . ."

What was good news at the Sloan was bad news at New York City Police Headquarters.

"If everything's on the up-and-up at that company, then all we've got is opportunity and means," the captain grunted when Inspector Giorni delivered the results.

"That's right."

"The DA isn't going to like this."

"It was his idea to charge Laverdiere so fast," Giorni pointed out diplomatically. "You wanted more time."

"They always flake out when there are big headlines," the captain said, freely libeling prosecutors around the country. "I suppose now they'll try to claim that Laverdiere flew into a rage when he found out Hunnicut set the fire."

Giorni was shaking his head with solemn deliberation.

"They may try, but it won't get them anywhere. I haven't told you the worst. We've been monitoring Hunnicut's credit-card charges and one of them was for gas up in northern New Jersey the day after the fire."

"Who cares where he bought gas that day?"

"That's what I thought, so I didn't give it any priority. But Sergeant Knudsen used his head when he saw the charge. He already knew that Hunnicut had been at work all day and at his fencing club all evening. There didn't seem to be enough free time for a hundred-mile round trip, so Knudsen drove over to check it out."

The captain was frowning. "And?" he demanded impatiently.

"Knudsen says he knew he was on to something the minute he saw where the gas station was. It's right off the George Washington bridge on the Jersey side, and it's one of those all-night deals. The owner said

Knudsen should talk to the kid who comes on duty at ten o'clock at night. Knudsen hung around and, sure enough, the kid remembered the whole thing. It was snowing when Hunnicut pulled in, driving one of those Audis with automatic all-wheel drive. The kid's father is thinking of buying one, so he asked Hunnicut how it handled and they gabbed some about the car."

The frown was beginning to carve deep trenches across the captain's forehead.

"Wait a minute," he objected. "Are you talking about the night they had the fire at Ecker?"

"That's the night it snowed. The kid says he'd been on for at least a couple of hours when Hunnicut arrived. According to the weather bureau, the snow started there shortly after midnight. It all fits in with the date on the charge slip."

"Then that would mean Victor Hunnicut left that Thai restaurant in Bridgeport, got into his car, and drove home. What about the identification? Is it solid, or does the kid just want to get his picture in the papers?"

Giorni reluctantly shattered this hope. "The kid mentioned it to the station owner as soon as Hunnicut's murder was on TV."

"Then why the hell didn't he mention it to us?" the outraged captain demanded. Veering in his assessment of the station attendant as a notoriety seeker to indifferent Joe Citizen, he proclaimed: "That's what's wrong with all these kids."

"He didn't know trips to and from Bridgeport were important."

"He should have read more thoroughly!"

Moved by some obscure compulsion to defend this particular member of the younger generation, Giorni said mildly, "The kid goes to college all day and works all night. I don't suppose he's got a lot of free time."

"All right, all right. What does the fire marshal up in Bridgeport say? Any chance of a timing device?"

"Nope. This was a real simple job. No fuses, no timers, nothing beyond a lit match. Victor Hunnicut had nothing to do with that fire. He didn't see who set it and he didn't do the job himself. He was home in bed."

The captain groaned.

"Wait until the DA hears this one. That leaves him without a shred of motive for Bob Laverdiere."

"Not to mention that there's a whole slew of motives at ASI, and their people were all at Javits, too. Besides, I've got another goodie for you. The guys manning the booths at the trade show were all wearing badges, which has been a big help tracking Hunnicut. That is, until we came across a security guard who remembered an ASI badge by the right freight elevator but claimed it wasn't Hunnicut. So we flashed a bunch of pictures at him and guess what? Wiley Quinn was there at just about the right time."

"Quinn?"

"He's the one Hunnicut was putting down when Laverdiere charged in."

Both policemen silently contemplated what an adroit defense attorney could do with that.

"If you ask me," Giorni said dispassionately, "I don't think the DA can get past a preliminary hearing."

"And yet Laverdiere has been covering something for all he's worth. In fact, he's been lying his head off."

The captain scrubbed his bald spot in vexation as he reached his conclusion.

"And there's got to be a damn good reason why."

Chapter

20

WHITE KNIGHT

Institutions invariably favor other institutions. As a result, the lowly mortals caught up in critical situations are often the last to be apprised of significant information. After the Winstead Group had chewed over the results of its investigation, after it had honored its obligations to the Sloan Guaranty Trust and the New York City Police Department, after its adjuster had held a long discussion with Bridgeport's fire marshal, Bernard Stillman finally realized that a certain courtesy call might be in order.

Tina Laverdiere did not exactly overflow on the phone.

"Thank you for letting me know," she said formally.

"And of course we'll be sending you a copy of the final report."

"I'd appreciate receiving it as soon as possible."

Then she cradled the receiver. After days of nerve-stretching anxiety, she should have been conscious of relief. But the overwhelming sense of constriction was still with her. There was only one way to end it.

With sudden decision she rose.

"I'm going over to see Bob," she told her secretary. "It may take a while."

Her husband, instead of being in his office, was floating around the plant, and the production area had never been Tina's natural home. Adding to her difficulties was the prevailing din. The high ceilings of the old mill echoed back the clank of equipment and the whir of motor belts so effectively that every question had to be shouted. And wherever she went, the story was the same.

"I'm looking for Bob," she yelled over the stamping presses.

"He was here a couple of minutes ago," someone shouted back. "I think he was heading over to toasters."

As her search continued past the clangor of milling machines and metal lathes, every exchange was audible to dozens of people. Even in the comparative calm of a wiring room, the women at the long bench were so intent that there, too, normal volume was useless.

"Edna."

No answer.

"Edna! Where's Bob?"

The longer her trip lasted, the more edgy Tina became. From floor to floor she trudged, her progress rousing considerable curiosity. The Ecker line was familiar with a cool, efficient Tina. They had heard talk from the accounting department of brief flare-ups. But cold or hot, she was always punctilious. This Tina was barely in control, confining herself to jerked-out phrases because she could not trust herself to say any more.

"Bob's gone?"

"He just left."

"Where to?"

She had covered the entire building by the time she spotted her husband in the farthest corner of the top floor. The mysterious warning system that exists in all workplaces had preceded her, so that the entire shift watched her stiff-legged approach.

Bob was deep in consultation with the foreman for coffeepots.

"I need you," she interrupted unceremoniously.

"In a minute, honey," he replied, barely glancing up. "Jed's got an equipment problem. Why don't you wait in—"

"NOW!"

Without another word she swung on her heel, to the fascination of all onlookers.

If Bob was slow to read the signs, Jed was not.

"I can take it from here," he muttered hurriedly.

Forced into a trot to keep his wife in view, Bob pattered down the stairs and followed her into his own office. The door was barely closed before she said tightly, "Winstead just called with the final results and we're in the clear. There's absolutely nothing wrong."

Caught off guard, he replied seconds too late: "Well, that's great, Tina. Of course we always knew it, but it's nice to have everyone else know it, too."

She made no attempt to match his forced gaiety.

"This would be a wonderful time for us to stop lying to each other, Bob."

"What are you talking about?" Glancing wildly around for support, he saw at least twenty interested gazes following events through his glass walls. "And we can't have a scene here. Everybody's watching."

"Tell them you're taking a long lunch," she directed grimly.

His excuses were to no avail. Totally inflexible, Tina was being as hard on herself as on her husband. She only knew that she could no longer deal with the careful omissions that now characterized their life together. By dint of remorseless pressure she managed to sweep him from the Ecker plant to the Laverdiere home.

"All right, you've been a Christian martyr long enough, Bob," she almost spat, plunking herself down at the kitchen table. "Suppose you tell me what's going on."

"My God, you know what's going on," he protested. "We agreed what I was going to tell the police."

His reminder was a mistake. "I should have my head examined for agreeing," she retorted. "We ought to have told the truth from the start."

"Are you out of your mind? As soon as the police found out you had the skewer, both of us would have been arrested."

"I went along with that at the trade show. We were rattled then, but at least we were normal with each other. It was afterward that everything went haywire."

"I don't know what you mean. And why are you carrying on this way now? Anybody would think we'd gotten bad news instead of good news. Don't you see this means I don't have a motive anymore?"

He kept pulling away from the real issue, but Tina would have none of it.

"You thought I killed Victor Hunnicut," she said dully.

He was appalled. "Don't talk nonsense. What would make me think that?"

"That's what I'd like to know!"

"You can't think of a reason, because it just isn't so. You've been so anxious about the Winstead audit that you've started imagining things."

She ignored his bluster. "But why, Bob, in heaven's name, why?"

He was trying to avoid her eyes, but every time he turned, she turned. Looking into that bottomless well of misery, she did not enjoy closing his escape routes, one by one. But something told her it had to be done.

"Why?" she insisted.

Finally his defenses crumbled.

"It was when they told us the fire was not an accident," he confessed wretchedly.

"You thought I was embezzling from Conrad?" She was dumbfounded. "For Christ's sake, Bob, have you gone stark raving mad? What was I supposed to be doing with all this money?"

Shamefaced, he shook his head. "It wasn't that."

She had clutched his hand during his string of evasions. Then it had been to prevent escape. Now it was to promise sympathy and understanding.

"You see, I got real shook up by what that bastard said at the trade show," he began.

"Go on."

"He claimed I was lousy at my job, and he said it as if it was obvious. Then the other guy from ASI didn't seem to think it was unreasonable. But I've always thought I was pretty good."

For once Tina was not interested in his self-esteem. "You're a fine production manager," she said perfunctorily.

"And the company's been doing so well, which seemed like proof positive. I was hanging on to that when the fire marshal told us the boiler house was torched. And you're the one in charge of the records. So I thought . . ."

Tina felt as if the weight of years had been lifted.

"You thought I was cooking the books to make you look good," she finished for him.

"Well, you're the one who knows what goes on there," he defended himself belatedly.

In moments of extreme emotion, human features become distorted. For once Tina Laverdiere did not look like a handsome woman. Her skewed smile made her seem more like a stroke victim than an affectionate wife.

"Oh, Bob, you're an idiot. I couldn't get away with that year after year. Don't you understand? There's a limit to what you can do with accounting. You can divert money from one section to another, you can disburse it to fake accounts, you can lose it in the computer, but you can't simply create it."

"I'm sorry, Tina, I'm really sorry. I wanted to talk to you but I was afraid, and the whole thing was tearing me apart."

She recalled an earlier misgiving.

"In Chicago I thought you might have told Virginia."

"Mother!" he gasped. "When has she ever kept quiet about anything?"

Tina realized that she should have known better.

"While we're at it," she said relentlessly, "I suppose I should admit that I was suspicious of you."

Under different circumstances his expression would have amused her.

"How could I finagle the records? I don't know anything about what goes on in your office."

"God knows you've proved that," she said weakly.

She had never believed for a moment that Bob had struck out in a fury because of anything to do with the Ecker Company. Bob was a good production manager, a dutiful son, a splendid father, but he had only one real passion in his life, and its name was Tina Laverdiere.

"You're so transparent, Bob," she expostulated. "You poured out everything Hunnicut said about you and Conrad and Alan. But you didn't mention a single word about me. And I was the one who'd gotten under Hunnicut's skin. When he tried tangling with me in Princeton, I cut him down hard enough to get him thrown out of the meeting."

"You never told me that."

"No," she agreed before falling into a reverie. She

had abandoned herself to the warm relief that was finally enveloping her.

"Maybe we should stop protecting each other," she said at last. "We don't seem to be very good at it."

Bob dismissed this piece of womanly weakness. Wrinkling his forehead, he pointed out this left the Ecker fire more of a mystery than ever.

"Who cares?" Tina said buoyantly. "The police have to worry about that one. That's their job. Maybe they'll be able to get on with it, once we tell them what really happened."

"Oh, my God!"

Inspector Giorni had the dubious privilege of hosting the conference between the Laverdieres, their lawyer, the DA's lawyer, and himself.

"So you met your wife on the floor of the trade show after you talked to Frayne and Ecker?"

"That's right."

"And you told her what had happened? While you were still mad?"

"Yes, I bumped into her while she was doing the rounds and of course she was a little upset but—"

"I was in a blazing rage," Tina interrupted evenly.

Her lawyer stirred into uneasy protest, but Giorni ignored them both and continued to press Laverdiere.

"You gave her the skewer?"

Only after a compelling glance from Tina did Laverdiere answer. "She said she'd be passing our booth and she'd take it back."

"So then what did you do?"

"I wanted to get my mind off the fight. I knew Conrad would handle ASI but I couldn't seem to concentrate on the show. Instead I decided to check things out downstairs—make sure the dollies and tools were ready, to dismantle the booth."

When they were off the subject of Tina, Laverdiere's replies came more easily.

"But you didn't take the murder elevator?"

"No, I was at the far side of the building. I used the freight elevators on the east end. But it turned out I couldn't spend much time in the basement because everything was in such apple-pie order. When I was through, I went to the elevator closest to the trucks. And you know what happened. The doors opened, I saw the body and I just panicked. I got the hell out of there as fast as I could."

The inspector had no difficulty filling in what had been left unsaid. One minute Bob Laverdiere had seen his wife, skewer in hand, furious at Victor Hunnicut. The next, he had seen Hunnicut practically skewered to the floor. He had drawn the obvious conclusion.

"And then the two of you decided to keep quiet? In spite of the fact that it left you the number-one suspect?"

"You'd just think we were in it together," Bob said sulkily.

"Like hell! You thought she'd done it."

"Not then, I didn't," Bob fired back incautiously.

Tina's clear voice ended the dialogue.

"That came after the arson report," she announced.

Giorni was not enthusiastic about either of the Laverdieres, but he had to admit that the wife was moving things along. It would have taken hours to extract a coherent account from her husband.

"So you thought she was fudging the books and Hunnicut got wise to her." Giorni examined his witness contemptuously. "Mr. Laverdiere, did it ever occur to you that your wife might have had a hard time killing Hunnicut? If she lost her head and raised a skewer, would he just sit still for it?"

It was an article of faith with Bob that his wife was

capable of succeeding at anything she set her hand to. Reflexively he produced the wrong encomium.

"Tina's in great shape."

"So was Hunnicut!" Giorni snapped. He was remembering the assessment from the Zichy Salle des Armes—quick feet, strong wrists, everything except the heart of a tiger. But nothing brings out the tiger in a man like defending his own life.

Having discharged at least some of his spleen, Giorni turned to Tina.

"Now you," he said harshly. "You carried that skewer across the floor to the Ecker booth."

"That's right," she said, sounding every bit as adamantine as the inspector.

"Did it still have a mushroom on it?" he barked.

Until now, he had received unhelpful replies to this question. Both Alan Frayne and Ken Nicolls had been unable to disentangle their memories of the skewer at the Ecker booth and the skewer across the concourse. Conrad Ecker had been too consumed with bellicosity to notice anything at all.

But Tina did not even pause to think. "At the beginning it did. It wasn't until I slammed down the skewer that the mushroom fell off on the counter." Then, continuing her policy of frankness, she added, "I was still pretty mad."

Giorni knew exactly how much that frankness was worth. "And I suppose it never crossed your mind that your husband might be guilty."

Tina lifted her chin.

"I read the arson report, too. Naturally I had moments of doubt," she admitted. "But thank God the Winstead people have put them to rest."

Tina's openness was directed toward emphasizing one particular point. Victor Hunnicut had been murdered for business reasons, not personal reasons. Her story was simple. Both Laverdieres had been thrown off balance by the discovery of arson, each had suspected the other of corporate shenanigans. Happily that was all.

"And now you both think you're home free," Giorni began on a threatening note.

His audience had the sense to remain quiet.

"What I'd really like to do is throw the two of you into the can for obstruction of justice, but," he continued regretfully, "I suppose that'll have to wait. We'll be checking up on your stories, the ones you're telling this time, I mean. For now I'm through with you, you can go."

The Laverdieres were eager to avail themselves of this permission, and their lawyer lingered only long enough to cast a gloss over the complete rout of his charges.

Whatever Giorni felt, the DA's man was sorry to see such promising suspects depart.

"She still could have done it," he theorized hopefully. "That mushroom could have fallen off anywhere."

Already rubbing his eyes in preparation for the days to come, Giorni shook his head. "Not on your life. When Laverdiere was waving that skewer around while he yelled at the ASI bunch, he was bending over the back of the booth. If it had fallen in their faces, they'd remember. And if it fell off while he was on the floor, it would have been trampled within seconds. There were thousands of people milling around. Besides, what bothers me about the wife is what's always bothered me about the husband. I don't think Hunnicut would have gotten into an elevator alone with either one of them. He'd have been too scared."

"He wouldn't expect an attack."

"I don't mean that." Giorni flapped an impatient hand. "He'd be afraid for his job. He'd just been chewed out by Gardner Ives and told to make everything sweet with Ecker. He was a boy who obeyed orders. He'd already gone one round with the husband. The skewer would have told him the wife knew all about the scene at the booth. Hunnicut couldn't afford another spat, no matter who started it. Of course there was no reason in the world not to go along with one of the ASI bunch."

The DA's man considered this new array of possibilities.

"Maybe not Quinn," he argued. "But Hunnicut was in hot water with Bradley and Pepitone."

"Yeah, but he didn't know it. According to that guy from the Sloan, Bradley said he'd fingered Hunnicut as the ASI troublemaker, but only after Hunnicut left."

"So you're saying one of those rumors about Bradley or Pepitone was right on the money and Hunnicut had to be silenced."

Giorni's glance would have flayed a less insensitive man. "No, I'm saying that *could* be what happened. I like a little proof of these motives before I go haring off, half-cocked."

He could see what was coming. The DA's office would be reluctant to drop charges against Laverdiere unless they could simultaneously level them against someone else. Laverdiere's lawyer, on the other hand, would be anxious to strike while the iron was hot. Crunched between these two parties would be the police department.

"You know," mused the DA's man, who had never noticed Giorni's barb, "I think we need an intensive investigation of the ASI people. And pronto!"

"Somehow I thought you'd say that," mumbled Giorni.

Chapter

MARKET CORRECTION

The Winstead report had repercussions in Princeton as well. There, Sparling Castings remained a source of concern, but the heavens had not opened. ASI's involvement with gunrunners and terrorists was still contained behind closed doors. Perhaps this was only the lull before the storm, but Gardner Ives actually took time to read the insurance company's final paragraph.

". . . and he thought it would be a good idea to have an informal dinner with Conrad Ecker," Tom Robichaux explained. "Just the four of us at his club."

"Now that Winstead has upgraded Ecker's financial rating and there's been all this free publicity, I suppose Ives wants to go forward with the merger," Thatcher hazarded.

"Panting at the bit, if you ask me," Robichaux said complacently. "But you know none of them can come right out with anything. According to Gardner, we're not talking merger, we're just getting to know each other better."

It was Thatcher's private opinion that this was no time to get to know Conrad Ecker. The continuing estrangement from his nephew had left him sore as a bear.

"Of course he's relieved to have some of the clouds roll by, but I don't know how he'll react to hours of stroking by Ives," he warned Robichaux. "He's defensive and he's touchy."

"Don't blame him. Can't say I'm looking forward to this shindig myself," said Tom, a staunch foe to any after-hours intrusion by his business responsibilities. "But we have to start somewhere."

"True," Thatcher said, "but even if Conrad doesn't blow up, it will be four hours of boredom."

Robichaux, casting around for some emollient, found only one. "The brandy at the club isn't half bad."

Conrad Ecker was the last to arrive and he had dignified the occasion with a perfectly respectable business suit. He still stood out. With the best will in the world—and there was no reason to suppose that any such force was at work—he could not achieve the sleek, tidily packaged look resulting from winter tans, custom tailoring, and nonstop massages. While everybody stared at him, and most recognized that familiar face from television, he examined his surroundings with frank interest.

"Haven't been in a place like this for years," he remarked, making it sound like a fortunate escape.

"You're a good way from the city," Gardner Ives replied. "One of the things I like about the Princeton location is that we're far enough out for daily purposes but the city is available when we want it."

Any fears Thatcher entertained about a headlong approach by Ives were quickly laid to rest. The man had obviously consulted all those articles about Conrad Ecker, home-spun millionaire. By the time drinks arrived, Ives was barely warming up.

"I always try to get away in the hunting season myself," he began.

His stomping ground, he went on to say, was in Maine. Wisely eschewing executive lodges and wine cellars, he genially discussed guns, ammunition and, of course, the ones that got away.

"The worst disappointment was two years ago," he said, comfortably launched.

Ives had been a lucky winner in the Maine moose lottery. Armed with state permission to help thin the herd, he had sallied forth expectantly.

"I spent a whole week at it and never even saw a moose," he chuckled.

Ecker simply reported that he himself always hunted in the White Mountains, but conditions there had changed a good deal.

Thatcher felt duty-bound to make some contribution—if only as a native of New Hampshire.

"They certainly have," he agreed, "but these days I'm only up there when I'm hiking."

"Don't suppose you do that in the season," Ecker remarked.

"Certainly not. From what they tell me, I'd be taking my life in my hands."

You were doing just that, according to Ecker, if you ventured into your own backyard anywhere north of Boston. "These city types are a menace," he growled. "They just spray bullets in a circle whenever a leaf moves."

As a small child Thatcher had heard relatives and neighbors inveigh against the invasion of hunters from the mill towns. No doubt these shafts had been aimed against young men from Bridgeport. Now, fifty years later, Ecker was the old-timer.

But some changes met Conrad's approval. In the early days his group had stayed at a ramshackle cabin owned by somebody's cousin. Now he and his friends expected not only electricity and furnaces, but all the support facilities of a four-star resort.

"It's not really my style, but it has its points."

There was a good deal to be said, he continued, for a heated indoor swimming pool in which to soak cranky, aging bones.

When Ives blinked, Thatcher deduced that an indoor pool was not among the amenities in Maine.

After the subject of hunting died a lingering death, Ives made a stab at other topics. But tax loopholes, foreign travel, and new corporate jets were not up Ecker's alley. Only when Ives desperately fell back on his family did he evoke any response. An Ives daughter had just qualified as a surgeon and the Ives son was in law school. Conrad riposted with Douglas Junior, a serious student of the cello. Not only was he enrolled at Juilliard, he had appeared at Tanglewood.

Curiously enough, this struck a chord with Robichaux.

"Tanglewood, eh? Hetty and I were up there last summer." In an aside to Thatcher, he continued, "Henrietta's big on music, you know."

Startled, Thatcher realized that yet another Robichaux wife had been divorced and a replacement ensconced without his noticing. There was this to be said for Tom's recent marital moves. They no longer involved his friends in ceremonial rice.

"Is she indeed?" he murmured politely.

"Hetty said the Brahms dragged," Tom repeated with simple pride. Then, punctilious about social obligations, he turned to Ecker. "But I'm sorry we didn't know about your boy."

Ecker came as close to bridling as a seventy-year-old man can.

"Can't guess where this music business came from," he said gruffly. "As near as I know, his father can't sing a note."

"Same thing with my daughter," Ives agreed. "The rest of the family can't stand the sight of blood."

"You're lucky," said Robichaux, retailing the experience of a worldly friend who had inadvertently produced a clergyman.

On this harmless topic, Gardner Ives managed to spin his way through dessert. Only when they adjourned to a lounge did he edge toward the reason for their gathering.

"I was very pleased to hear the result of Winstead's study," he proclaimed. "Although we already knew the company was very strong."

Waving away the waiter bearing a tray of cigar boxes, Ecker fumbled in his pocket. "I'm glad it's over," he rasped. "Pain in the neck while it was going on. Now we can get back to work."

Given Ecker's performance so far, Thatcher would not have been surprised to see him flourish a corncob pipe, but he achieved almost the same effect by producing a battered pack of Camels.

"Yes, indeed, Winstead must have been disruptive," Ives said soothingly. "And I quite see how you would want a few days to pull yourself together."

For the first time he struck the wrong note. He could have been encouraging a convalescent after a nasty bout in the hospital.

"Oh, we're pulled together. Sometimes I think people are crazy," Ecker said largely. "We've been making the best coffeepot in America for years, and now thousands of customers are rushing in to buy it because they saw a picture of me in a funny hat."

The message was clear. Conrad Ecker, vis-à-vis ASI, was in the catbird seat and he knew it.

"Splendid," Ives forced himself to say.

"Even so, I guess we could all use a little rest while we see how things work out," Ecker said deliberately.

"But what else is there to find out? I know that technically there are still some charges against your production man, but they're bound to be dropped. So everything will be all right."

Gardner Ives, Thatcher saw, had not yet factored in the inevitable consequences of Bob Laverdiere's exoneration.

Very slowly extinguishing his cigarette, Ecker shifted forward in his vast club chair and explained the facts of life.

"You see, the cops haven't found a motive for Hunnicut's murder at my company. So now they're bound to look at yours."

Gardner Ives goggled.

It did not help when Tom Robichaux, mellowed by the brandy snifter he was cradling, nodded sagely.

"Stands to reason," he remarked in unfortunately sprightly tones. "Particularly the way Hunnicut was lipping off."

Thatcher hastily intervened in order to give Ives breathing time and to cloud the issue. "There is, of course, no suggestion of complicity by ASI. But there is always the possibility that one individual may have been endangered by Hunnicut and no doubt that is an area that will receive official scrutiny."

But Conrad Ecker had not driven down from Bridgeport to wade through mists of obscurity.

"The point is, which individual?" he retorted.

Gardner Ives was still in shock.

"But it's absurd to think my executives are running around stabbing people," he blurted, involuntarily revealing a fine distinction between his employees and Ecker's.

"Thought the same thing myself when they arrested Bob," said Ecker, mentioning his nephew with an effort. "But somebody did kill Hunnicut. You can't get away from that. And I don't want him running around my company with a skewer."

Groping for an answer, Ives could only say, "It will probably turn out to be a motive from his personal life. An old girlfriend or something like that."

By now Conrad Ecker had gone as far as he was prepared to go. He conceded that police suspicions might easily prove to be wrong, just as they had in the case of Bob Laverdiere.

"I'm even willing to say that I still like the sound of the merger, always assuming the numbers reflect our growing market," he continued blandly. "I've got nothing against some preliminary talks, so long as we aii know where we stand. And that's simple enough. Nothing gets signed until this murder is straightened out."

By the time Gardner Ives disjointedly called an end to the evening, Thatcher thought that Conrad Ecker could congratulate himself. Two major points had been made with brutal clarity. The Ecker Company was worth more money with every passing day.

And, from now on, it was ASI that was on trial.

Chapter

SETTLING DAY

What Conrad Ecker began, the *New York Times* finished.

"Good God!" Gardener Ives sputtered over his first cup of coffee the next morning. A paroxysm of sneezing convulsed him but Mrs. Ives took her cue from his right hand. Whenever Ives was affronted by a news item or an editorial, he poked it with a martial forefinger. Now, as he groped for a handkerchief, she slid the paper into position where she could read for herself.

" '. . . Sparling Castings, a division of Aqua Supplies, Inc., which is headquartered in Princeton, New Jersey, was indicted yesterday . . .' Oh, dear."

Her hopelessly inadequate response coincided with a sinus-clearing honk from across the table.

"And that means it will be in the *Journal*," Ives said thickly, shoving back his chair. "Probably on TV, too."

"Aren't you going to finish breakfast?" she twittered. "You know you'll get a headache if you don't eat something."

"I've already got a headache," Ives informed her.

Mrs. Ives was not surprised. "You got in awfully late, and you tossed and turned all night."

Since she did not have to clean, cook, or run errands, Mrs. Ives channeled her nurturing instincts into semi-professional health awareness. Usually this was acceptable to her husband, but not today.

"I had a very, very disappointing meeting with Conrad Ecker," he complained, overtaken by an earlier grievance.

But Sparling and ASI on the front pages instantly reclaimed him. The telephone in the hall rang. In Ives's absence, his wife buttered toast and replenished his cup.

". . . just a mouthful before you rush off," she urged when he returned. "No, don't wolf it down, Gardy. You'll give yourself indigestion."

"That," Ives announced, "was Tom Robichaux. He thinks it could have been worse."

Despite having heard about Robichaux for months, Mrs. Ives had no idea who he was. Nevertheless she scented an ally.

"You see? The trouble with you, Gardy, is that you don't know how to relax."

Ives, who agreed that he was a paragon of responsibility, preened slightly, then declared, "I'd better get over to ASI."

"To do what?"

It was a good question, but Ives was not around to hear it.

Ives descended on ASI like a fireman answering the bell. His whirlwind bustle initially focused on the trackers who had misled him about the eye of the storm.

"Some stringer in Muncie put it on the wire, and

Dow Jones picked it up," said one of them, peering at his computer screen. "Look, Gardner, I want to get these releases out before noon."

The lawyers were even less satisfactory. "Once you get into district court, somebody's bound to notice," they philosophized. "But we're filing for a continuance, and if we can settle in the meantime, there won't be much of a follow-up. Let me get back to you after I've talked to Livada."

Balked at every turn, Gardner Ives raged impotently at fate. To have ASI, good corporate citizen and friend of public television, tarred in the *Times* and the *Journal* bit deep. Robichaux & Devane could take the long view, but Ives found stories about infractions of the criminal code as repugnant as exposés in the *National Enquirer.*

Nor did he share his wife's opinion that there was little for him to do except field incoming calls with statesmanlike double-talk. For most of the day he fussed around aimlessly, racked by fears that ASI and Sparling would preempt network programming on three television channels and cable. When that bugbear failed to materialize, relief set in, but only moderately.

Elsewhere, a firmer grasp on reality prevailed. The wider ASI family, geared up for a publicity bloodbath, assessed the situation with a collective sigh of relief.

"What's six inches in the *Journal,* and four inches in the *Times?*" asked a staffer largely. "Particularly when they're all about rules and regulations that nobody understands?"

He spoke too soon. The following forty-eight hours produced a flurry of scattered coverage. *Barron's* ran a short piece depicting Sparling Castings as a sinkhole of depravity. ASI was described by some business journals as stodgy, complacent, and lumbering. On the other hand, *Time* and *Newsweek* barely noticed while late-night comics stuck to Washington for laughs. The security analysts sniffed the air, consulted their tea leaves, and rendered a split decision. Prudential Bache said hold, Goldman Sachs said sell, and Bear Stearns said nothing.

Throughout the crisis, Gardner Ives suffered visibly. Instead of the prescribed eight-hour sleep, he began snatching catnaps. After years of steering ASI along well-trodden paths, he found himself waiting for the next blow to fall. Again and again, he had to beat down an impulse to seek advice and comfort from Phil Pepitone. As a result, Ives's stab at morale building was unimpressive.

". . . appreciate all the extra hours you people have put in," he said with scripted thanks to the foot soldiers. Then, before they got carried away, he improvised, "I'm still afraid that none of this will do ASI much good. We're just going to have to wait and see how the pension managers react."

In all the excitement, he had quite forgotten Victor Hunnicut. So he was looking for trouble in the wrong direction.

Reading about large sums of money is a national pastime. For little old ladies in supermarkets there are mansions in West Palm Beach and alimony everywhere. Sports fans can revel in sinfully large multi-year contracts. Expenditures by rock stars, TV evangelists, and First Ladies—foreign and domestic—are universal crowd pleasers.

At the same time relatively few people lust for details about the national debt, the corn-hog ratio, or Eastman Kodak's latest restructuring plan. The optimists at ASI and Robichaux & Devane had some justification for thinking that their moment in the sun was too brief and esoteric to attract salacious attention. Unfortunately for them, there was a small minority fascinated by the Sparling revelations, and it happened to be uniquely positioned.

The New York Police Department convened a veritable seminar on the subject. Among those in attendance was Inspector Giorni. What he learned from the assembled pundits did not strike him as immediately germane.

". . . sure, I understand Sparling mislabeled and shipped to Libya by way of Germany," he said, consulting notes. "But where and how does ASI fit in?"

This earned him a lecture on corporate structure, with special reference to wholly-owned subsidiaries and legal liability.

"In fact," said his instructor, soaring to theoretical heights, "ASI might, just possibly, seek remedy from the courts by claiming that there was concealment at the time of the sale."

"Give me a break," muttered Giorni, detaching himself from these intricacies. His search for Victor Hunnicut's murderer was already complicated enough. Sparling just added a new wrinkle.

Giorni wanted information to factor into his investigation, not a post-graduate course. For his purposes, the authorities available to the department knew too damn much.

"But it's all out of books," he complained with fine contempt for intellectual prowess. "What I want is someone who knows the score."

At ASI, there were probably dozens of them. But too many figured prominently on Giorni's newly revised hit list.

Robichaux & Devane was out, too.

"They're in bed with ASI," said Giorni, continuing the process of summary elimination.

Then he reached the Sloan Guaranty Trust.

* * *

"Well, yes, I've been spending a lot of time at ASI," said a puzzled Ken Nicolls. "Tell me what you want to know, and I'll do my best."

"This ASI-Sparling business," said Giorni bluntly. "I've got a feeling it might have a bearing on the murder. Trouble is, I don't have a real feel for ASI, and you've been hanging around there for days."

"They're all buzzing about Sparling," said Ken. "They're saying that Pepitone's screwed his pitch with this one."

Giorni pounced. "Pepitone wasn't mentioned in the papers. Do you mean he picked Sparling, too?"

Nicolls felt he was being towed out of his depth.

"Look, I can't vouch for any of this. I work with the peasants over there. I'm just repeating what I heard."

Ken was still explaining his inability to confirm or deny when the door opened.

"Oh, sorry to interrupt," said John Thatcher. "I didn't know you had a visitor."

Before he could withdraw, Nicolls said hastily, "This is Inspector Giorni, who's in charge of the Hunnicut investigation. He's been asking me about ASI and Sparling."

Thatcher did more than sanction cooperation with the police; he pulled up a chair.

"Good afternoon, Inspector. How can we help?"

Giorni, when he discovered he had landed a big fish, brightened and transferred his attentions. "Did all this flak about Sparling come as a surprise to *you*, Mr. Thatcher?"

"Yes and no," said Thatcher. "These criminal charges were a bolt out of the blue. But long before they surfaced, we at the Sloan had reason to believe that Sparling was not one of ASI's successes. Now, at least, we understand why."

"I don't follow," Giorni confessed. "What do the two have to do with each other?"

Thatcher tried to boil down the complexities. "The Sparling people wanted to sell their company at a good price. So, to make their books look good, they indulged in the illegal sale of arms. And represented the earnings as part of normal operations. ASI was the sucker who bit."

"Nicolls, here, says that Pepitone's to blame for the whole mess."

Before Ken could protest, Thatcher did so for him.

"No, he's telling you what some people at ASI are saying. It's only natural to blame someone when things turn out badly. But the decision to buy Sparling must have been reviewed by many people and, more to the point, Sparling's books were examined by experts. ASI was not the only one fooled. There was the state of Indiana, the U.S. government, and Price Waterhouse."

"But Pepitone could still have stumbled across something," said Giorni, dismissing paperwork. "In which case the talk Hunnicut stirred up would have scared the bejesus out of him."

Privately Thatcher thought Pepitone was aiming at the presidency of ASI, not shortsighted gains.

"It sounds unlikely to me," he said, addressing Giorni's hypothesis. "Ordinarily I'd say you were asking for not one, but two coincidences. However, I admit that with Hunnicut shooting so many arrows into the air, one of them could have landed somewhere."

"Sure," said Giorni sourly. "The problem is narrowing the field."

It was obvious that he was not impressed by the Sloan's contribution to his endeavors.

"Well, if there's nothing further I can do," said Thatcher brazenly.

Collecting the file he had come for, he left Ken Nicolls to the police and retreated. But since there is no rest for the wicked, Miss Corsa simply handed him the phone.

"Ah, Conrad," said Thatcher. "No, you're not inter-rupting. "I've just wrapped up a—what was that? Spar-ling? What about Sparling?"

After some excited cracklings from Connecticut, he replied, "Yes, I agree that the *Christian Science Monitor* is generally accurate. But if you read carefully, you'll see that Sparling does not materially alter—"

Another outburst from Conrad.

Firmly, Thatcher intervened. "ASI is still in position to make a very attractive offer. That is the assumption under which the Sloan is proceeding, as I think the Ecker Company should."

The following ten minutes tried Thatcher's patience considerably.

"Two monomaniacs," he said to Miss Corsa once he could unburden himself. "Neither of them would care if Sparling shipped poison gas to Fidel Castro. Instead, Giorni seizes on Sparling to help catch his murderer. And Conrad . . ."

Conrad Ecker was joyously expecting Sparling to knock Gardner Ives off his high horse.

Conrad's glee suggested other uses for Sparling.

"Look," said Alan Frayne persuasively. "Conrad's getting a big kick out of watching ASI take the heat. After what Ecker went through when they arrested you, it's put the cream in his coffee. So the time's ripe, Bob. Just take the first step, do some stroking, and we can all get back to normal."

But the sweet breeze of vindication was still buoying up Bob Laverdiere.

"Me apologize to Conrad? Forget it," he said with unimpaired cheerfulness.

Frayne was not the only one trying to restore peace.

"You should make it up with Bob, Dad," said Doug Ecker after a blow-by-blow telephone account.

"I'm not the one who has to crawl," his father thundered. "Unless Bob straightens up, he's on his way out."

Doug treated this empty threat seriously. "You can't do that."

"Why the hell not?" Conrad demanded.

Doug welcomed the opportunity to revise some of his father's thinking.

"Because . . . you . . . need . . . him," he said deliberately.

For once, Conrad was speechless.

"Bob's a good production man, and he's—"

"Production managers are a dime a dozen," Conrad snapped. "Particularly now."

"This is the ideal time to sell out," Doug rolled on. "You're riding the wave of great publicity. Bring in a new man, and you'll lose all your momentum. You and Bob have got to get your act together."

By way of reply Conrad delivered a lengthy, hot-tempered diatribe.

Unlike her male counterparts, Alice Ecker knew that a face-to-face meeting of the adversaries was doomed before it started. The new Bob Laverdiere was too exhilarated to backpedal for anybody. And Conrad would choke on his own bile before he made a friendly gesture.

Happily, there was an alternative.

"I asked Tina to drop in for coffee," said Alice, flattening Conrad with a fait accompli.

The peace conference was informal but effective.

"You see, I was afraid there really might be something wrong, Tina," said Conrad, finally shuffling into a shamefaced apology. "I should have known that wasn't possible—not with you keeping an eye on the books."

With her husband out of danger, Tina could afford to be generous.

"I'll tell Bob what you said," she told Conrad, making it easy for him.

"You do that!"

At the Ecker Company, at least, the hostilities were over.

Chapter

RANDOM TESTS

When he left the Sloan, Inspector Giorni realized that his next step had to be a frontal assault on ASI. This time he would be going, not to learn about Victor Hunnicut, but to learn about his murderer. Furthermore Giorni knew just where to start. Phil Pepitone might be linked to criminal activities at Sparling. Wiley Quinn certainly had been sighted at the freight elevator. Under these circumstances, Sam Bradley had the least to lose.

But nobody at ASI was more conscious of the shifting sands than Bradley, and he was a born poker player. Overnight he had busily calculated the odds. There was virtually nothing to be gained by joining the legion arrayed against Phil Pepitone; becoming his sole ally might pay off in the future. And they both stood to gain by maintaining that Victory Hunnicut had never posed a real threat.

"I'm glad to help in any way I can, Inspector, but

I've already told your people what happened at Javits," he began in mild protest.

"Let's start earlier than that, say with your finding out Hunnicut was the source of all the talk here. Is that why you went up to the Ecker Company?"

"Of course not," Bradley lied easily. "I'm sure you realize that any merger would mean an integration of both research facilities. I was a little worried about that, because Ecker's such a small, idiosyncratic operation. The thing to do was to take a look. And I'm glad I went. Even prepared, I was surprised at Conrad Ecker's work habits."

Giorni refused to be sidetracked.

"But you already knew you were being smeared?"

"Oh, yes. Naturally I assumed it was the first step in another power struggle. They have them here about once every three months."

His indulgent tone was an invitation to Giorni to join in amusement at ASI's corporate follies. But Giorni had other things on his mind.

"You're saying you thought it was some kind of big shot—someone like Pepitone."

Bradley shook his head solemnly. "Phil and I aren't in competition. If you must know, I was thinking about some of the technical people out in the divisions. One or two of them resent having research centralized." Carried away by a speech he had often made to Gardner Ives, he continued, "They don't realize that the more you blinker your research people with compartmentalization, the less likely you are to get the benefits of cross-fertilization."

Giorni's opinion of ASI was sinking steadily. If this kind of gobbledygook had protected Bradley's position, in spite of his dismal record, then almost anything could be pulled off here.

"But you knew all this talk sprang up at the same

time the Ecker acquisition got hot?" he asked, bringing them back to earth with a thud.

"A lot of things were happening then, Inspector. I didn't make the connection until I found out what Hunnicut was up to. And I was lucky there. Nobody had told Bob Laverdiere my job at ASI and he repeated some of Hunnicut's slurs on my work. With that to go on, I came back here and discovered he was behind all the rumors."

"Why didn't you do something about it right away?"

By now Bradley's fingers were steepled and he was examining them as if judiciously weighing laboratory results.

"I didn't really satisfy myself until just before the trade show and I was still hesitant. Hunnicut was so junior, I thought he might be acting for someone else. Then I overheard him with Quinn at the Ecker booth, and it all became clear. He was trying to sabotage Ecker because some other assistant would get the job."

"Then why go to Pepitone? You had just as much at stake."

There were at least some aspects of the corporate ethos that Bradley respected.

"In Fred Uhlrich's absence, Phil was the proper person to discipline Hunnicut," he replied gravely.

"Sure," Giorni grunted. "And Pepitone blew his top when you told him?"

Well aware that his conversation with Pepitone had been witnessed by others and possibly overheard, Bradley had long since provided himself with an answer.

"He was more outraged than anything else," he said, producing a wry smile. "The arrogance of an assistant trying to deal himself into company policy stuck in Phil's craw. So he was going to straighten Hunnicut out. That's all there was to it."

It did not escape Giorni's notice that this rendition accomplished two ends. It reduced the entire problem of Hunnicut's conduct to insignificance and it distanced Bradley from any subsequent confrontation.

"And what about you?" the inspector demanded. "You told that guy from the Sloan you were going to get rough with Hunnicut."

"Oh, I'm not denying I was annoyed. If it had been left to me, I would have considered firing him."

After this, further questions were futile. Bradley had established the general outlines of his position. Hunnicut's scandal-mongering was a piece of self-interest that had gone astray. The charges against Pepitone and Bradley were ridiculous. Even more absurd was the suggestion that Hunnicut might accidentally have hit a bull's-eye. Almost as an afterthought Bradley denied hearing any rumors at all about the Sparling acquisition.

After this polished performance, Inspector Giorni found it a relief to turn his attention to Wiley Quinn. Quinn was braced for an inquisition. His body was stiff, his face tight, and his voice carefully controlled. Like Bradley, he began by declaring that he had told the police all he knew about events at Javits.

Too clever to attack from the expected direction, Giorni said casually, "Never mind about the trade show. Suppose you tell me the details of all the talk Hunnicut started."

"I've told that, too," Quinn responded. "While Vic was at the booth, he smeared everybody at Ecker and made a big thing about Sam Bradley and Phil Pepitone being rotten at their jobs."

Giorni shook his head. "I don't mean what Hunnicut himself was saying. I man how people here took his digs and ran with them."

"My God, you're not wasting your time on that, are you? The talk was plain crazy. You've got to realize that everybody was bored, and it had become a game. They were trying to outdo each other in coming up with wild theories. I mean, after they finished trashing Pepitone and Bradley, they even went to work on Gardner Ives. They would have—"

Frowning, Giorni barked his interruption. "Wait a minute! What are you talking about? What do you mean, they were bored?"

"I thought you were asking about the fund-raiser."

Quinn sounded as if he regretted his outburst, but under prodding he described the evening and the fanciful charges that had been tossed about.

"And how much of this stuff filtered back to the company?"

"Too much of it," Wiley admitted. "But some of it was so way out, it couldn't stand the light of day."

Giorni wondered if he had hit pay dirt. An entire evening devoted to imaginative calumny might have scored one real hit.

"Any of this talk involve Sparling Castings?"

A fleeting look of surprise crossed Quinn's face. This was not the line of questioning he had feared. "It came up at the TV station, but that's the last I heard of it. People had forgotten Sparling until that gun-running stuff hit the papers. Now, of course, everybody's saying that when Phil Pepitone recommends a company, it's the kiss of death. First Ecker gets us knee-deep in a murder, now Sparling has us cheek-by-jowl with terrorists."

"Is that all they're saying?"

"Believe me, around here that's enough."

Little by little, Quinn's tone had become almost normal. As long as they were discussing the fund-raiser or reactions to Sparling, he felt safe. No one knew better than Inspector Giorni the stress imposed by alternating between relief and tension.

"So what Hunnicut said at the Ecker booth was nothing new," he began, accelerating his tempo. "You'd heard it all before and you knew what he was up to."

"That wasn't hard to figure out. With Vic, it was always himself."

"You mean he saw you had a chance for promotion and he was busting a gut to torpedo the deal."

"Put it that way if you like."

"That's the way it was," Giorni shot back, pleased to see Quinn back on the ropes. "And you decided to do something about it. You wanted that job."

"Sure I did. What's so damned strange about that?"

Giorni had been rattling along like a machine gun but now he paused, allowing Quinn's discomfort to mount. Then, as if he had reached the only reasonable conclusion, he said softly, "So you decided to settle Hunnicut."

"That's not so! It wasn't that way at all."

"Oh, yeah? You think we don't know about your movements? After you finished at the ASI display, you started roaming the floor, trying to track somebody down."

"Look, you've got to understand—"

"You want me to understand, you'd better stop lying your head off."

Cornered, Quinn rubbed the flat of his hand over his head. Little though Giorni knew it, half his work had already been done by Mrs. Wiley Quinn. Breakfast that morning had featured a heated exchange.

"You can't keep quiet about this anymore, Wiley."

"We've got a mortgage and a baby. What do we do if I'm on the unemployment line?"

"What do we do if you're in jail?" she had retorted.

The prospect did not rouse in Wiley Quinn the transcendent glow of self-sacrifice that had sustained Bob Laverdiere.

"Oh, God, I'm stuck no matter what I do."

"Maybe not. Sparling has changed things."

He had been afraid to hope, but she remained adamant.

"Wiley, no job is worth being front runner in a murder investigation."

These words were still ringing in Quinn's ears as he began a halting explanation.

"I learned a lot from the way Bob Laverdiere handled Vic. The creep would fold if you tackled him head-on. On top of that, his name was going to be mud for causing trouble with the Eckers. Then I heard that Phil Pepitone was looking for Vic."

"So you realized that Bradley had blown the whistle on Hunnicut."

But Quinn disagreed.

"No, I'd gotten it all wrong. I saw old man Ecker come busting over to our display, and I thought Phil was on the warpath because of that. It seemed like the right time to tell him what else Vic had been doing. Now, of course, it doesn't look like such a bright idea," he concluded sadly.

"Let me get this straight. You claim it was Pepitone you were trying to find?"

"There's no claiming about it. For Christ's sake, I asked people."

Giorni adopted a stance of heavy disbelief. "And just where are you supposed to have tracked him?"

"All over," Quinn said evasively.

"We have a witness who places you right by the murder elevator."

A dull-red flush stained Quinn's cheeks.

"All right, all right. Yes, someone told me Phil had been heading in that direction. When I went over to take a look, he wasn't there. I never did hook up with him."

"Come off it. The only reason you've dreamed up this story is because you're scared."

"Oh, for God's sake, what difference did it make at the trade show? It all seemed cut and dried. One minute Laverdiere was waving a skewer around, mad as hell. The next, we're told somebody has stabbed Vic with it. It didn't take a genius to guess what happened."

Giorni hooded his eyes in thought. If Bob Laverdiere, faced with much the same progression, had assumed his wife killed Hunnicut, it was not unreasonable for Quinn to draw the same conclusion about a virtual stranger.

"If it was so damn irrelevant, what was the harm in telling us?"

"Plenty of harm," Quinn snapped, irritated. "If I'd put Phil by that elevator for no good reason, what do you think would have happened to my career? Even if my job didn't go down the tube, I could kiss good-bye to any promotion. Phil would have his knife into me."

"You think he's going to love it now?"

But Wiley, having finally done the unthinkable and placed Phil Pepitone at the scene of the murder, regained his confidence.

"These days Phil doesn't cut much ice in the front office. He's got other things to worry about."

This assessment was confirmed before Inspector Giorni ever reached his last suspect. Questioning Sam Bradley and Wiley Quinn had not entailed penetrating ASI's front office. But Phil Pepitone could be approached only past the safeguards that protected the high and mighty. Every security guard and receptionist who was part of the process greeted Giorni with avaricious interest. Nobody was going out of his way to protect Phil Pepitone's image. Only his personal secretary, the final bastion, evinced a different reaction. And she looked worried.

"I'll tell him you're here."

Pepitone himself was making no pretense of being above the battle.

"You're all I need," he welcomed the inspector in a basso growl.

There was no point in preliminary sparring.

"We've placed you by the freight elevator at Javits," Giorni said starkly.

Pepitone did not flinch.

"So what?" he challenged.

"You didn't mention that little fact."

"Damn right I didn't. Why go looking for trouble?"

Giorni settled more deeply in his chair. Nothing could have suited him better than this readiness to take on all comers. If Pepitone was defying him to do his worst, he was ready to oblige.

"Well, trouble is what you've got now. It makes a neat little timetable. First Bradley tells you that Hunnicut is responsible for all the smears that have been circulating. Then you go off to settle his hash. The last we hear of you, you're right on the spot where Hunnicut gets himself killed a few minutes later."

"Sure I went looking for him, but I never found him. Try and make something of that."

Giorni knew exactly what was moving Pepitone to all this belligerence. Unlike everybody else, he had been given no respite. First there had been all the speculation about money changing hands over the Ecker deal. Then the Sparling acquisition had blown up in his face. The man certainly knew that behind countless closed doors, people were discussing the future of Phil Pepitone. It must be a relief for him to have an adversary actually sitting across the desk.

"Oh, I can make something of it," Giorni replied placidly. "You admit you'd tracked Hunnicut to the freight elevator. Now you're telling me you didn't follow through and take it?"

"That's right. Nobody told me he took the elevator. Some girl had seen him go down that corridor, so I checked it out and he wasn't there. I never even considered the elevator. There was no reason for Hunnicut to go to the basement. He was supposed to be finding

Conrad Ecker. I just went on searching the floor and I missed him."

The inspector had already discovered that the more tranquil he became, the more aggressive Pepitone became. Almost offhandedly, Giorni remarked, "That story could be shot full of holes."

"Just try it. You can look all you want, you won't find anybody who saw me get on that elevator. And even if I did, what's the big deal? I was simply going to chew the kid out. You don't stab an assistant manager because he steps out of line."

"Not usually, no," Giorni conceded. "Not unless his big mouth is getting everybody too close for comfort."

"Jesus! You're not digging up that garbage about a bribe from Ecker, are you? They just couldn't get a handle on anything reasonable to accuse me of, so they had to start singing looney tunes."

"Actually I wasn't thinking about Ecker. I was thinking about Sparling."

Pepitone stared, then erupted in a contemptuous snort.

"Sparling! So now you've got me as some kind of gunrunner. Am I supposed to be huddling with Libyans? Where do you pick up this tripe?"

"It's been suggested that you greased the wheels of the Sparling purchase."

"That's a new one, but why should I be surprised? By now they've probably got me pegged as a child molester. Let me straighten you out on some basics, Giorni. Sparling has turned into a lemon and everybody's busy finding a fall guy. They think they've got me nominated. Well, that's the kind of thing you expect around here and I know the rules. But this load of shit you've dragged in here is something else again. I'm not sitting still while they try to saddle me with a murder. Who the hell have you been talking to?"

Giorni was impassive. "You know I'm not telling you my sources."

"I don't give a damn about you," Pepitone shot back. "In fact I'm through talking to you. You want any more, make an appointment with my lawyer. But I'm settling things around here."

His witness was lost, Giorni realized, when Pepitone stabbed the intercom.

"Tell Ives I'm coming in to see him," he ordered.

The secretary's breakdown was now complete.

"Oh, I'm not sure that's such a good idea, Phil," she moaned despairingly.

"Well, I am!"

Pepitone was already on his feet, speaking more to himself than to Giorni. "If I find out that Gardner is behind this, that stuffed shirt is in for the roughhouse of his life. By the time I get through with him, every single member of the board is going to realize how Sparling was his wonderful baby."

Abandoned unceremoniously, Inspector Giorni was left to review the reactions he had provoked. Sam Bradley, so insistently a spectator rather than a participant, had committed the ultimate absurdity of trying to join Giorni as another outsider looking in at ASI. Wiley Quinn was so rattled, he could be hiding anything. And Phil Pepitone found the burdens he was carrying, whatever their nature, so onerous that he was ready to seize any opportunity for open combat.

But in the end, like most policemen, Giorni preferred facts to personalities. Sam Bradley might conceivably have a motive to kill Victor Hunnicut. Quinn undeniably had opportunity. Only Phil Pepitone looked as if he could qualify on both counts.

Chapter

EXTRA DIVIDENDS

Gardner Ives never knew what hit him. Two hours later he was still white and shaken, shock waves were reverberating through ASI, and Phil Pepitone was crowing to his secretary.

"Relax, Irene. Ives is going to find another patsy," he announced. "He's agreed that it won't be Philip S. Pepitone who carries the can for Sparling."

Irene was overjoyed to hear this, and so was Sam Bradley when he burst in shortly thereafter.

". . . and I've got something else you ought to see," he exclaimed.

Pepitone was still savoring his moment of triumph. "If it's more trouble, I don't want to hear about it right now."

"Just the opposite." Bradley flourished his copy of the Winstead report. "I thought all you people studied the insurance company's review of Ecker."

"Days ago," Pepitone agreed.

"Well, you missed the most important part."

"What the hell do you mean?" said Pepitone narrowly. "Winstead proved Ecker's sound as a bell financially. What's more important than that?"

Bradley was practically licking his lips. "You should have read the footnotes about the test lab. Frayne never breathed a word to me when I was up there, but it looks as if Ecker has made a real breakthrough. They could be on the verge of producing a digital reprogrammer."

"Suppose you talk English," Pepitone growled.

Putting a curb on his enthusiasm, Bradley obeyed. "Digital programmers screw up if there's a power outage. You can set the microwave, but all it takes is a momentary glitch in the current for you to find a burned-out roast or a hunk of raw meat."

Now that Pepitone knew what they were talking about, he was ready with objection. "But that's on the market now. It's a necessity for production lines."

"Those devices are for heavy industrial applications. They're complicated and they cost more than a whole kitchen. Ecker is cracking the consumer market with something much smaller."

"And simpler, I suppose."

"It's so simple, it's elegant," relied Bradley, his technical appreciation displacing commercial considerations. "I can't get over this. It's unlike anything Conrad Ecker has ever done before. That old geezer is really something. He's going out in a blaze of glory."

Pepitone began to share the excitement. "You'd better go up to Ecker to check it out and make sure it isn't pie-in-the-sky. Get everything you can out of Frayne. This could be damned important."

"Exactly," said Bradley, beginning to lecture. "You realize, Phil, that this defuses your Ecker problem, too. Nobody can question your judgment now."

"Yes, Sam, I realize that," said Pepitone, who had

already figured this out. "But it's bigger than that. If you can call back and tell me everything's kosher, I'll be able to light a fire under Ives. We're going to have to move fast to keep ahead of the pack."

"I shouldn't have any trouble. By now Frayne must know the cat's out of the bag." Bradley rose to leave, then, with Southern courtesy, added, "Phil, I can't tell you how pleased I am the way things are turning out."

Once again Pepitone was ahead of him. Sam Bradley was not the man to rejoice in the victories of others. If he was seeking allies so eagerly, he expected to need them.

"I wasn't sure whether you'd be willing to talk," Bradley said to Alan Frayne when he reached Bridgeport.

Now that Conrad Ecker and the Laverdieres were reconciled, now that orders were pouring in, now that another Ecker triumph was waiting in the wings, Frayne was his old self.

"I wouldn't have a month ago," he said cheerfully. "And I wasn't crazy about letting in the Winstead team. We were still trying to keep it under wraps. But while we were all running around in circles with the police, my crew ironed out the final bug in the production process. We're home clear now. The patents are filed, and we'll be turning these things out before you know it."

"What a shame you didn't have the reprogrammer in time for the show."

Alan Frayne's smile threatened to split his face. "This one sells itself. We don't need all the hype. Would you like to see a demo?"

Bradley accepted the offer and, afterward, overflowed with congratulations.

"You know," he said as he was preparing to leave, "everybody's been on my case because of ASI's research. There's been static about funding, about security, about project selection. But I'm beginning to think the trouble is that I don't have somebody like Conrad Ecker."

Bradley had barely cleared the premises when a familiar figure entered.

"Lord, not again," Frayne groaned.

Inspector Giorni politely requested a few minutes time.

"That's one way of putting it," Frayne grumbled, leading the way back to his office. With the door closed, he launched into complaint.

"When is this going to stop?"

Giorni was mollifying. "There's no need to get hot under the collar. Now that the charges against Mr. Laverdiere are being dropped, we hope you people here can help out with a timetable for the trade show. I've already spoken with the others."

Even as a witness rather than a suspect, Frayne wanted to see the last of the police.

"Nobody likes having us around, but don't forget that you've got a big stake in getting this thing cleared up," Giorni said persuasively.

"Oh, all right. Fire away."

"Let's start when Mr. Laverdiere complained to you and Conrad Ecker about Hunnicut."

Frayne, expecting the familiar questions about Bob's rage, temporized. "The Laverdieres have already admitted they were mad."

"I want to know what time you think that was."

"Time?" Frayne said blankly.

Patiently Giorni tried the usual promptings. Had Frayne eaten lunch, and did he remember when? How long until Ken Nicolls had surfaced? Could he estimate the length of the indignation meeting with Bob Laverdiere?

Giorni covered every minute until the confrontation with Gardener Ives, then commented, "That's all pretty hazy. Can you be more specific about what you did afterward?"

"I decided to do my job. We have two reasons for going to the show. We display our own goods, and we keep an eye on the competition. I'd already covered some of the exhibits in the morning. After Ives I did the rest."

"So you went directly from ASI to a tour of the hall?"

Now that he had been put through the process of reconstruction, Frayne worked harder on his replies.

"Well, not directly. I'd done my best to soothe Ives's ruffled feathers, but Conrad had still been boiling when he left. I thought I'd try my pacifying technique on him, too."

"You wanted him calmed down for the famous apology he was supposed to get?"

Frayne was amused. "Hell, no. Hunnicut wasn't important to us. But Conrad meets a lot of people at the show who are. I wanted him in fighting trim for all those big customers. That's why I swung by our booth. But it was a washout because Conrad wasn't there. In fact, there wasn't anybody there except Phil Pepitone, and I'd had my fill of ASI, so I ducked out."

"Now I want you to think carefully, Mr. Frayne. Did you see anybody from Ecker or ASI as you were circulating around the floor?"

His brow wrinkled, Frayne concentrated. "I don't think so. In fact, I couldn't have. Obviously, if it had been anybody from Ecker, I would have stopped to talk. And, as I say, I was gun-shy of the ASI team, so I'd remember them."

"Mrs. Laverdiere says she was doing the rounds about then, too."

Frayne was not bothered by this. "No reason for us to bump into each other. I'd already done the right-hand side of the hall, so I stayed on the left. And some of the booths had a real crowd."

"And when did you hear about the murder? Were you still on the floor?"

"Depends what you mean. I was at the Black and Decker booth when someone said there'd been an accident. We could see guards and people hurrying to the rear of the buildings. But it wasn't until I came back to our display that I heard Ken Nicolls had found a body. Even then, I didn't know it was Hunnicut until the police began questioning us."

Giorni had deliberately introduced neutral subjects to act as a buffer before the next turn in his interrogation.

"All that may be helpful, you never can tell," he said, pocketing his notebook and leaning back casually. "Now I'd like to consult you as an expert."

"An expert about what?"

"I want to talk about the problems of stealing ideas from a lab."

Frayne was silent for a moment, then he asked unhappily: "This is about Sam Bradley, isn't it?"

"I see you people have heard the talk," Giorni commented.

"Conrad's been keeping tabs on ASI. You can't blame him, with the merger and everything, but that doesn't mean there's anything to what Hunnicut was saying."

"I realize that. I haven't forgotten he said the Laverdieres were crooks and you were covering for Ecker's senility."

The mere repetition of these charges raised Frayne's hackles.

"Not one word of which is true," he ground out.

"We know the guy was flinging around anything he could dream up, but the talk still has to be checked out.

In Bradley's case the starting point seems to be that his lab hasn't produced anything his company could use."

"Which could just be a run of real bad luck. Inspector, let me say one thing. We're a very successful outfit and we've introduced a bunch of good products. Yet, at a rough guess, two-thirds of Conrad's ideas bit the dust and don't go anywhere. Even so, he's practically a legend. You talk to anybody in the industry and they wonder how we can do it. Because everybody knows that most ideas, for one reason or another, never make it to market. It's unfortunate that ASI hasn't come up with at least one new development, but it doesn't prove anything."

Giorni duly noted that these were the kindest words about Sam Bradley that he had yet heard.

"Like I said, we're just checking," he rumbled. "Another one of the accusations was that Bradley doesn't run a tight ship. That's really what I want to discuss. I suppose a lab has to take some precautions. Otherwise, what's to stop one of Bradley's young scientists from realizing he's got something worth a mint and simply pocketing it?"

Frayne spread his hands in a gesture of helplessness.

"I'm the last person to ask. Of course you're right fundamentally, but we don't have those problems here. Bradley's sitting on top of a big operation with a lot of hired hands. If it's like most big outfits, there's a fair amount of turnover. ASI must do something to protect itself, but I don't have a clue how they work it. Over here, it's a different ball game. Conrad Ecker *is* our R and D operation. There's no question of riding herd on a pack of his assistants."

Alan Frayne clearly wanted to avoid attacking Sam Bradley, but there was still merit to his position. Giorni was willing to concede that Ecker and ASI were different animals. Returning to his chief concern, he said, "Okay, let's forget about how someone might steal the stuff. Let's go on to what he'd do with it once he had it. I suppose he'd sell it?"

"Well, that would be the name of the game, wouldn't it?" Frayne asked cautiously.

"Yeah, but I don't understand exactly how he'd go about it. I suppose companies buy ideas."

"All the time," Frayne agreed, "and at every level. Most companies have a program where they pay employees for cost-cutting ideas. It can be fifty dollars for a simple improvement up to thousands for a biggie about production. At the opposite end, you can go off and buy another company to get its ideas. That's basically why ASI is after us."

Giorni knew he was not getting what he wanted, but it took him several moments to analyze the inadequacy.

"That's not what I'm talking about," he said at last. "In both those situations the buyer actively wants something and is trying to find it. But what about the reverse? When the seller is trying to find a buyer?"

"I see what you mean. Well, the world is filled with people who think they've got a better mousetrap, and the mail does bring offerings from crazies. But there are more commercial ways of going about it, and every now and then you hear of an established company buying an idea. I don't really know how it's arranged."

"The Ecker Company has never bought an idea through the commercial system?"

Alan Frayne froze. Then, with an angry flush, he burst forth: "Look, is all this just a roundabout way of getting back to that bullshit about Conrad being senile? Let me tell you, he's just come up with another miracle. Hundreds of people have been after this one. And I'm not talking about guys fooling around in garages. Conrad's beaten out a pack of big R and D outfits. A year from now the stores will be filled with our digital reprogrammer and the industry will be yakking about the Ecker magic all over again."

Abandoning his casual posture, Giorni snapped upright. "What's this about a new product? This is the first I've heard of it."

"We were sitting on it until the Winstead people picked it up while they were nosing around here."

"Was ASI one of the outfits working on this idea?" Giorni demanded bluntly.

Frayne stared. "How the hell would I know? Off the top of my head, I'd say not likely. It isn't in their line. But then, they're trying to expand out of their line."

Entirely new possibilities were jostling and thrusting within Giorni's mind. Trying to stay on top of his churning thoughts, he deliberately slowed the pace of his questions.

"Let's take this one step at a time," he said. "That fire you had here. It wasn't just the financials that went up in smoke, was it? There were lab books there, too?"

Giorni's habit of hopping from one subject to another again disconcerted Frayne.

"Sure. That's all in the fire marshal's report."

"And there's no way you can tell if it all got burned or if something was stolen?"

"No, but I don't see where this is leading."

"What if somebody was after your new product, and the fire was just a cover?"

"But that doesn't make any sense. For Chrissake, Inspector," Frayne exploded, "just because I said we don't have the same problems as ASI doesn't mean we don't have any security at all. Those were old lab books. Everything current is kept right here in my lab in a nice fireproof safe armed with all those anti-burglar devices. We don't send material over to records until a new development is fully protected or until it's turned out to be a dud. There wouldn't be any point to stealing from records. Everybody knows that."

Silently Giorni provided an addendum to Frayne's last remark. Everybody *at Ecker* knows that. Was it possible that someone who had not been present during ASI's inspection had made a natural error?

"My mistake, it was just a passing thought," he muttered. Then, with another of his sudden veers, he continued, "So let's go back to your movements at the show and see if we can fill in any blanks."

As Inspector Giorni left, he was reflecting on the universal misconception about what was useful to the police. Virtually everybody at Ecker had ended his session by apologizing for an inability to pinpoint times and places at the trade show. Tina Laverdiere had provided a notable instance. She remembered glimpsing Sam Bradley at one of the exhibits, but could not recall its name, its position, or the time. All she retained with any clarity was her spasm of irritation at the clothing worn by a woman demonstrating the rotisserie.

"They had outfitted her in a pink ruffled apron, a teased hairdo, and the highest heels I've ever seen. No woman has looked like that at a barbecue since World War Two. But then," she had smiled ruefully, "that's not the sort of thing you want to know."

On the contrary, this was exactly what Giorni wanted to know. Armed with these details, he would have no trouble determining all those specifics that Tina could not supply. In a similar manner, Conrad Ecker had contributed a previously unknown reference mark. He admitted that, after his bout with Ives, he had purchased a roll of antacid tablets and consumed two on the spot.

"They claim those things work right away, but it took ten minutes for them to kick in. Honest to God, if I advertised my products that way . . ."

There followed a sweeping indictment of antacid claims, including a few of the pithy comments with which he had favored the salesperson.

But Alan Frayne remained the most egregious example of public naïveté. He, too, had excused his performance, in blissful ignorance that he had placed Phil Pepitone by the Ecker booth—at exactly the right moment to steal the murder weapon. And his disclosure of Conrad Ecker's new brainchild provided the first light on a nagging problem.

If Ecker's finances were irreproachable, why had the records office been torched?

Snapping his seat buckle into place, Giorni nodded with grim satisfaction.

"I always knew there was some connection."

Chapter

BULLS AND BEARS

Thanks to Inspector Giorni, the next day was a landmark at the Sloan Guaranty Trust. For once Miss Corsa gave an unscheduled visitor priority over John Thatcher's work in progress.

"Without an appointment?" Charlie reproached her. "Rose, you must be losing your touch."

"It's Conrad Ecker," she said, explaining and condoning.

"Send him in," Thatcher said. Then, recalling the possibility of outriders, he added, "He's by himself, is he?"

Conrad Ecker, his wiry hair bristling, was quite alone when Miss Corsa ushered him in. A forceful tweed jacket enhanced his aura of peppery consequence.

"Nice girl you've got there," he said grandly when Thatcher rose to greet him. "Glad you can see me. I suppose I should have called ahead."

During the niceties that followed, Thatcher saw that

Trinkam was ready to be entertained by Conrad's quirkiness. Everett, of course, had always been an avowed devotee of the Ecker yogurt maker. Thatcher would have been willing to let them sit in, despite the risk of hearing them described as nice boys, but it was obvious that Ecker was champing at the bit.

Nevertheless, after Charlie and Ev took themselves off, Ecker fidgeted uncomfortably. Finally he found his tongue: "I've got to talk to somebody," he said in a gust.

Formula dictated a soothing *That's what I'm here for.* But Thatcher had not reached his current eminence by impersonating a medical caregiver.

"The pressure seems to be on ASI these days. What's bothering you at Ecker?" he said, plunging in.

"The police are back at our place," Conrad told him.

At first Thatcher misunderstood, but Ecker went on to dispel the notion of renewed suspicion.

"No, they claim they're after us this time as witnesses. But what they're really doing, whether they admit it or not, is picking our brains about ASI. And I don't like what they're asking."

"Well, they do have to find out who murdered Hunnicut, after all," Thatcher argued.

This vapidity triggered sound as well as fury.

"I don't give a damn about Hunnicut," Ecker retorted. "I care about the Ecker Company."

Thatcher persisted. "Conrad, as long as the police are working, they're bound to say things you don't like."

Ecker glared at him. "It's not the police who bother me. You saw how sick Ives looked when I told him Ecker was getting more valuable. And we all know why. My God, I thought our troubles were over when the police zeroed in on ASI. But now, everything they come up with over there makes my company look less valuable. And, Thatcher, I don't think this is all an accident."

When Ecker was talking about shenanigans in a Sloan negotiation, he had Thatcher's full attention. "You think Ives is deliberately denigrating Ecker to discourage other buyers?"

"Or to drive our price down. He needs every bargaining chip he can lay his hands on. I don't begrudge him that, but once he starts playing dirty, I draw the line—even though I don't see exactly what I should do. That's why I'm here. And don't advise me to lie down and keep quiet."

"No, no," said Thatcher hastily. "But there's a middle ground between playing dead and going public."

"What's that?" Ecker demanded.

That was the usual huddle to clear the air. If peace did not ensue, the combatants would at least have established their rules of warfare.

"Miss Corsa," said Thatcher, pressing the button. "See if you can get hold of Gardner Ives for me, will you? If it's humanly possible, I need to see him today."

Luck was on his and Miss Corsa's side. After ruthless telephone forays she discovered that she would not have to dispatch Thatcher to New Jersey.

Gardner Ives, fortunately, was already in town.

". . . conferring with Tom Robichaux, which we could have expected," said Thatcher, leading the way up Broad Street. "ASI's had one headache after another lately."

"Pfa!" said Ecker, magnificently unsympathetic to any distress but his own.

He was, it developed, one of the world's many Manhattan haters. Stalking along beside Thatcher, he loathed every face in the crowd, every taxi blocking a crosswalk. "How you can live here beats me," he muttered.

Thatcher, refraining from witticism about the haunting charm of Bridgeport, replied, "I'm taking you to one of our local beauty spots."

Robichaux & Devane, that ancient and honorable investment bank, had over the years become a museum piece. Period furnishings and rare Orientals were intended to convey an impression of untouchable superiority. Yet, despite the surrounding grandeur, Gardner Ives and Robichaux looked bewildered and apprehensive.

At sight of his prey, Ecker bore down on Ives.

"Aha!" he growled, ignoring Robichaux, who half-rose in agitation.

"Afternoon, Tom, Ives," said Thatcher sedately.

With a cockfight imminent, Robichaux regarded this as inadequate but he valiantly tried matching Thatcher's aplomb.

"Good to see you, good to see you," he babbled. "Understand you've got something you want to talk about, Ecker. Sit down, make yourself comfortable."

His relief, when Ecker complied, was palpable. Thatcher, on the other hand, remained confident that blood was not going to fly. His man might be up to it, but Gardner Ives looked like a spent force.

Although Thatcher did not know it, Ives was in fact a three-time loser. First he had been put through the meat grinder for trying to duck responsibility in the Sparling debacle. Then Phil Pepitone had gone on to ram the digital reprogrammer down his throat. Now, with Ives's very survival resting on a speedy and amicable merger, here was Conrad Ecker pawing the ground.

Wanly Ives greeted Thatcher, then turned. "I hear you've got something on your mind, Conrad."

For a dedicated hunter, Ecker exhibited unsportsmanlike behavior.

"You're right about that, at least," he began challengingly.

At this Thatcher stirred. As a rule he found it wise to give his principals their head. What this cost in coherence and relevance was usually balanced by sops to the egos involved. But letting an unrestrained Conrad Ecker loose on Ives, in his present condition, would amount to a dereliction of duty.

"Perceptions tend to get distorted once the police start burrowing around," Thatcher intervened. "Conrad's been getting some strange feedback, so we decided to discuss the whole subject with you."

His careful circumlocution was too much for Ecker.

"First they claimed that Pepitone had to be paid off to choose Ecker—"

Tumult broke out before he could proceed.

"Utter nonsense!" rumbled Tom Robichaux, who had himself been part of the selection process.

Thatcher chimed in with a weightier authority. "The Winstead report makes it abundantly clear that Ecker had no need to—"

Ives, already suffering from battle fatigue, opted for appeasement.

"Of course I don't know a thing about what the police are doing," he said. "It goes without saying that we at ASI regard any such charge as ridiculous. Ecker is far too strong a company to need to bribe anyone."

The chorus of praise was futile. Conrad Ecker, as Thatcher could see, had barely scratched the surface.

"Of course it's ridiculous," he spat back. "And when it didn't work out, you came up with a real beaut."

This silenced everyone except Thatcher who, with considerable courage, said, "Perhaps you might explain what you mean, Conrad."

Ecker could barely form a sentence. After several false starts, he finally forced the words out: "They're claiming I stole my ideas from ASI."

Robichaux, never at his best when startled, unwisely chose to treat this as humor.

"Ho! Ho! Ho!" he chortled unconvincingly. "That's a good one."

With rising choler, Conrad blasted him. "Oh, yeah? What about this guy Bradley? The cops started by asking what Hunnicut said about him back during that inspection trip. Now Bob tells me they're on a new tack. They want to know how easy it would be for Bradley to steal developments from ASI."

Ignoring a strangled bleat from Ives, Thatcher came to Robichaux's defense. "But, Conrad, what does that have to do with you?"

"Plenty," Conrad told him. "Because then, by God, they want to know if Ecker ever buys ideas that outsiders are trying to peddle."

Ives was gasping like a fish out of water when Ecker crescendoed: "Where do you think this leads? Somebody's saying Bradley sold stuff to me. Me?" he choked. "Me, stealing from ASI! Hell, they haven't produced anything new for the last ten years. I've come up with product after product, and good ones, too. Why would I try to get hold of their junk? Compared to Ecker, ASI's a joke."

Tom Robichaux turned to Gardner Ives. Thatcher, too, expected a blistering retort to this wholesale barrage. But Ives, blinking furiously, was absorbed by private outrage. For five years he had been Sam Bradley's chief advocate. It was too late to disassociate himself now.

"What are *you* complaining about, Conrad?" he yelped. "If any of this is true—which I doubt—it's ASI that's being ripped off."

Thatcher wondered if Ives would ever stop concentrating on himself long enough to recognize that ASI might be harboring a murderer. Or, for that matter, to notice that his response had infuriated Conrad Ecker even further.

"You think I don't understand what's going on?"

Ecker shouted. "The minute you hear about my digital reprogrammer, the word goes out that I might have stolen it. That kind of scenario a six-year-old could understand. You're trying to scare away other buyers."

John Thatcher might be one of the last to hear about the digital reprogrammer, but he was quick to appreciate its implications. Another lucky strike like this one, and it would be Ecker buying ASI.

Ives, however, was thunderstruck. Torn between astonishment at the charge, fear of losing Ecker altogether, and insulted dignity, he blustered helplessly: ". . . never heard of such a thing . . . not a word of truth . . ."

Then, pulling himself together, he reverted to type. "Ecker, I assure you that ASI would never stoop to such despicable tactics. We're proud of our reputation for unblemished integrity."

But Ecker was still foaming.

"From what I read about Sparling, you're not a bunch of choir boys over there."

With Ives reeling and Robichaux goggle-eyed, Thatcher had no alternative.

"Now wait a minute, Conrad," he said firmly. "The police are asking general questions. They want to know if it's possible for Sam Bradley to steal ideas. They want to know how he'd sell them. But did they ever actually ask if Bradley sold anything to Ecker?"

Ecker resented cross-examination.

"Not in so many words," he said after a long pause.

Thatcher was implacable. "Did they—or anybody else—specifically link Sam Bradley to your digital reprogrammer?"

Losing steam, Ecker said with reluctance, "Well, no."

"Then," said Thatcher severely, "this spate of innuendo is all in your own mind."

Ives grasped what might be his final opportunity.

"You're being a little harsh, Thatcher. Naturally Conrad is very concerned by the mere possibility of such a suggestion. The Ecker Company *is* Conrad's good name. But that's so self-evident that the police would never dream of impugning his personal ability."

Ives's well-intentioned contribution took them from bad to worse. Suddenly, with all the fight knocked out of him, Conrad Ecker was left with the one question he did not want to recall.

"Then why are they asking if I'm getting senile?"

Chapter

RENTS AND ROYALTIES

Inspector Giorni's activities in Bridgeport had left him as discontented as Conrad Ecker.

". . . so we've got Pepitone placed right next to that damned skewer," he complained to Sergeant Gwendolyn Belliers. "What good is that if he doesn't have a motive anymore?"

It was late at night and Giorni's desk was littered with the debris of sandwiches and coffee. He himself had slumped down in order to study the ceiling.

Wendy Belliers, who had spent the day at ASI, nodded briskly.

"Right now, Pepitone's parading around, reminding everybody that he was the one who picked Ecker."

Giorni was a last-ditcher by nature. "Okay, so Pepitone wasn't bribed by Ecker. Was he bribed by someone else? Where does he stand with Sparling?"

There was little joy there, either.

"In the first place, it was Ives who really chose Sparling. Then it turns out the Sparling people cooked their books, and the outside accounting firm didn't catch it. But we're talking highly technical fraud here. If Sparling bribed anyone, it was the accountants. That lets Pepitone out.''

''Then what about Wiley Quinn?'' Giorni continued doggedly.

''I don't see it,'' she said. ''He wasn't being accused of anything that could land him in jail or cost him his job. Sure, Hunnicut was getting under his skin. If you ask me, Quinn was more likely to deck him than anything else.''

This was exactly the conclusion that Giorni had reached, but he liked to clear away the underbrush as he went along. Now he signaled an end to the preliminaries by tilting upright and sweeping the crumpled wrappings from his desk.

''What's more, a Sparling bribe to Pepitone or a quarrel between Quinn and Hunnicut doesn't explain that fire at Ecker,'' he began. ''But when we come to Sam Bradley, we've got a fighting chance for a connection.''

With a frown, Wendy said, ''I thought Frayne claims the digital reprogrammer was never in any danger.''

''Ah, but what about earlier work from his lab?'' Giorni asked, formulating his theory as he proceeded. ''Bradley's had a no-show record for a long time. And we've already heard of one case where a product scrubbed by Ecker was brought out by another firm. Suppose Bradley managed to buy one of their rejects from a file clerk? He's planning to bring it out as his own, when, bang! suddenly he finds out that ASI's going to buy Ecker and those old lab books could be dynamite.''

Wendy, who had been following intently, grinned. ''Here's an even juicier twist,'' she offered. ''Suppose Bradley finally did come up with something good, decided to steal it, and sold it through a go-between to Ecker. A merger with Ecker would really throw him for a loop. He'd have to destroy the old lab books, not because of what they contained, but because of what they didn't contain."

"I like them both," Giorni said, nodding appreciatively. "And there's a plus with your version. At Ecker they get uptight if you suggest that everything didn't originate with Conrad. I can understand the old man being sensitive about his age, but even Frayne saw red when I asked if they ever bought outside ideas. Still, the main thing is that both of us have found a way to link the fire with Hunnicut's murder. There's only one hitch."

This banished Wendy's grin. "We don't have a guru," she said, her voice tinged with incredulity. "Not a single one."

The New York City Police Department is justifiably proud of its specialists. But somehow the long list did not include an expert on the marketing of ideas.

"And yet there have got to be professionals around," she reasoned. "I read an obituary the other day of a man nobody's ever heard of. But he spent a long life selling ideas to the *Fortune* 500. There must be some sort of system for doing that."

Giorni regarded his subordinate indulgently.

"So it's a business," he said, his face creasing into a slow smile. "What we do is call a guy who knows all about business."

John Thatcher was not quite that omniscient, but he never doubted that the resources of the Sloan could produce the right man for Inspector Giorni. As it happened, the search went no farther than Charlie Trinkam.

"Sure," Charlie said instantly. "Art is the man you want to talk to."

Like the inventor whose obituary Wendy Belliers had read, Arthur Hanscom Cherniak was a man few people had heard of. Nevertheless, the sale of his ideas provided funds that had made him an investor worthy of the Sloan's attention.

"He's been at it fifteen years now, and he's only forty-five," Charlie expanded.

"Do you think he'll be willing to drop by and speak with Inspector Giorni and us?"

"Oh, sure, he's an obliging sort of guy. All we have to do is pry him loose from that log cabin of his."

Thatcher's eyebrows rose as he rapidly revised his preconceptions. "He lives in a log cabin?"

"Well, it's the kind that's got three bathrooms. But it's way the hell out in Putnam County. As if that isn't bad enough, it's at the end of a private road through the woods with about a hundred bird feeders drooping off every limb."

"It sounds as if he's not our standard client," said Thatcher, looking forward to the coming session.

Within minutes of his arrival at the Sloan, Arthur Cherniak demonstrated that he, too, enjoyed broadening his horizons.

"I was glad of the chance," he replied when Inspector Giorni thanked him for coming. "I've never met a homicide detective before. It must be interesting work."

Giorni modestly replied that most murders required only slogging routine.

"And very few of them are the kind people like to read about," he went on, having met this form of enthusiasm before. "If it isn't gang-related, then it's a barroom brawl or a domestic dispute."

The newspapers, Cherniak protested wistfully, regularly produced something more complicated than that. Giorni, now that he had taken the measure of his man, sensibly deferred his own goal in order to create goodwill. Art Cherniak lapped up every detail of a recent domestic shooting. Even Charlie Trinkam allowed himself to be sidetracked.

"Faking a burglary is for dummies," he said, suddenly emerging as an arbiter. "All those wives who claim they shot hubby by mistake have the right idea. Admit everything except state of mind."

Thatcher gave full marks to the inspector for concealing all signs of impatience. The reward came when Cherniak, after a lingering sigh, voluntarily returned to the topic at hand.

"I hear you want to know about the sale of ideas."

Giorni nodded vigorously. "Yeah, it's come up in a current case, and I'd like to hear how somebody goes about it."

"The answer is there are a lot of variations, depending on what's being offered and who's offering it."

Thatcher knew they had to pussyfoot before Giorni would name names. But to edge them forward, he said, "What about giving us a general overview, Art? We can get down to specifics later."

"Well, most people who succeed are basically employees and ex-employees of the industry they cater to. They've been working for an electronics company, say, or an automotive company. Then they get an idea that's the direct result of a need they've spotted. They know the firms that are likely to be interested in their baby, they've got personal contacts all over the place, they can rattle off the commercial arguments for their product. Naturally they have a built-in advantage."

Charlie waved proudly toward his client. "That's how Art got started. He was working for a manufacturer of X-ray equipment."

"God, that's right. I'd almost forgotten." Cherniak seemed to be peering back through the mists of time. "But it's a different kettle of fish for the guys who come up with an idea out of the blue. You've got to realize that it's hard for a buyer to recognize the value of something that doesn't solve an existing problem. You're asking him to take a leap into the unknown. Personally, I've never understood how the first zipper was sold when everybody was happy with buttons. But this is where we come to a fundamental consideration. If you're dealing with a small gizmo designed for the consumer market, you can begin by selling it yourself. That is, you demonstrate that there really are customers out there. Those are the mail-order guys who run magazine ads and TV spots. Then, if that works, they show up at the trade shows to try for some commercial accounts. If they get the thing off the ground, they can sell the whole kit and caboodle. Some of them manage it, but only with an item that doesn't cost much to produce. You can go that route with a better knife, but not with a better airplane.''

Thatcher knew all about the barrier raised by cost of entry into a field, but he saw another distinction as well. "And that system is only feasible when you're targeting the general public."

"Absolutely. And probably most ideas are directed toward the production process. There are big bucks in a better knot-tying machine."

Inspector Giorni was more curious about the traceable activities of inventors than about their financial rewards.

"Okay, but I suppose the first step for all of them must be getting a patent."

Cherniak was sorry to puncture the notion that a simple trip to the patent office would solve anything.

"I'm afraid not," he said. "Getting a patent at the start is a risky business. In the first place, it takes a hell of a long time—three years isn't unusual and somebody can beat you to the punch in the meantime. Then, you can kill yourself by not having exactly the right claims on your application. If you apply before your concept is completely realized, your claims may not be broad enough to give you adequate protection. Even worse, if your claims aren't narrow enough, the patent examiner will disallow you. These days people often deal with an idea as a trade secret. They sell it on that basis, requiring the buyer to get patent protection after the dust has settled."

His audience was startled to have the entire elaborate patent system relegated to the sidelines.

"Then what is the first step?" Thatcher pressed.

"Persuading a prospect to let you in long enough to give a presentation. That's not easy the first time at bat and it's pretty nerve-racking. God, I can remember getting a haircut and buying a new suit so they'd have some faith in my cost figures. I don't bother about that anymore."

The final statement was scarcely necessary. Not many visitors found their way into Thatcher's office wearing blue jeans and jogging shoes.

"Between being excited at getting somebody to listen to me and being afraid I'd blow it, I didn't know what I was doing," Cherniak continued, lost in a nostalgic glow. "The whole thing was a blur."

Charlie Trinkam was always indulgent to youth.

"Well, you must have done something right, Art. You sold your gizmo."

Cherniak beamed. "Not that time, I didn't. It was the second time out that was a success."

The information emerging was less and less to Inspector Giorni's liking. "Look," he said, frowning, "the guy I'm checking on seems to fit your first category. He's in the business, he'd know what firms to approach and how his idea would fit their product lines. But, if he's stolen it from his company, he's not going to go around presenting it himself, is he?"

"Hell, no," said Cherniak, taking crime in stride.

"There's too much risk that he'd run into someone who knew all about him and his employment. He'd use an agent."

"I thought agents in this field had a bad reputation," Thatcher ventured. "That they were simply hucksters exploiting innocent simpletons."

Cherniak snorted contemptuously. "Oh, that bunch. There are hundreds of them circling the patent office. But there are some real agents who perform other functions. Max Steele, for instance, negotiates contracts for me. Then, if I don't know the right firms, he finds a sales rep experienced in the field. The thing is, good agents don't take just anybody. They demand a track record or its equivalent."

"Would my man qualify?" Giorni asked. "Always assuming the agent didn't know he was stealing."

"Oh, I think so. From what you say, he could easily demonstrate that he was a serious prospect. He'd submit a professional presentation, accompanied by a list of the most likely buyers with an analysis of their product lines. Not to mention that he'd know what agent to go to."

Now that a hopeful road was appearing, they had reached a watershed.

"Then it would really be useful to find out who those agents are," Giorni said suggestively.

"I can help you there, Inspector, but you're going to have to loosen up," Cherniak warned. "At the very least, I've got to know what field we're talking about."

Giorni had seen this one coming, and he had no doubt what the result would be with such a dedicated reader of crime news.

"Probably small kitchen appliances?" he began slyly.

"Say, are we talking about that stabbing at the trade show? Well, I'll be damned."

"Or possibly a digital reprogrammer."

The crime buff disappeared, to be replaced by the inventor.

"For the consumer market?" Cherniak exclaimed excitedly. "Now which genius came up with that one? ASI or Ecker?"

"Apparently Conrad Ecker," Giorni said slowly, watching for signs of disbelief. "Although they tell me it's not the sort of thing he's done in the past."

But Art Cherniak evinced only respectful admiration. "Nothing that old bastard did would surprise me," he said, bestowing the accolade of one professional on another. "Well, with this info, we can get started. If you like, I'll call Max and ask him to put together a list of the agents who were probably approached by your man."

Cherniak was as good as his word, calling Washington on the spot. After triumphantly announcing that the work would begin immediately, he refused an invitation to lunch. True to Charlie Trinkam's description, Cherniak was already yearning for his woodland retreat. Within minutes he was rushing off to catch a train.

As soon as the door closed, Giorni dropped the veil of anonymity. "Of course it isn't going to be that easy. Sam Bradley wouldn't use his own name."

"Don't let that bother you, Inspector," Thatcher said reassuringly. "You say there's a limited list of ASI projects that failed to come to anything. Find an agent who's handled one of them, and you'll have a starting point."

"Then you can blow the alias out of the water," Charlie proclaimed with gusto.

Giorni favored his companions with a disenchanted gaze. "Look, when banks ask questions, people answer whether they want to or not. It doesn't work that way with the police. These people in Washington will probably start yapping about confidential information."

"I don't see how. After all, these agents are hired

precisely in order to publicize the achievements of their clients. Their business is letting people know what's for sale. And that's all you're asking to know. The rest will be a matter of tracking backward.''

Insensibly Giorni was cheered by Thatcher's analysis.

"You mean, if the right product's there and they give me the name of the client, I'm home free."

"Sure," said Charlie, weighing in. "Nine chances out of ten, the client will be something called General Equipment Corporation at a P.O. box number. The signatures will be provided by a straw man."

All those experts back at headquarters were finally going to pay their way.

"If there's one thing our Fraud Squad is good at," Giorni said, nodding happily, "it's getting behind a straw man."

Chapter

PAYING THE PIPER

While John Thatcher huddled with New York City Police and inventors from the backwoods, Miss Corsa set about tabulating the latest arrears. By the time Inspector Giorni departed, she was reordering all immediate priorities. As a result, the following morning found John Thatcher back on his normal bland diet. Impeccable Wall Street credentials were required before anyone gained access to him. Fourth-quarter reviews, alternating with first-quarter estimates, crowded murder and mischief off his docket. At spaced intervals he was permitted light relief in the form of good gray Everett Gabler.

Mercifully for Thatcher, this unnatural state of grace was abruptly terminated by a frantic telephone call from Tom Robichaux. Miss Corsa, despite well-founded suspicions, could scarcely deflect one of the Sloan's traditional peers.

"Tom!" Thatcher said with rare pleasure. "What new convulsions have you got from ASI?"

Where the police are concerned, reciprocity is seldom the reward for services rendered. Thatcher did not expect Giorni to keep him abreast of the search for illicit moonlighting by Sam Bradley, but any discoveries there would be convulsing ASI. Tom Robichaux could never be considered a reliable source, but during Thatcher's stint of forced labor he was, at least theoretically, available.

"ASI?" said Robichaux, drawing a blank.

With resignation, Thatcher reminded himself to smuggle in Ken Nicolls when Miss Corsa was not looking and asked, "What's on your mind, Tom?"

"Henrietta wanted me to make sure you haven't forgotten about tonight," Robichaux replied.

"Certainly not," said Thatcher, upborn by the conviction that Miss Corsa would remember what he did not.

She briefed him later. "You're due at seven-thirty, in the Grand Ballroom of the Waldorf Astoria."

"It will make a nice change," said Thatcher.

He was tweaking the wrong taskmaster. Miss Corsa truly honored the sacred wellsprings of private charity.

A Musical Evening with Friends of the Julliard met standards loftier than hers, if a thousand dollars a plate was any criterion. Fully rigged out in white tie and tails, John Thatcher surveyed the usual gala scene—favor-laden tables, convoluted floral arrangements, and a Cunard-level bar—as well as the usual faces. He was engulfed by brilliant gowns, smiles, and diamonds.

As a rule, putting a check in the mail sufficed for the reigning Mrs. Thomas Robichaux and her pet project. Over the years Thatcher, and half of Wall Street, judging from the acquaintances he sighted, had Saved the Rain Forest, Built the National Cathedral, and

Preserved New England Antiquities with cold cash. But one consort in recent memory had actually required supporters of nonrepresentational art to view the sorry stuff. Now the current incumbent, a Friend, had deputized poor tone-deaf Robichaux to corral a live audience.

Without high expectations, Thatcher deferred his quest for modest entertainment amidst this organized festivity in order to consult the program. Coming events (brought to him with the compliments of Robichaux & Devane) included brief remarks by assorted luminaries, then a musical interlude.

Appended to this chilling text were some explanatory notes. Since *moderato ma non troppo* simply confounded his ignorance, Thatcher moved on to more intelligible code words. Despite recent changes in the tax laws, "patron" still stood for princely munificence. For "associate member," Thatcher and his fellow initiates read pittance throughout.

He was approaching the middle range of respectable contributors like the Chase Manhattan, Paramount, and the Sloan Guaranty Trust, when a top-tier name jumped up at him. There, big as life, was the Ecker Company, sandwiched between Dupont and Ford.

Before Thatcher could decide how to interpret this temerity, his attention was claimed.

"Long time no see," said the voice in his ear.

Slewing around, Thatcher encountered Charlie Trinkam. Predictably, Charlie had a decorative brunette on his arm.

"Ah, good evening, Mrs. Laverdiere," said Thatcher. With a nod toward the Sloan's ranking bon vivant, he flourished his program at Tina. "You're just the person to help me out. Tell me about this extraordinary generosity of yours to Juilliard."

Tina, radiant in a draped Grecian gown, was impersonating a dear little dimwit. "Oh, it's not my generosity," she fluttered. "It's all of us. Ecker's really rooting for Juilliard, and tonight we've all turned out to prove it. Why, Doug and Gloria have come up from Florida, and at this time of year, that's something."

"Of course," Thatcher agreed politely.

But Tina's prattle had alerted Charlie. "I see you two have already met," he charged.

"We're old, old friends," said Tina with an artful throb.

Charlie, who rarely encountered playfulness to equal his own, was prematurely hopeful. Then Bob Laverdiere spoiled his party.

"Yup, it's a great night for all us Eckers," Laverdiere sang out, enveloping Tina in a boozy hug.

"That does it," murmured Charlie sadly. His code, elastic about husbands, proscribed business after hours. Once the lovely Mrs. Laverdiere was identified as part of the Ecker Company, she was off limits. With regret for what might have been, Charlie moved on to greener fields.

"Why's he going away?" demanded Bob plaintively.

Despite these distractions, Thatcher continued delving into the Ecker Company's big-time commitment to the arts.

"And are Conrad and Mrs. Ecker here, too?" he probed, improbable as this vision appeared.

"With bells on," Tina told him. "Alice is wearing the dress she bought for Betty's wedding."

"Betty's second wedding," said Bob lugubriously. Then a long sip from his glass revived his spirits. "Say, this champagne's really good. Let's get the name and buy a couple of cases, Tina."

"Fine," she said, sharing the joke with Thatcher. "One drink and Bob starts buying cases. That's why I'm the designated driver."

"But it's special," her husband protested. "Here,

have a taste. Better yet, I'll get you a glass. I'll get both of you a glass. Just wait right here."

With fuzzy determination he tottered off—past several tray-bearing waiters—in the approximate direction of the bar.

Instinctively, Thatcher braced himself. Like Charlie, he had no innate fear of husbands as such but, too often, when they got tipsy, they strewed tight-lipped mates in their wake. Coping with enraged females had never been Thatcher's forte.

But Tina continued to bubble.

"As you can see, we're all celebrating," she said cheerfully.

Apparently the extended Ecker clan was presenting a united front. Thatcher was willing to accept this as gospel but he still wanted to know why.

"Douglas, Junior," Tina explained as if the whole world knew.

Junior, Thatcher suddenly recalled, was Conrad's gifted grandson. More to the point, tonight he was the family star.

". . . at Juilliard, where he's doing brilliantly," Tina continued. "That's why he was chosen to conduct. Of course that's a tremendous honor, but on the cello, Junior's already a concert-caliber soloist."

Thatcher, no slouch at small talk, knew his limitations. Precocious genius, on or off the cello, reduced him to generalities.

"No doubt you're all very proud of him," he said. Even if Junior was a budding Mozart, that should be safe.

"Ye-es," said Tina slowly. "Doug and Gloria are simply bursting. *That's* why Ecker's gone overboard for Juilliard. But there's a downside, too."

"There always is," said Thatcher, shifting automatically from one romance to another. In family firms as in family farms, only one happy ending is permissible—

handing over the reins to the rightful heir. A sale to strangers is not a commercial transaction, but the death of a dream.

And, as Tina demonstrated, a dream that is easily misinterpreted.

"Of course it'll be a thrill to have a superstar in the family," she mused. "But in many ways it would have been so much easier if Junior were just a nice ordinary kid, who could take over when others leave off. Of course we all understand that Junior has to do his own thing."

Silk, satin, and dangerously high levels of perfume in the atmosphere usually caused Thatcher to suspend his critical facilities. Tonight some compunction for Junior moved him.

"But, Mrs. Laverdiere, it is Doug himself who introduced the discontinuity. His retirement created the gap."

For his pains, he received a sharp jab.

"You sound just like my mother-in-law," said Tina. When Thatcher's jaw dropped, she relented slightly. "Bob's mother's got a complicated idea of the Ecker Company. But actually, Mr. Thatcher, the future's always been very simple. It was going to be Junior—or nothing. We just expected Doug to last longer."

"Poor, poor Doug," crooned Bob, popping up again. He had, Thatcher noticed, progressed from champagne to Scotch. "You know, you've got to feel damned sorry for poor Doug. Of all the lousy luck! Stuck down there in the swamp, miles and miles away from Ecker, where he really belongs. And where he's a somebody. Oh, sure, he's got money enough for all the toys he wants. But what good is that? He's awful damned young to get stuck on the shelf, twiddling his thumbs."

Tina the wife swung into action.

"Forget about poor Doug," she directed crisply.

"We'd better do something about you, Bob. Otherwise you'll be flat on your back before Junior takes a bow."

Tactfully, Thatcher left the Laverdieres to their own devices and began circulating. On the principle that brief remarks and musical interludes always entail too much sitting, he made it a practice to keep moving until the last minute. Nimble footwork took him past clumps of stationary guests and many other husband-and-wife teams. As chance would have it, Tom Robichaux's Henrietta was occupied elsewhere.

". . . but she's overjoyed at the crowd," Tom reported. "And, John, she particularly wanted me to thank you for coming."

Thatcher, who would not recognize Henrietta if she fell into his arms, yielded to temptation.

"I'm delighted," he said. "And are you enjoying yourself as well, Tom?"

Robichaux's internal struggle boded ill for his continued conjugal felicity, but he was always a gentleman. "A very delightful evening," he said, daring Thatcher to do his damnedest, "and a worthwhile event."

The Ecker table, when Thatcher stopped by to chat, featured marriages made in heaven. Mr. and Mrs. Douglas Ecker were such proud parents that it was impossible to contemplate other facets of their union.

"The kid wouldn't let us come backstage," Doug boasted to Thatcher, "Says he's got stage fright."

"Horse—" Conrad began, before crumbling, "—feathers."

Wedged between his wife and his daughter-in-law, he was a far cry from the holy terror last seen. He was, however, in noticeably fine fettle. And Douglas Ecker certainly bore no resemblance to the lost soul of Bob Laverdiere's vaporings.

Even the singleton at the table beamed with confidence.

"Oh, Junior always claims he's nervous," Alan Frayne began affectionately.

"But once he's on stage—wow!" Conrad jumped in.

Junior's triumphs had become a family ritual.

"Did I tell you that Betty sent the most beautiful flowers again?" said Gloria to Alice Ecker.

"Oh, I'm so glad," Alice exclaimed.

"Sis never forgets," Doug chimed in.

Approbation of thoughtfulness from California hummed around the table, and as far as Thatcher could see, Alan Frayne joined in.

However, happy families are no place for outsiders. Thatcher was ready when a minatory tinkle sounded through the ballroom.

"I'd better see where they've seated me," he murmured.

The Eckers, he was convinced, never missed him.

Thatcher's table, when he located it, offered a mixed bag. There were Francis and Mrs. Devane, devout Quakers as well as Robichaux partners. The Devanes rendered unto Caesar when they had to, but they preferred to discuss gardening. The other philanthropist awaiting him was Hugh Waymark. Waymark never left the bond market far behind, but Mrs. Waymark overrode him with a running critique of all the dishes served.

". . . a pinch of cardamom—I think. But I can't be absolutely sure."

On the whole, Thatcher was not unhappy to have the formal program begin.

An hour later, he was on his feet, cheering lustily. This was not solely attributable to the madness of crowds, although the din around him was contagious.

". . . as authoritative as Christopher Hogwood!"

"And the *lento!* Have you ever heard such a *lento?*"

". . . wonderful new talent right here in America. Why keep importing Russians?"

Thatcher, who made no pretense at being one of the cognoscenti, simply clapped. While the finer points of the performance were, no doubt, wasted on him, he had responded to the bravura that Juilliard's students brought to their task—and to their endearing intentness. Their *Carmen* Suite might not be the most polished to which he had ever been subjected, but the aspiring artists were far more pleasing to look upon than their jaded Philharmonic cousins. In fairness to the musicians' union, it had to be added that gleaming hair and glowing complexions made the ensemble more attractive than their audience, too.

But, although beguiling, the performers were not perfect. Like their elders, they succumbed to calls for an encore.

It was, whispered Mrs. Hugh Waymark after the opening bars, Samuel Plummer's beloved "Song of the Middle Border."

"Plummer," she enlightened him further, "is one of Juilliard's most distinguished alumni."

As far as Thatcher was concerned, that was no excuse. The waves of relentless Americana enveloping him did what the *lento* could not. Thatcher relaxed his heroic wakefulness and let his thoughts drift away from the homespun score. But, like Samuel Plummer, he stuck to nuggets from the national repertory of quaintness.

"Mother knows best," he reminded himself while the violins tugged vainly at his heartstrings. That, of course, depended on what Mother knew, and which mothers one was talking about.

Then there was the ancient prescription beloved of coos, codgers and sots: "Nothing like a drink to kill the pain."

But had Bob Laverdiere been hurting while he burbled on? Thatcher rather doubted it.

He was reviewing "If it ain't broke, don't fix it" when the soggy finale arrived.

In spite of the provocation, Thatcher's music-loving neighbors responded with another rousing ovation. The conductor stepped to the front of the stage, bowed from the waist, and waited for silence.

Watching a black-suited back was not Thatcher's notion of entertainment, even when long arms were coaxing and bullying violins and woodwinds into a harmonic whole.

But, with the maestro facing him, Thatcher discovered Junior, and another ancient saw.

Acorns, he had always been told, do not fall far from the tree.

Obviously, perfect pitch was not the only genetic anomaly about Junior. Taller by at least a head than his father or grandfather, golden blond, he was—although nobody had bothered to mention it—gloriously handsome.

Every swan hatched by barnyard ducks seems destined to become a superstar. But this awful fate had yet to befall young Ecker. Not quite an adult, but no longer a boy, he was still modest, confident, and appreciative to a fault.

". . . personally thank my mother and my father."

Wild applause.

". . . and Grandfather and Grandmother Ecker."

Mrs. Waymark was still going strong. Hugh began fumbling for a cigar.

". . . wonderful friends Tina and Bob, who've always been real sympathetic."

Junior should already have stopped. After parents and grandparents, most crowds cease empathizing and start fidgeting.

". . . and last, but not least, my Uncle Alan."

The polite patter was drowned out by the rustling that herald departure. Thatcher remained seated, while escorts went for wraps, makeup was repaired, and families ringed the performers, who were leaving the stage clutching instruments like trophies. For several long minutes he sat still, testing another hoary old saw for contemporary relevance.

"Out of the mouths of babes . . ."

Chapter

28

A USUALLY RELIABLE SOURCE

John Thatcher's call from the Waldorf Astoria propelled Inspector Giorni into a whirlwind of activity. Within forty-eight hours he had what he wanted: nevertheless he was still too late. Alan Frayne's plane had already landed in Zurich, Switzerland.

Determined to exact a pound of flesh somewhere, Giorni stormed across the Ecker compound to disrupt a high-level conference. Ignoring John Thatcher, Tom Robichaux, and the Laverdieres, he bore down on Conrad Ecker.

"You tipped him off," he rasped accusingly. "I could nail you for that."

Conrad's response to any display of aggression was reflexive.

"I'll do as I damn please!"

"You realize you've let a killer get off scot-free?"

"If you'd done your job right, he'd have been behind bars a long time ago."

Thatcher's sensitive ear detected a false note in Ecker's vigorous ripostes. Say what you would about him, he usually kept to the point. Fortunately Tina Laverdiere, who had been listening with a faint air of amusement, was willing to solve Conrad's dilemma. Before Giorni could demolish the last digression, she broke in:

"Oh, for heaven's sake, Inspector, can't you see that Conrad didn't warn Alan? Alice is the one to blame."

Conrad, whose appetite for combat was insatiable, cast her a resentful glance.

"That's no business of his!" he declared before turning to Giorni and issuing a splendid ultimatum: "And I'm not having you drag my wife into this."

"She's the one who dragged herself in."

The outthrust jaws, lowering brows, and rapid-fire exchanges might have gone on forever if Tina had not suddenly choked on a spurt of laughter.

"If you really want to track her down, I can tell you where to go," she said merrily. "Alice is having her hair done at Gaston's Salon on South Water Street."

For the first time Giorni's resolution faltered.

"Think you're pretty damned cute, don't you?" he said, scowling at Tina.

Thatcher's sympathies were with the inspector. It was one thing to bellow threats at Conrad. It was quite another to tackle a white-haired grandmother in the midst of whirring blow dryers, mincing stylists, and a spellbound clientele.

But Tina recognized the worth of other approaches besides unremitting defiance.

"Oh, come on, Inspector," she coaxed. "I couldn't believe my ears when Conrad told us that Alan had hightailed it. We're all dying to find out what's been going on. So why don't you just tell us?"

Still bent on causing discomfort to someone, Giorni

snapped: "Why not ask Thatcher? It was his bright idea."

Tina, Bob, and Conrad turned to Thatcher expectantly. Tom Robichaux, however, shook his head.

"That's no way to treat a client, John," he criticized.

This opinion was not shared by Conrad Ecker. He was too annoyed at having been beaten to the finish line.

"Don't see how you could come up with Alan. You probably picked his name out of thin air," he said with all the graciousness of a sore loser.

"Oh, it was easy after your performance at Tom's office," Thatcher replied with malice aforethought. "You're the one who started us on that hare about Bradley stealing from his lab. And once anyone looked at Bradley, the next logical step was Alan Frayne."

Bob Laverdiere took over. Casually reaching for Conrad's pencil, he rapped it sharply on the table.

"We'll never get anywhere this way," he announced. "Suppose you start at the beginning."

Thatcher was momentarily distracted by an insight into the new force at Ecker that had been steadily emerging all afternoon. Conrad might be sitting at the head of the table; Laverdiere was calling the shots.

"Actually it all became clear at the musicale," Thatcher began again. "For weeks we had all been dealing with ASI's reaction to your firm. Given the number of relatives here and the informal chain of command, it was only natural that they should consider Ecker as a cozy family unit. But, until the Juilliard concert, I never realized how much you people accepted that fiction."

"Fiction?" Bob queried.

"Alan's always been part of the family," Tina protested.

"I never treated him differently than anyone else," Conrad added.

The last contribution sparked memories for Bob Laverdiere.

"Sometimes a lot better," he recollected.

Thatcher held up a hand to stem the tide. "Oh, I realize you were all continuing habits formed a long time ago. That's what was so confusing. You overlooked the fact that Alan Frayne, in one important aspect, ceased to be part of the family the day he got divorced."

"Nobody blamed Alan for that. It was Betty who . . ." Tina began hotly before having second thoughts. "What exactly do you mean?"

"Money," Thatcher replied succinctly. "When Conrad announced his decision to sell the company, nobody doubted his underlying motive. He was planning to provide for his family."

"Of course." It was Bob who answered. "When Doug was forced to retire, that became important."

Thatcher shook his head. "You misunderstand me. Nobody doubted that Conrad's munificent share of the sale would descend along the bloodline to his children and grandchildren."

This was one subject guaranteed to rouse Tom Robichaux.

"Only way to go!" he trumpeted. He rarely had a bad word for the system that had stood him in such good stead.

"And it's what most people do," said Laverdiere, striking a more detached note.

"Of course," Thatcher agreed. "But look at it from Frayne's point of view. For years the future was taken care of. Half of Conrad's estate would ultimately enrich Frayne's wife and children, and they would all be wealthy. Then Conrad's daughter divorced him and, almost as important, she moved to California."

Tina was puzzled. "I see the inheritance problem—

Alan would no longer benefit from it. But why should Betty's leaving be a big deal?"

"Because it obscured the issue. If Betty had been nearby, the change in Frayne's role would have been patent. She and her children would have been in and out of her parents' home, and her second husband would have become established as the son-in-law at all family get-togethers. Frayne would either leave the company or settle for being a close colleague."

"I see what you mean," Tina said slowly. "I suppose we did pretend that nothing had happened."

"It's not altogether surprising," Thatcher went on, "with the family's center of gravity here in Bridgeport. Nonetheless, I was startled at the Waldorf by the degree to which things had, on the surface, remained the same. Frayne was the familiar figure at Junior's concerts, while Betty was the one who had drifted away. Junior clearly considered Uncle Alan as the permanency in his world. If Frayne had remarried, I got the impression his wife would have become Aunt Sally. The ties seemed as close as ever."

Now it was Bob nodding acknowledgment.

"So, when Conrad decided to sell out, Alan had to face facts. It must have really shaken him. God, it took me a while to adjust," he confessed. "And, with our twenty percent, we'll be millionaires."

"Frayne didn't wait that long," Thatcher replied. "The moment Doug Ecker retired, Frayne foresaw dramatic changes down the road. And there was more than the vanished inheritance to goad him. Bear in mind that you and your wife have transferable skills. Production managers and accountants are needed everywhere. But Frayne was running a test lab for a research department that consisted of one person. He could never duplicate that. On the other hand, as soon as he considered ways to redress his grievance, he must have realized that he had one enormous asset—a credit balance of trust that had been accumulating for years. So he simply advised Conrad that one project would cost too much to produce, then went out and sold it on the open market."

Bob Laverdiere could not believe his ears.

"That can't be all there was to it," he objected, involuntarily turning to his uncle. "There must have been some sort of check."

Conrad, faced with a choice between blaming his son or blaming himself, did not hesitate. "There was. Doug reviewed Alan's decisions. I just let that lapse after Doug left. I never once thought about Alan double-crossing me."

A dull-red tide suffused Bob's face, and possibly for the first time in his life, he sounded dangerous.

"Let me get this straight," he grated. "For two solid years you've wanted us to treat every one of Doug's systems as sacred, no matter whether it was production, sales, or record-keeping. And then, behind our backs, you casually scuttle one of the most important?"

Conrad did not burke the issue. Shamefaced and awkward, he stumbled into a long-overdue apology. "Didn't want anybody doing what Doug did," he mumbled. "It was a mistake. I should have had you take over from him."

"Yes, you should have," Bob said evenly. For a long moment that seemed to be all. Then, tempering justice with mercy, he added, "I never would have doubted Alan's honesty either."

Benignly, Thatcher observed this honorable attempt by both parties to meet halfway on a tricky and tortuous path. Inspector Giorni, however, was only too pleased to emphasize flaws in Conrad's conduct.

"So you practically invited Frayne to steal this kitchen cleaner of yours," he remarked smugly. "What the hell is the thing, anyway?"

"Ah, not the cleaner," Tina sighed. "Conrad had a

real winner there. It mechanically washes your kitchen floor and then really dries it."

She sounded enthusiastic enough to be a potential customer.

Meanwhile Giorni was nodding to himself. "I figured it couldn't be a mop, not the way it's going to be priced by the outfit that bought it from Frayne."

This offhand remark threatened to derail the entire conversation.

"What are they planning to charge?" three voices demanded in unison.

When Giorni told them, Tina and Bob groaned aloud. Conrad was made of sterner stuff.

"The bastards are going to cut corners," he ground out.

"You can see why Frayne felt safe," Thatcher commented, neatly seizing the opening. "Long before he took to crime, another company happened to bring out a cheap version of one of Ecker's rejects. You would all assume the same thing had occurred again. And none of you would have the same proprietary interest after the Ecker Company was sold. Still, when the anticipated merger became a reality, when Pepitone and Hunnicut appeared in the flesh, Frayne did not want loose ends lying around. Old lab books were still being automatically shipped to records, and anyone who studied them would realize that Frayne's conclusion about the kitchen cleaner was at variance with the facts. A fire in the boiler house seemed the perfect solution."

"Damn fool," Conrad argued. "He should have known it would never pass as an accident."

"You're underestimating Frayne," Thatcher retorted.

"You sure are," Giorni agreed. "If he hadn't gone on to kill someone, the fire wouldn't have raised such a stink. And he had bad luck with it, anyway. First, the alarm went out too soon. If the fire hadn't been discovered until the night watchman came back, it would have been harder to tell that some lab books had been gutted. And the acetone he used is water-soluble, so there's a good chance you'll miss it with the spectrometer. Besides, Frayne made damn sure this was a nontechnical fire. He didn't monkey with the sprinkler heads, he didn't use a detonator or timer."

Thatcher did not regard Frayne's plan as beyond criticism.

"Not using a timer was an error," he pointed out. "The Laverdiere home in Westport was the number posted for the fire department. They had to be home to take that call but Frayne was not notified until the following morning."

Recalling the hectic atmosphere of that predawn emergency, Bob agreed. "I thought of calling Conrad, but not Alan. And even if I'd called him from the plant, he would have had time to get home."

"In spite of the confusing element introduced by Hunnicut's presence in Bridgeport that night," Thatcher continued, "the most likely people to burn Ecker records were always the people at Ecker. That's why Frayne bent over backward to make it seem as if the financial books were the target of the blaze."

Tina was no longer amused. "So having made sure I'd be chief suspect, Alan could relax and proceed happily."

"Certainly he had every reason to congratulate himself on his foresight when Sam Bradley showed up, frankly asking to see the material on rejected ideas. But near misses can be tension-inducing and Frayne's luck ran out at the trade show."

"You mean something happened there we don't know about?" Bob asked.

"Far from it. In fact, you and Gardner Ives unwittingly conspired to convince Frayne he was facing a deadly peril."

The old Bob Laverdiere reemerged.

"Me?" he gasped, reviewing his behavior at Javits. "I didn't do anything; I was done to. Hunnicut unloaded that pile of garbage on me, and I was thrown for a loop. As for Ives, I never even saw him."

"But your rendition of what passed between Quinn and Hunnicut was misleading. Mind you, Ken Nicolls was confused, too. At first he thought Hunnicut's remarks about the sale of ideas from the lab related to Ecker rather than to Bradley. Your version encouraged Alan Frayne to make the same mistake. On top of that, you assumed Hunnicut was the man who would be handling Ecker for ASI. When you transmitted that alarm to Frayne, he would have remembered Hunnicut's wide-ranging questions in Connecticut."

"They had me confused, too," Tina admitted. "After the inspection trip and the session in Princeton, I didn't know where Victor Hunnicut stood at ASI."

"To make matters worse, Frayne could not get satisfactory answers to his questions from Gardner Ives."

Again, Tom Robichaux stirred to life.

"I've had that trouble with Gardner myself," he said chattily. "The man wanders all over the place."

And when Tom complained about divagation, thought Thatcher, things were really bad.

"Ives simply wanted to end the encounter," he said hastily, "but to Frayne it seemed as if ASI were evading any discussion of Hunnicut's status. So there Frayne stood, with a Hunnicut who was going to be established at Ecker, with a Hunnicut who already suspected what Frayne had been up to. The danger was self-evident and Hunnicut had to go."

It did not look that simple to Tina. "I still can't get over the risks Alan took," she said. "When the police suspected us, it seemed so absurd. Imagine doing something like that at a crowded exhibition hall."

"I'm sure he took normal precautions," Thatcher

reasoned. "He didn't grab the skewer from the Ecker display until Pepitone had left. And, as nobody has come forth as witness, he must have been careful when he steered Hunnicut to the elevator. Of course Frayne had to chance what he'd find when the elevator doors opened in the basement. God knows what he would have done if some innocent trucker had been standing there."

These days Bob Laverdiere could afford to joke about that.

"Instead Alan got clean away and the innocent trucker saw me."

"Yeah, but that same elevator always made you look like a wild card," Giorni announced, confessing earlier doubts. "That's why I moved so fast the minute Thatcher suggested following up on Frayne's list of rejections. As soon as you had a motive for him, he stuck out like a sore thumb."

This time Conrad suspected Monday-morning quarterbacking rather than pure dumb luck. "Why should Alan stick out more than anybody else?"

"Because Hunnicut was told by his boss to find you and apologize," Giorni said promptly. "The easiest explanation for the elevator was that somebody told him you were in the basement and offered to take him there. The only one likely to pull that off was Frayne. And he was a little too casual about putting Pepitone by the skewer at the right time. As soon as I thought that one over, I realized he was taking out insurance."

"He must have been incredibly nervous when you began to ask about Bradley's chance to steal from ASI's lab," Thatcher pointed out. "It would take only a slight redirection of thought for you to realize how much easier it would be for Frayne. After all, Bradley headed a facility that crawled with scientists and lab assistants and clerks who knew what was in the works. Furthermore they had such a poor record that anything likely to be a success would attract mass attention. But Frayne was not only sitting next to a prolific source of good ideas, he was the only person who saw the results of both his test people and his costing people."

The reference to that prolific source did not escape Conrad.

"I may have had more good ideas than I realized," he said reflectively.

Thatcher had been wondering if this possibility would occur to him, but Bob was mystified.

"What do you mean, Conrad?"

"You want to bet that Alan didn't burn *all* the lab books. He probably took the ones that were promising. The next thing I know the discount stores will be importing my ice-cream maker from Switzerland. Ah, well," Conrad continued with uncharacteristic resignation, "it's time for me to put all that behind me, now that I'm retiring."

Thatcher felt that Giorni deserved an explanation. "Conrad was on the phone to ASI this morning. The merger is going full steam ahead."

"It'll sure go a lot faster now that Pepitone's in charge of it," Conrad said peppily.

His attempt to bully Pepitone, Thatcher knew, had met with the kind of resistance he appreciated. Poor Gardner Ives had never been any fun at all.

"So Pepitone's now a white-haired boy at ASI," Giorni concluded.

"If you ask me, he's going to be sitting in Ives's chair before many months go by. But I'm not the one who'll have to deal with him. I'm letting Bob take over from now on."

Giorni was singularly uninterested in Conrad's acts of contrition. "Then, if Bradley manages to hang on, everybody comes out of this fine, including Frayne for the moment."

"Do you think Alan will be caught?" Bob asked, seeing more headlines in his future.

"Depends on how much money he's stashed over there, and how savvy he is," said Giorni realistically. "Interpol has been alerted, but none of this would be necessary if Mr. Ecker, here, hadn't blabbed to his wife."

This was one charge from which Conrad demanded vindication. "I never said a word to her. Alice overheard me on the phone agreeing to get that list for you, and she added everything up. Then she put Alan wise to what was going on."

For some extraordinary reason, Robichaux was moved by this tale. As a man who went through in-laws like boxes of Kleenex, he regarded Alan Frayne's tenure in the Ecker family as a record-breaker.

"Fifteen years," he murmured, awe-struck. "She must be devoted to him."

"She is not!" Conrad shot back witheringly. "She was just thinking about the kids. Alice says she's not having her grandchildren grow up with a father who's a convicted killer, not if she can help it. If he's just another guy on the run, she says he'll be forgotten."

Tina was curious about something else.

"Never mind what she said. What in the world did Alan say when she warned him?"

"Haven't you got it clear yet? Alice didn't warn him, she ordered him to go. Of course I gave her hell for that."

Giorni, as the symbol of authority, nodded approval. "And so you should have."

This was enough to make Conrad reverse in his tracks.

"I'm not so sure now. I don't deny I'd like to get my hands on Alan's throat, but Alice is probably right. Why the hell should the rest of us have to live with this? Let him scurry around Europe trying to sell my rejects to schlock outfits. No, what burned me up was that she didn't tell me until this morning. She said she wasn't going to have me interfering."

If Conrad expected support, he was in for a rude surprise.

"Good for Alice," Tina applauded.

Conrad frowned. "The truth is, Alice is getting a swelled head with this cookbook of hers."

"Cookbook?"

"Didn't I tell you? She's been fooling around, trying to bake and make pastry in a microwave. When she finally figured out how to do it, she wrote down the directions, and damned if some publisher isn't going to bring it out!"

ASI had merely noticed, and resented, all the free publicity flowing to the Eckers. Thatcher was pleased to see that Alice and some enterprising publisher intended to exploit it.

Ecker, meanwhile, was continuing to detail his wife's efforts. "Of course it wasn't easy. She had to do a lot of experimenting. She just got stubborn about making the damned thing do what she wanted it to do . . . seems some fool who never tried baking a cake did the design . . . don't see why it has to be that hard . . . why juggle the ingredients? . . . why not change the design?"

As Conrad continued, his gaze focused on a point far away and his voice became fainter and fainter. Tom Robichaux and Inspector Giorni quietly peeled off for a discussion of ASI. But Bob and Tina Laverdiere remained so rapt that Thatcher sensed he was part of a privileged band.

He was watching inspiration descend—on a client of the Sloan Guaranty Trust.

ABOUT THE AUTHOR

Emma Lathen is the pen name shared by Mary Jane Latsis, an economist, and Martha Henissart, a lawyer. Their first book written together was published in 1961.

HarperPaperbacks *By Mail*

MYSTERIES TO DIE FOR

THE WOLF PATH
by Judith Van Gieson

Low-rent, downtown Albuquerque lawyer Neil Hamel has a taste for tequila and a penchant for clients who get her into deadly trouble. *Entertainment Weekly* calls Hamel's fourth outing "Van Gieson's best book yet — crisp, taut and utterly compelling."

THE RED, WHITE, AND BLUES
by Rob Kantner

From the Shamus Award-winning author of THE QUICK AND THE DEAD. P.I. Ben Perkins takes on a case that strikes too close to home. When babies begin to mysteriously disappear from the very hospital where his own daughter was born, Ben embarks on a macabre trail of corruption, conspiracy and horror.

PORTRAIT IN SMOKE/ THE TOOTH AND THE NAIL
by Bill S. Ballinger

HarperPaperbacks is proud to bring back into print, after thirty years, a special two-in-one edition from the Edgar Allan Poe Award-winning author the *New York Times* dubbed "a major virtuoso of mystery technique." In PORTRAIT IN SMOKE, second-rate businessman Danny April is haunted by a beautiful woman. So is magician Lew Mountain in THE TOOTH AND THE NAIL. And both are involved in mysteries that seem impossible to solve.

RUNNING MATES
by John Feinstein

From the *New York Times* bestselling author. Investigative reporter Bobby Kelleher has just about given up the hope of ever landing the "big hit" —the story that will make him a star. Then the governor of Maryland is assassinated and things start to change—quickly and violently.

EVERY CROOKED NANNY
by Kathy Hogan Trocheck
In this high-caliber debut, Trocheck introduces Julia Callahan Garrity, a former cop who now runs a cleaning service in Atlanta. Sue Grafton calls this novel "dust-busting entertainment," and *The Drood Review* picked it as a 1992 Editor's Choice selection.

BLOOD SUGAR
by Jim DeFilippi
In the tradition of the movie BODY HEAT, this gripping suspense novel has just the right touch of sex and a spectacularly twisty ending. Long Island detective Joe LaLuna thinks he knows what to expect when he's sent to interview the widow of a murder victim. Another routine investigation. What he gets is the shock of his life. The widow is none other than his childhood sweetheart, and now, he must defend her innocence despite the contrary evidence.

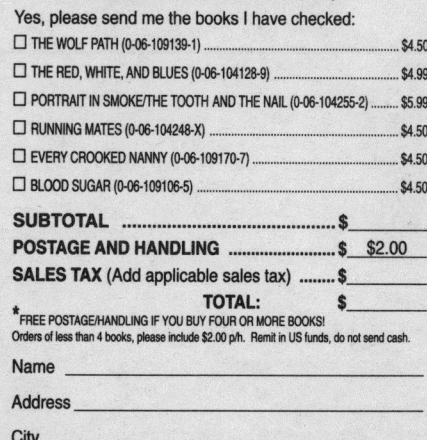